Rachel Morris

Rachel Morris's first novel, *The Fringe Orphan*, was published in 1992. She lives with her husband and children in North London.

SCEPTRE

Also by Rachel Morris

The Fringe Orphan

Ella
and the
Mothers

RACHEL MORRIS

SCEPTRE

Copyright © 1997 by Rachel Morris

First published in 1997 by Hodder and Stoughton
A division of Hodder Headline PLC
A Sceptre Paperback

The right of Rachel Morris to be identified as the Author of
the Work has been asserted by her in accordance with the
Copyright, Designs and Patents Act 1988.

10 9 8 7 6 5 4 3 2 1

All characters in this publication are fictitious and any
resemblance to real persons, living or dead, is purely coincidental.

A CIP catalogue record for this title is
available from the British Library.

ISBN 0 340 66010 4

Typeset by Palimpsest Book Production Limited,
Polmont, Stirlingshire
Printed and bound in Great Britain by
Mackays of Chatham PLC, Chatham, Kent

Hodder and Stoughton
A division of Hodder Headline PLC
338 Euston Road
London NW1 3BH

Ella
and the
Mothers

SCEPTRE

He came to see her one evening as she was packing up to leave. She was kneeling on the floor with clothes and shoes and books and papers strewn helplessly around her. She had taken some of the books and built them up into towers and now she was taking a book from every tower and reading the first page before she put it in a box. She had been there an hour and a half and the box was not yet full. Martin stood and watched. He was wearing new Doc Martens and a white, linen suit that she hadn't seen before. He was looking nervous but shiny as well with all his new love. It was eight weeks since he had run off with Angelina – thus acquiring this unfamiliar look of grandeur and dignity and joyousness – and four weeks since they had put the house on the market. Now Martin was so happy it was all he could do not to ring up Madeleine every day to tell her all about it.

He had brought round a form that he wanted her to sign. But it seemed that mostly he had come to assure her that really Angelina was good-hearted. He began to pace the room. 'It was her idea that I should come and see how you were getting on,' he said. 'Really sometimes she's extraordinarily mature. I forget how young she is. And she wants to be friends with you,' he said, and he sat down on a chair with his knees apart, his elbows on his knees, a look of shining contemplation on his face.

He was a big, clumsy-looking man who wore his crumpled, linen suit and open-necked shirt with an awkward air as if he feared that he might move suddenly and tear them. But though his body was clumsy his face had a clever, mild, ironic expression.

He had fair colouring and almond-shaped eyes and a hooked nose and lips which were full and sculptured-seeming.

Madeleine was kneeling on the floor. His Doc Martens were only inches away from her nose. She was holding a pencil in one hand. I could leave some graffiti on those shoes, she thought, Something to remember me by. And then she looked up and caught his eye. 'Mind you,' he added with a flash of truth, 'I can see that the evidence is against her good nature.'

Is that an apology? thought Madeleine. But no, he didn't really mean it, because no sooner had he said it than he began to pace the room again with the same daft look of love upon his face. He peered at the CD titles on the shelf.

'You must take some more of the CDs,' he said, because it was Martin's plan that everything should be divided between them with scrupulous care. When they had been a couple they had distributed the qualities between them and Madeleine had got courage but Martin had got sweetness. Now that he was so happy he wanted more than ever to be good to Madeleine. 'You must take more of the CDs,' he said again, but Madeleine wasn't listening. She was thinking up insults beginning with the letters of the alphabet: Alligator, Bumface, Cockbrain, Dumkopf. Her vague expression began to irritate him. 'I want you to keep the ring, Madeleine,' he said, and at that Madeleine jumped. 'Good God,' she said, genuinely startled. 'What would I want with that old thing?'

Madeleine badly wanted to cheat upon her ex but each time she took more than her due he offered it to her anyway, thus undermining her with his generosity. Even when leaving, thought Madeleine, he still wants it all: Angelina and my blessing as well. Elephant-legs. Fart-face. Gargoyle-guts.

She was being difficult in every which way she could imagine. She wasn't returning his calls, nor answering his letters, and when he brought round documents for her to sign she read them with exaggerated care and queried everything and then forgot to sign them anyway. She spilt a cup of coffee over one document and took another to the bathroom to read it where she flushed it down the toilet. By accident, she had said on that occasion, and Martin had stared at her in bafflement and she had stared back at him with the same expression, because quite genuinely she couldn't understand any of this. Except that he had run off with a French girl half his age, so let him do the work of unravelling it all: the house, the mortgage, the insurance and so on.

He gave her the form that he wanted her to sign. 'Two signatures,' he said, 'here and here,' and then he left her to it and went out through the kitchen door into the twilit garden. She stood at the window. She watched the glimmer of his pale trouser legs as he drifted along the herbaceous border. He'd only been gone eight weeks but the garden had already taken on an unkempt air, the grass growing long and the ivy entangling itself in the roses. He reached up to touch a blossom and she thought, that must be because he's sorry to be leaving this place. But when he came back in again he didn't look sorry at all: rather he looked dreamy and contented.

He went past her up the stairs and into the double bedroom. She followed him up and saw him with his back to her, looking out of the window. She stood in the doorway, sighing loudly. 'I don't feel well,' she said.

'Perhaps you should see a doctor,' he replied, not bothering to turn round.

'I don't like doctors,' she said sulkily, and he answered absent-mindedly, 'Ah no, you never did,' and she felt that though he was kind he was essentially indifferent, as if the eye of his love were elsewhere. Which of course it was.

He leant forward until his nose was pressed against the glass. Outside there was a crescent moon, a skinny, decorative creature, perched in a flushed, translucent sky. Madeleine wondered if Angelina was out there in the car, waiting for him.

Martin said, 'You know our holiday?'

'What about it?' asked Madeleine.

Way back in February they had booked and paid for a holiday beside the Italian lakes.

'We were wondering if you were going to use the tickets?' Martin asked.

'I don't know,' said Madeleine and she added, bitterly, 'I've rather gone off holidays.'

'In which case,' he said – and he was very smooth and hardly embarrassed at all – 'perhaps Angelina and I could buy you out?'

'What for?' asked Madeleine stupidly, and Martin answered simply, 'Because we want a holiday.'

Madeleine didn't answer. She sat down on the bed. She closed her eyes. The form lay unsigned beside her. She was thinking that insofar as she had thought about the holiday at all she had assumed that they would return to the travel agent and get their money back, because surely neither of them would want to take a holiday without the other? But it seemed that she'd been wrong. I must still have the habits of a wife, thought Madeleine, because how else to explain her assumption that what was in her head must be in his head also? I loved you, thought Madeleine, I listened to your problems. I promoted your career. How could you have done this to me? And yet he had, and not only that but he was going to get off scot-free because what was tormenting her – which was the memory of their past together – he had forgotten as blissfully and as completely as if it had never happened.

He had forgotten – she knew it – the dinner party where they had first met, and the houses they had bought together and the books she had encouraged him to write, and the holidays they had taken. And he had forgotten – she knew this also – his admiration for her brains and her energy and even her bossiness (because in those days he had thought himself pretty smart and thus that he understood the Zeitgeist and that the Zeitgeist was powerful women). All through the seven years that they had lived together they had been laying down their memories like clothes in a drawer, thinking that they'd last for ever. But we were wrong, thought Madeleine – because only eight weeks ago Angelina had turned up in their lives and, like a house-clearer, had simply thrown the past away.

Now he stood looking out of the window with a dreamy, daffy expression. In this twilit room the shadows in the folds of his new suit were as black as shadows in the snow.

'The form, Madeleine,' he said, but Madeleine wasn't listening. She was wondering if Angelina had bought this suit for him?

'You've got a new suit,' she said, 'a snow suit,' and at that Martin turned round, with a confused, impatient look.

'The form, Madeleine,' he said again.

Oh you bastard, Madeleine thought. Her fingers, lying at her side, curled round the edge of the form, and quietly and surreptitiously they drew it onto her lap where – before he could stop her – they began rhythmically to tear it into pieces.

2

This was Madeleine Kingdom: a skinny, somehow sinewy-looking young woman, with neat features that fell just short of prettiness, snapping, dark eyes and dark hair cut short and bleached to the colour of straw. She had a darkish complexion which gave her face a shadowy look and red-painted lips to match her painted toenails. She taught twentieth-century literature at London University, in which cloistered world, where the smallest gesture seems hugely magnified, she wore a leather jacket to work and was thought of by her boss, Professor Atkins, as an angry young woman.

Professor Atkins didn't like her. She was clever and hard-working and gave interesting lectures – but what were these virtues compared with her vices? Which were that she interrupted him in the middle of his sentences; that she queried his decisions and stirred up his students against him and once even went to the Dean when she didn't like something that he was doing; and that she gave fancy lectures which made him feel old – on subjects like 'The Detective: A History of the Genre' – and that more students went to her lectures than went to his.

Professor Atkins was a curious-looking man. He had a huge head and a great, square face around which his coiffed, grey hair was curled in tendrils. But from his shoulders down his body tapered, past narrow hips to little, dainty feet and turned-out toes and a shimmying walk. The summer that Martin left Madeleine she was quarrelling with Professor Atkins over next year's timetable, which she said was unfair to the second years. She raised the subject with him at every meeting. She wouldn't let up. She even waylaid him in the corridor and outside lecture rooms, waving the timetable under his nose as if, he thought irritably, all she had to do was to get him to see some obvious truth and straight away he'd give in.

Each time she had a go at him he would blush and smile with rage, shifting nervously from foot to foot, his eyes zooming in every direction, clocking her curious, modern looks. And he would say to himself angrily, She's haranguing me. Although that's not how it seemed to Madeleine. She didn't feel that she was being troublesome or aggressive or unreasonable, simply that the matter had to be sorted out and she couldn't rest until it had. And each time she had a go at him, he would think to himself, how impossible young women are these days – because he had been young in the fifties and remembered well that time when women were women, with waists and bosoms and ankles, those days of sex and sin and adultery, that time of Lucky Jim-mery.

He didn't know that Martin and Madeleine had split up. He had met Martin once when Madeleine brought him to a staff party, and had thought him a nice enough man, cultured and with a good job. So why can't he keep her under control? the Professor would think, when at last she'd stopped haranguing him and had gone away and left him to stare helplessly at his feet.

When the students saw the two of them quarrelling they always took Madeleine's side. Madeleine was popular with the students, because she worked hard for them and was loyal to them and looked after them, although always in an Oh-for-God's-sake-impatient-older-sister way. They even admired her clothes, although this was unheard of in the relationship between students and lecturers. Madeleine favoured leather jackets, ruffled shirts, peaked caps, high-heeled shoes, short, flounced skirts and painted toenails, all of which she loved because they were raffish and Bohemian and because she liked the way they looked when she walked with her quick, brisk step, because she could cut a dash in them, as her mother would say. Madeleine got her clothes from the market or from expensive little boutiques in Covent Garden, run by androgynous-looking women. On a good day, Madeleine looked like an Elizabethan boy-actor dressed up as a girl. Or perhaps it was a girl-actor dressed up as a boy?

Either way, after Martin left her, her clothes grew even more extraordinary. It was a point of pride with her that she should dress as confidently as ever. 'Don't let the bastards grind you down', was Madeleine's motto.

After the house had been sold and whilst she was deciding what to do next Madeleine went to live in a block of flats not far from Mornington Crescent. These flats had been taken over by a housing association and had been let out mostly to single people, to students and drifters and loners – hippies, her mother would call them. Madeleine had one room, a kitchen and a bathroom, sublet to her by one of her students. The day she moved in she left most of her belongings at her mother's house, bringing with her to the flat only two suitcases of clothes, her computer, her work and some of her books, all of which she unloaded by herself – box by box and bag by bag – from the car and carried up to her flat.

When she had closed the front door behind her she looked around at where she was going to live. The bed-sitting room was painted a dirty white, with linoleum on the floor and a mattress in one corner and posters on the wall. The bathroom was long and narrow with an avocado-coloured suite. The kitchen, on the far side of the living room, was long and narrow also. All the windows were plate glass and curtainless. Madeleine's heart sank. She had no idea how to make this flat more habitable. She was not at all domestic. In the past it was Martin who had done that kind of thing.

She went across to the living-room window and saw that it looked down onto quiet, stony streets, unrelieved by greenery. It was nine o'clock at night and the sun – which was enormous and the colour of a poppy – was sinking through a cloudless sky in a glory of gold. To Madeleine it had a weary look about it, as if for two pins it would finish things here and now and not rise at all the next morning. And yet it would of course. Unless she did something the sun would rise every morning and shine down on Madeleine Kingdom, alone and abandoned.

Some of her students lived in this building. On her way to work the next morning she passed them standing outside on the pavement. They smiled at her and chorused, 'Hello, Madeleine.' The young men wore their hair greased back until it glinted in a carbonised way, like coal in the sunlight, whilst the girls wore skirts like flowers and kicky boots, the toes of which resembled old root vegetables. The students knew that Martin had left her and they felt sorry for her. The men were trying out on her unfamiliar feelings of pity towards a woman, stretching and making tender these feelings like little children stretch out rubber bands. But I've never been left by a man before, thought Madeleine, rushing past them with her nose in the air. Don't think I'm the kind of person who often gets left by a man. She was still quite gob-smacked by Martin's defection.

Two of the students fancied her. When she came home from work on the first day they popped out from the dark corner beside the lift as if they had been waiting for her. They were pretty men with dark shades and tanned legs and sawn-off jeans. One of them had rosy cheeks and dark, curly hair. The other owned a car which she had already noticed the night before, rushing off down the road, packed to bursting-point with their friends and with a brightly-coloured stream of music flying out behind. 'Hi, Madeleine,' they said, and they smiled at her speechlessly, jauntily, admiringly. They got into the lift with her and when she got to her floor they got out with her and fell into step beside her, saying, very daringly, 'We liked your lecture, Madeleine. Would you like to come to dinner?' At which she looked startled and proud and shrugged her shoulders. 'Perhaps,' she said.

She let herself into her flat. She took a bath and then she went across to the off-licence to buy a bottle of gin and some tonic. As she crossed the road she heard a man's voice in the sky. Perhaps it's Him, she thought, siding with Fart-face against me? But when she looked up she saw that it was only a couple of workmen on a roof, calling out to each other.

Back in the flat she went out onto the balcony and saw –

below and to the left – the two students sitting out on their balcony, with their knees drawn up quietly, listening to music and waiting for her. When she looked at them from this distance she felt as she did when she discovered a new poem or saw a pair of shoes she really liked: it was a greedy, gobbling feeling, a I-have-to-have-it, have-to-taste-it feeling. I must be growing old, she thought, to be eyeing up young men like this. Is this what Martin felt when he first set eyes on Angelina? And yet she knew that when she came up close to them their speechless admiration would depress her. She kept remembering scraps of conversation from her years with Martin. She missed that ease of conversation, the feeling that Martin had been her equal, not superior to her but not inferior to her either.

I should go and join them, thought Madeleine, and then, again – ten minutes later – I should go and join them. But she didn't and a part of her knew she wouldn't, because of course she was still too dumbstruck by Martin's defection. It was this astonishment that was making her bump into furniture and trip over kerbs, sending her sprawling with a terrible clattering and shattering of her wits, because for all these years she had assumed that Martin was as fixed in her life as the kerb on the pavement. She kept hearing his voice and seeing his face and if she tried to imagine touching a man then the memory of Martin would interpose between them so that for Madeleine, although these students were so pretty, they were as inappropriate as Christmas presents in July.

During her second night in the new flat she woke twice, at the insomniac's hours of one o'clock and four o'clock. She got up and made herself a cup of coffee. She fiddled with the lock on the balcony door and opening it she stepped out. On this fine summer's night London had a spaceship look about it, as if each tall building, bedecked in lights and invested with strangeness, had just landed from some distant planet. There Madeleine stood, with concrete under her bare feet and feeling small and skinny and baby-naked, although she was dressed in her pyjamas. It was as if by his defection Martin literally had diminished her.

She began to clutch at her achievements in order to console herself. I am Dr Madeleine Kingdom, she thought, a BA (Hons), MA, PhD in Edith Wharton, with a good job and numerous published articles on the early modernists (although lately she'd fallen in love with thirties' detective novels); a feminist? – 'Of course,' says Madeleine, 'what else is there to be?'; and with a head stuffed full of heroine-worship. For Madeleine loved the courage and independence and achievements of women and had thought that Martin loved these things as well. He had made her feel confident – 'Too confident,' said Madeleine bitterly, because she never saw it coming.

4

It was the wanting of children that did for Martin and Madeleine. For three and a half years they had been trying to conceive. Blindly they had pursued the object of their desires, although between them their experience of children had amounted to almost nothing. But they felt how time flowed onwards towards the inevitability of children, houses, mortgages and family holidays; and Martin wanted to do what all their friends were doing, which was to make a family unit which he could nourish and support. Whilst Madeleine looked at childless friends and saw how the mind, with its energy unconsumed, would diddle and dawdle and churn the empty air, seeking an object on which to expend itself. 'I don't intend to grow old like that,' said Madeleine.

And so after two years of trying to make a baby by themselves they began to attend a private clinic in North London where, although the prices were high, the results were good. Madeleine couldn't bear to go to the bottom of a NHS waiting list when what she wanted was a baby now. It was how she was used to living, with everything planned and fixed; this year the PhD, next year the book, the year after that promotion.

The clinic stood in a quiet, suburban street at the back end of Golders Green. There were gardens on every side of it. On the ground floor behind tinted glass was a day clinic and the doctors' rooms and the waiting and reception areas, furnished with low leather armchairs and pot plants that seemed to snap carnivorously and glossy magazines with pictures of Middle Eastern cities. On the floors above, opening out from quiet, carpeted corridors, were bedrooms and labour rooms and ante- and post-natal rooms and a surgical theatre.

Their gynaecologist was called Mr Kalotheou. He was a tall and slender man with hair that receded from a high forehead and the mouth of a forties' movie star. He wore the kind of clothes that villains wear in certain, well-dressed gangster movies where you know that the artistic director has a degree in fashion design. His long, loose jacket swung from his elegant shoulders and like all the best jackets hardly touched his back at all, except at the points of his classy shoulder blades. His trousers were cinched in around his narrow waist and, being ever so slightly too long, gathered on the tops of his shoes in a most Italian way.

On meeting her he liked to shake Madeleine's hand and to address her as 'Doctor Kingdom', which made Madeleine think 'Smarmy bastard', because his air of paternal superiority had a way of driving her bananas. She used to tell herself that she would not fall prey to his absurd Mills-and-Boonery. Sometimes she tried to hurt him by querying his success rate or questioning his procedures. But although Mr Kalotheou bent he would not break. Instead, he smiled at her sadly and, if she persisted in abusing him, he questioned – with a touch of sharpness – her scientific knowledge and pointed out – but courteously – that the experiments she was citing against him were ones that he himself had carried out.

On the walls of his study were photographs of all the IVF babies that he and his partner, Professor Williams, had conjured into this world with their potions and their medicines. There was also a photograph of Mr Kalotheou's three children and his wife, a pretty woman with dark, chocolatey eyes – an edible hausfrau, thought Madeleine. It was painful to think that Mr Kalotheou and his wife probably knew more about children than she did. Not to be able to conceive is a humiliating experience and it was this that was making Madeleine so particularly bad-tempered.

When Martin and Madeleine first went to see Mr Kalotheou he outlined the tests that he would do upon them: a sperm assessment test to check on the number and mobility of Martin's sperm; blood tests to see if Madeleine was ovulating properly; a post-coital test to check on Madeleine's cervical mucus; sperm tests to see if Martin's sperm were penetrating Madeleine's eggs; an ultrasound to examine the state of Madeleine's follicles and a biopsy to look at the state of Madeleine's womb.

Whilst he talked Martin and Madeleine held hands. Martin was looking at Mr Kalotheou but Madeleine was looking at Martin and feeling little rushes of tender pity towards him, because privately she was convinced that she knew what the problem was – Martin's sperm, which would be neither strong enough nor fast enough to fertilise her eggs. Poor Martin, thought Madeleine, but she kept her mouth tight shut because she didn't want to upset him.

And yet as it turned out it was not poor Martin but poor Madeleine, for after nearly six months of tests Mr Kalotheou discovered that Madeleine's tubes were blocked. He recommended them for in vitro fertilisation. He said he was really very hopeful that they would get their baby but by this time it was too late for their relationship, because after two and a half years of trying to make a baby Martin and Madeleine were quarrelling daily.

They quarrelled in the car on the way to the clinic. 'Fuck, fuck, fuck,' Madeleine would say, 'why don't your sperm swim more strongly?'

'Why are your eggs so tough?' Martin would answer sulkily, 'and anyway, it's nothing to do with eggs or sperm. Your tubes are blocked, you know that's what the trouble is.'

'I know that's what he says the trouble is,' said Madeleine, referring to Mr Kalotheou. 'I hate gynaecologists. What kind of man is a gynaecologist, anyway?'

'A man who wants to make a lot of money,' said Martin bitterly, and then he added, 'but someone has to do it and he is quite good at his job.'

'He thinks I'm not conceiving on purpose. He doesn't like women like me.'

'How do you know? He's an intelligent man. He knows that the mind is one thing and the body another and that the two things are not necessarily connected.'

'If you were ever to leave me,' said Madeleine, 'he'd say, "Good for you, Martin, she was clearly an impossible woman."'

But Martin had stopped listening. The more their relationship foundered the more clearly the subversive male voices spoke up inside him in protest. 'Blue stocking,' said these voices, 'my wife is a blue stocking.' And Martin wondered where the phrase came from and why if she were a blue stocking her legs were so bare and so sinewy-looking.

'Who would say that?' asked Martin in confusion.

'Mr I-have-an-amazing-bedside-manner-Kalotheou,' said Madeleine.

'Shit, Madeleine,' said Martin, 'I don't talk about us to your gynaecologist—'

'*Our* gynaecologist,' said Madeleine.

'—and anyway, I'm not going to leave you,' said Martin in astonishment. 'I love you, Maddy,' he said, although even as he said it he knew it wasn't true. But Madeleine wasn't listening. 'Fuck, fuck, fuck,' she said. 'I want to have a baby.'

And they quarrelled after seeing Mr Kalotheou. After their first attempt at IVF failed, Martin wanted to give up but Madeleine told the gynaecologist that they were continuing with the treatment. Out in the corridor afterwards Martin said, 'I thought we were going to stop all this?'

'I want to have a baby, Martin,' said Madeleine, banging through a swing door.

Martin banged after her. 'You don't even know any more why you want a baby, do you?' he said. 'You just want one because you can't have one.'

Madeleine stopped short and stared at him. 'Because I don't want to grow old like my mother, do I, smart-arse,' she said.

'Oh, there's no fear of that,' Martin assured her. 'How come you're so childish when your mother isn't?' he asked her, and this so annoyed her that she stalked off down the corridor again, so that he could shout after her retreating back, 'And why do you always walk off in the middle of a discussion?'

And they quarrelled in front of their friends, drawing them into the drama of whether Martin Jenkins and Madeleine Kingdom could conceive a baby.

Sometimes they quarrelled in front of Sally, who was Madeleine's best friend. Sally was a journalist of twenty-five or so, not very tall, with long dark shaggy hair and a thick fringe with flashing, sliding eyes beneath. She had a way of leaning back in her chair, of wearing her chiffon shirt and high-heeled boots, of tapping with her cigarette box upon the table, of looking at you with lips apart, of blowing out her smoke at you.

Sally was an urban pirate who planned to live for ever by answering back and wearing the best clothes and by pinching the best jobs from under the men's noses. She was a feminist of the kind that wants no favours, no positive discrimination, no talk of 'Don't stab me in the back, darling, I'm a woman also'. Sometimes she and Madeleine met up in a fashionable café in Camden Town where the music's beat runs on and on and the waitresses half dance as they go about their work. Madeleine, who was a straight-up-and-down feminist would order herself a beer, but Sally would order herself a cocktail and then they would settle down to discuss their careers. Sally always asked after Madeleine's boss because Sally paid attention to elderly men, knowing full well that it is with them that most power in this world resides. Madeleine, on the other hand, paid them no attention at all. Sally should have been called Mercedes. It would have suited better her sexy intelligence.

They talked about jobs and men and sex and money, but they never talked about babies, nor how much Madeleine wanted one, because Mercedes-Sally couldn't believe it, not even after Madeleine began IVF. Mercedes-Sally had noticed that with mother-love there comes a weakness and a mushiness of spirit and if there was one thing she couldn't stand it was the mushiness of motherhood. Babies were the big thing that came between them, with Mercedes-Sally on one side and Madeleine on the other, with those whose stomachs turn over irrationally at the sight of a small child, with those who feel they are always being followed by phantom children, children who don't exist but ought.

One day they quarrelled in front of Mercedes-Sally about whether or not Mr Kalotheou was sexy. Martin thought that with his looks every woman must surely fancy the gynaecologist. 'Why?' asked Madeleine, and Martin seemed puzzled to know how to explain it. 'Well, he's wonderfully gentlemanly,' he said, and Madeleine snorted. She said that she knew that already.

Only the other day she had been arguing with Mr Kalotheou

over whether or not women should be allowed to sell their eggs. Mr Kalotheou had been shocked.

'A woman's fertility shouldn't be for sale,' he said.

'Don't be stupid,' Madeleine had answered brutally, 'men do it all the time, selling their sperm for £15 a go. Don't you use that service here?' And at this Mr Kalotheou had blushed, which was the first and only time that Madeleine succeeded in making him do so.

'He's a gentleman,' said Martin.

'Gentleman, schmentleman,' said Madeleine scornfully. 'He believes in women as Madonnas. In fact, babies without fucking is exactly what he's after.'

Mr Kalotheou was always sweet to Madeleine – asking after her health and enquiring after Martin and worrying about the side effects of the drugs he had to give her – but Madeleine was humiliated, and indeed puzzled, by not being able to conceive, and humiliation made her bad-tempered, so that the sweeter was Mr Kalotheou towards her, the ruder was Madeleine to him.

One day Madeleine burst into tears in front of Mercedes-Sally.

'I want to have a baby,' she said.

'I don't understand why you're torturing yourself about all this,' said Mercedes-Sally, 'I used to think that you and Martin were the perfect couple. Careers, money, each other. What more could anyone want?'

5

A week before he left her, Martin and Madeleine were in the bedroom back home, getting ready to go out. Madeleine was sitting at the dressing table, putting on her make-up, whilst Martin was perched on a low chair, lacing up his shoes, with his knees pushed up uncomfortably around his waist – because he was a big man – and his trousers twitched up to show a pair of pure white matching socks. These plus his braces, added a dapper touch to his anxious, ironic air.

Martin was thinking about sex. Since his relationship with Madeleine had reached its latest lowpoint he had found himself assailed by images of women that he fancied: women on the tube, secretaries in the office, newscasters on the television, actresses in late-night pornographic movies, women's faces on the fronts of magazines, the girls who brought the sandwiches in at lunchtime on trays slung round their necks – and the receptionist at the fertility clinic.

There Martin and Madeleine would sit, side by side, on low leather armchairs, waiting for their appointment, whilst Madeleine marked essays and Martin eyed up the woman behind the desk. She was of Middle Eastern origins with vast, dark eyes which swam too close together in a delightful, cross-eyed sequence. When she walked she sank down on her four-inch heels into soft, expensive carpet. When she sat down she crossed and uncrossed her legs as if unzipping herself with a flash of metallic light – and each time she did so Martin felt his own hard exterior unzipped to leave his soft insides exposed.

It seemed to him that this receptionist was an Arabian princess bedecked in jewellery, and that although her jewellery – like everything else about this clinic – was probably worth a fortune, it didn't look it, and so in his mind she became a delightful, cheapskate, bargain-basement Arabian princess.

Martin felt it was many years since Madeleine had so stirred his imagination, albeit with such a cheap and tinkling vision, and his prick together. And then through his fantasy he heard Madeleine's voice, saying, 'What will we do if we don't have children, Martin?'

'What?' he said, 'I don't know. Live, work, I suppose, grow old together.'

'But you'd make a good father.'

'Yeah. Well. We don't always get what we want, do we?'

'Why not?'

'What?'

'Why don't we get what we want?' asked Madeleine in a restless, stroppy voice.

'Oh, for God's sake, Madeleine,' he said, and she replied, 'I think babies should be given out as rewards for hard work.'

'In which case, it would be good for you, but hard on other people.'

'But the present system's not fair,' said Madeleine.

He didn't bother to answer. Whoever said that life was fair? There she goes again, he thought: twisting and moulding life as it is to turn it into life as it should be. It was a week before he ran away and his mind had started to splinter and break up into separate personalities, some of which were still faithful but others of which were faithless and faithlessly commented on the loved one's deficiencies.

The party they were going to that night was held in a tall, old-fashioned house beside the canal at Little Venice. It was a fine evening and the reflections of water were rippling on the ceilings of the house, adding further to the delights already carved there, of scrolls and pleats and vine leaves.

Martin and Madeleine stood beside the dips. The party, which was a black-tie affair, was something to do with Martin's work as an architectural journalist and so he was casting his eyes over the crowd in a working kind of way, but Madeleine was looking on sombrely, thinking that the men here looked boring and the women old-fashioned. Madeleine was tired but high as well,

because she'd just won a battle at work and now she was all
fired up with the excitement of this battle and wanted to share
it with Martin. 'Martin?' she kept saying, but Martin was looking
out over the sea of people and wasn't listening because he had
just seen his boss – a little, jaunty man with a mind as coarse
as a scrubbing brush – winding his way through the crowds
towards them. 'What a dickhead,' said Madeleine, referring to
her professor. 'What?' said Martin in alarm, because Martin's
boss fancied Madeleine no end and sometimes she took his
flirting in good part but sometimes she was withering in her
contempt for him. Oh God, thought Martin, because it seemed
to him that Madeleine was unpredictable and that she had no
sense of hierarchy nor of the deference that junior members of
staff were expected to render to their seniors.

Oh God, thought Martin again and he shut his eyes. He
thought that all the other wives here were like plump, soft
cushions (if more than forty) or like a dab of lipstick (if they
were younger). The plump, soft cushions were not sexy but
they were at least reassuring. But Madeleine was neither of
these things. She was dark and narrow and intense and when
Martin pictured her he saw her as a knife blade, a long, sharp
edge presented to the world. He ducked his head forward and
the gesture made him think of Charles I going to the block. In
his mind's eye he saw his neck with a curve grown into it, as if it
were bent permanently into the shape of a question mark, and
it came to him then that it was as a knife blade and a question
mark that he and Madeleine went out together.

How can I sleep with my wife, the knife? thought Martin, I'm
absurdly afraid of castration, and with this thought he knew that
their relationship was over.

'Martin?' said Madeleine again, impatiently, and now Martin
turned and smiled at her sadly, because although he was not a
bad man he knew that he was no better either than he had to be,
and that he was a little cunning as well, because how else was he
to survive in this villainous world? Madeleine was bad-tempered
and would-be-heroic, but cunning she wasn't.

A week later Martin ran off with a French nanny whom he met in Golders Hill Park. He had been to look at a suit in Golders Green but it hadn't suited him – it had been too big and made him look fat and uncertain – and afterwards he felt lonely because Madeleine had refused to come with him, saying she had too much work to do; and so, out of a kind of gloomy masochism, he went to the café in Golders Hill Park, although it was a place he normally avoided, it being so full of children.

The nanny sat at the table opposite, smiling at him. She had a little boy upon her lap. Martin saw a white blouse, a single strand of coral, a gold watch strap, the glisten of olivey skin. He saw a French girl, trained at her mother's knee in how to please a man. He saw generations of French women in lace and black Sunday best, bourgeois yet sexy. She smiled at him, showing the catch in her lower lip and her teeth like shiny grains of rice, and Martin saw a neat and sexy manipulativeness towards men, such as Madeleine has never shown, thought Martin with a sudden, fiery uprush of resentment towards his partner of seven years.

They walked together towards the playground. The path took them under tall trees, blowsy with summer heat, where the sunlight fell prosperous and dappled on the tarmac. Out beyond the trees they came to ornamental flowerbeds and the magnolias and the miniature lake. From where they stood they could see the bandstand on the hill, built like a baby Greek temple. 'Do you have bandstands like that in France?' Martin asked.

'Of course,' she said. Her feet had a placid, slightly flat-footed look about them which pleased him enormously.

The little boy sat in his buggy. His white hair stood up on his head like a cockerel's crest. He had blue eyes and a shine on the skin of his face like the shine of light on a thick, transparent rind of cheese. He was watching the geese and how they waddled their big, feathery bottoms across the grass in search of shade. The little boy looked up at Martin. He waved his hands like a couple of flags and Martin thought, I should have something like that so that people would look at us and say, 'What a chip off the old block that little one is'.

They stopped to feed the ducks. The little one threw his bread all in one go whilst Martin and the nanny looked on. The nanny smiled at Martin. 'Your shoelace,' she said, and when Martin looked down and saw that it was undone he thought that this girl would care about his appearance in a way that Madeleine never had.

Afterwards, with hindsight, when the girl had long since ceased simply to be 'the nanny' but had become Angelina, whose ways of eating and talking and wearing her underwear were utterly familiar to him, Martin looked back and thought that this moment, when they stood together feeding the ducks, was of great significance. For it was then that he realised that he and Madeleine were never going to have a baby, that nature had meant Madeleine to be single, to live and die unduplicated, the pattern of the genes that had descended with such effort from one generation to the next, stopping short in Madeleine because they knew she was no more than a cul-de-sac. And it was now that he finally decided to abandon Madeleine, a huge decision and yet it was achieved so easily – disgracefully easily, thought Martin, ashamed of the speed with which he abandoned his partner of all these years – for as he made the decision he felt only the smallest of bumps, as if he'd driven over a branch in the road.

He stayed away that night and when he went home the next day to the house in Tufnell Park it already had a foreign look about it, uncomfortable and unfamiliar. He had been rehearsing all his resentments, drawing them up in a list which included not only what Madeleine was but what she would have been anyway. 'A lousy mother,' he kept saying to himself, remembering the jokes that their mutual friends had made about who would look after the baby when Madeleine was out drinking with her students. 'A lousy mother,' he was thinking as he stepped into the house, and then because Madeleine was waiting for him and because he felt guilty and her face was so reproachful and he was so full of resentments, he laid straight into her.

'You never loved me,' he told her. 'You just used me to give you a baby. And you never even knew why you wanted one. You just wanted one because you couldn't have one and you couldn't bear to be deprived of anything that you wanted. Think about it, Madeleine. It's your own fault,' he assured her. 'Everything that's happened. Because you won't acknowledge any distinction between the world as it is and the world as it ought to be.'

Madeleine was writing an article called 'The Passions of a Nineteenth-century Feminist'. He was shouting at her now and the pleasure was intense. 'Passions,' he shouted and she jumped because she hadn't followed his train of thought and because she was so utterly astonished at what he was telling her that she could only stare back at him in thunderstruck amazement. 'Passions,' he shouted again, 'That's a bloody joke. You're no more than a puritan.' That'll hurt her, he thought with satisfaction as he began to throw his clothes into a suitcase. She hated to be thought of as a puritan. He was speeding round the room now, scooping up books, papers, shoes, work, as fast as he could. His anger was fading rapidly, to be replaced by a dropping sensation, as if she'd slipped straight through his fingers. It was a wonderfully light and buoyant feeling that left room in his head for not one scrap of regret.

7

But Martin got Madeleine wrong. The maternal instinct flourishes like a flower – or a weed – in all kinds of places, and Madeleine wanted a child. She couldn't imagine a baby of course, never pictured herself changing its nappies nor how she would feed it, but she could picture a little girl – of course it would be a little girl! – and all the places they would go to together – Florence, to see the paintings; the Mediterranean; Latin America – and the life of excitement and adventure that they would share and all the different ways in which she, Madeleine, would fight to protect her daughter. Madeleine knew of feminists who wouldn't touch the in vitro fertilisation clinics – all those men compensating for their own inability to bear children by tinkering with women's insides – but Madeleine was the daughter of an academic and for all her big talk she'd been reared on the sober practice of hard work. For Madeleine, conceiving a baby was like passing a particularly hard exam and she was prepared to work as hard as need be to get it.

She'd already endured one course of in vitro fertilisation – the cocktail of drugs taken daily to promote ovulation; scans every other day to follow the development of the follicles; a laparoscopy to gather up the eggs; the transferring of the fertilised embryos back into the womb; the constant blood tests to check on her progesterone levels and the endless drugs to keep the hormone levels high. Having endured all this the lack of a partner seemed but the smallest of obstacles. She had £3,000 put away in a building society. She would undergo another course of in vitro fertilisation but this time using donor sperm.

She went to see Mr Kalotheou. It was a couple of weeks since the sale of the house and she was now living in the borrowed flat in Mornington Crescent. She told the gynaecologist what she wanted. 'But mind,' she added, 'I don't want any old donor sperm. He has to be university-educated and from the top two per cent of the population when it comes to his IQ. And if you get it wrong,' added Madeleine for good measure, 'I'll take you to court.' She believed in inherited intelligence. That her child should be bright mattered to her enormously.

Mr Kalotheou regarded her over his steepled fingers. He said, 'We are bound by the rules of the Human Fertilisation and Embryo Authority and will act accordingly. You of course are the principal patient but we are also obliged to consider the good of the embryo and to ensure that as far as possible it will be born into a suitable environment. You may not like it but society takes an interest in how you conceive your baby.'

'There's nothing in the rules against donor sperm,' said Madeleine sulkily, to which Mr Kalotheou replied, 'No, but it is normally given to couples where the husband's sperm is inadequate. However,' he added grandly, 'having treated you now for more than a year I am absolutely certain of your commitment to any child you might have,' and Madeleine, who had opened her mouth to protest at his superior tone, had to close it again out of gratitude for his decision.

'Now,' he said briskly, 'the laparoscopy. If you remember, it is an operation that requires a general anaesthetic so we would expect you to spend the night before in the clinic. Healthy and well-rested. That's how we like you to be. Quality of eggs is what we're looking for and it's an interesting area of research because we're finding that calm and happy mothers give the best eggs.' He smiled his classy smile. It was clear that he believed that he'd got the upper hand. 'Eggs, eggs,' he said, 'that the eggs should be so important to the process is one of the things that make me believe in the ascendancy of women.'

Creep, thought Madeleine, and because she was determined that he wouldn't get the better of her with his honeyed display of knowledge, she asked him, 'So how do you define "best"?' Mr Kalotheou gave her a hard look. It was the look that her teachers used to give her at school – admiring of her brains, weary of her stroppiness. When he answered her his voice was equally sharp.

'By "best",' he said, 'I mean the eggs that yield the best results and after nearly fifty successful in vitro births I think I am the best judge of that.' At which Madeleine subsided, so that once again Mr Kalotheou came out on top.

Madeleine hadn't felt well since Martin had left her. She felt tired and despairing, frayed around the edges by his loss, not paint-fresh any more. And the weather didn't help – such a steaming, baking summer – the days intolerable and the nights no better, so that when you rolled against your partner you sprang apart again, recoiling from all that steaming flesh – although this of course was not a problem for Madeleine who, for the first time in years, was sleeping on her own. Every morning she was woken at four o'clock by the heat and light, and by her despair. Every morning she stepped out onto the balcony and saw the cloudy darkness start to thin and clear, as in a fortune teller's ball, to reveal – what? – why, the failures of her life, of course. Grimly she would make herself a pot of coffee. Grimly she would chant to herself, 'I will survive. I will survive. I will not be defeated. I will not be defeated.' She was consoling herself with her usual dreams and fantasies: of the race of sassy women; of women as eighteenth-century pirates and women dressed as boys, roaming the world in search of adventure; of women as war correspondents, rescuing children from war-torn cities; of herself as an eight-year-old child, a large-brimmed hat shading her face, a gun in one hand, its barrel pointing accusingly – 'OK, tarbaby,' she says to her mother, 'I'm a spy, right, and you haven't seen me,' and herself as an elegant old woman, intelligent, formidable, alone, a fighter who fights the good fight, a beacon to other women.

Let him have some French girl, thought Madeleine defiantly, a girl who knows nothing and who demeans him by her youth and her ignorance. She, Madeleine, would have the books and the ideas and the career and the friends. And on top of that she would have a baby also. So she went on trying to shorten the gap between the world as it is and the world as it ought to be. Just as Martin had accused her, the day that he left.

8

On her way back from the clinic after she'd asked for donor sperm Madeleine went to see her mother. Dr Kingdom senior was an academic, a Doctor of Literature, a one-time Fellow of Girton College, Cambridge, and then a professor at Liverpool until her retirement. She was a tall, straight-backed woman with a head full of stern principles and austere passions: for sixteenth-century women poets, for seventeenth-century mid-wives, for eighteenth-century visionaries. She lived in a house not far from the Finchley Road which she had inherited from Madeleine's grandmother and which had been falling down around her ears unhindered for more than forty years. All around it were trees and shrubs which after nightfall gave the darkness a shiny, evergreen Victorian tint.

The day that Madeleine came to visit her she drifted round the kitchen making her daughter a cup of tea. She wore a full skirt and a white blouse. Her grey hair was tied up in a bun and the light flashed off her glasses. As she searched for the sugar bowl, she looked like a stiff-legged, long-legged, wading bird, hunting for food.

Madeleine's mother was practical in small matters but unworldly in large. She didn't understand about mortgages and overdrafts and the cost of living. She thought that Madeleine was absurdly extravagant and if she ever came to meet her down in town she always came dressed in thin, neat, cheap clothes with a carrier bag of her possessions beside her, and seemingly shrunk in size to a little, old woman. She also thought that Madeleine was absurdly argumentative. All through the marriage she and Martin had been united in an alliance of the reasonable against Madeleine's rebelliousness. 'Now, dear,' she used to say, 'remember that Martin works very hard. Don't take advantage of him.' To which Madeleine – for whom it was not possible to be anything other than a rebellious child – would silently respond, 'But you're *my* mother, not his.'

Now Madeleine sat on a stool and drank her tea, whilst her mother looked on with pain and anxiety. She knew of course that Martin had gone but not that Madeleine was trying to conceive by donor sperm. *That* had seemed like a confession too far. Now what's she thinking? Madeleine wondered, eyeing up her mother sideways, and then her mother opened her mouth.

'I don't know why you want a baby so badly?' she said.

'Didn't you want me?' asked Madeleine piteously, because she wasn't used to failure and a whiny self-pity would keep creeping in.

'Of course I did,' said her mother, 'but only after you came. Before that you were a hypothesis. You can't want something so badly that you've never had before.'

'Well, a hypothesis is what I want,' said Madeleine sulkily.

'You know, you mustn't neglect a man just because you want a baby,' said Madeleine's mother. And Madeleine thought, *my* fault; I suppose, *my* fault that Martin left me? And she began to ponder furiously why it was that with regard to her work her mother was so capable and confident, and yet with regard to men she was so childlike and obedient; and besides, thought Madeleine, didn't she let go of my father? Didn't she let him fade away some time during my childhood.

He had been an architect who all through the years when Madeleine was little had come and gone – although mostly he had gone. Occasionally, he had stayed overnight, hanging up his jacket on the back of a chair and jingling the coins in his pocket and eating supper with them in the kitchen. Sometimes when Madeleine had crept into her mother's bedroom, she had seen him rising up like a submarine, shadowy and insubstantial, from the bedclothes, whilst her mother slept beside him with her hands on her breasts, laid out as if for death in her best white nightgown. When Madeleine was older she had met him with her mother in parks and bookshops and had glimpsed him once through the window of a train. Her mother had given him money and he had blushed and smiled his thanks but with each reappearance he had grown more faint until when Madeleine last saw him drinking whisky in a pub not far from the British Museum – and it was sheer chance that she happened on him there – he looked so faded that she could hardly make him out at all, although his surroundings struck her very vividly – the claret-coloured upholstery on which he sat, the wooden floor under his feet, the ruby light which came in through the stained-glass window behind him. 'That's my father,' said Madeleine to the girlfriend she was with. 'What? the good-looking man?' asked the girlfriend. 'No, the old man next to him,' said Madeleine.

After that he disappeared entirely. You couldn't have said his disappearance was tragic. It was too insubstantial an event for that. And yet he left behind him an air of sadness that hung over the British Museum and its neighbouring streets, a sadness that was quite palpable to Madeleine, although Martin never felt it. Neither Madeleine nor her mother reported his disappearance. They never felt that anything dreadful had happened to him, simply that he'd lost what hold he had on family life and had faded away in the night, although later, when she grew up, Madeleine decided he could only have gone with the greatest reluctance, because to an architect with a hundred thousand books, a big house with nothing in it must be very heaven. And perhaps her mother was always expecting him back, because Madeleine once found a stash of money in one of the drawers, and who else could that be for, except her father?

And that's another thing, thought Madeleine, sitting in her mother's kitchen and drinking the tea her mother had made her – for lately her mother's Vichy-like capitulation in the face of men's needs had grown even more accentuated – whatever they wanted you had to give them, for fear that they might run off. 'Their egos aren't that fragile, mum,' said Madeleine, but her mother, having made her a cup of tea, had drifted off across the kitchen, wiping down the surfaces as if to leave all neat and clean – for God's sake – when she died, and Madeleine couldn't tell if she hadn't heard, or had heard and didn't agree.

The truth was that to Madeleine her mother seemed like a childless woman, a woman who couldn't multiply, who couldn't produce excess and extravagance, and who couldn't hold on to other people because she had a solitary gene, which perhaps she had passed to Madeleine – and this was why Madeleine wanted children so badly. I don't want to grow old like my mother, Madeleine thought.

Madeleine's mother's eyes lit upon her daughter's clothes. She was seventy now and she could no longer grasp the big tragedies of life and yet she could still grasp its details. And so she worried about the way that Madeleine dressed and cut her hair and the kind of shoes she wore, the more so since Martin's defection. Today Madeleine was wearing a sleeveless leather jerkin, a flounced skirt, a skinny vest, shoes with chunky heels and a flower on the front of each. 'You mustn't dress too eccentrically, darling,' she said. 'Men don't like to be embarrassed.' And Madeleine snorted and swore under her breath – 'Oh fucking hell' – because wasn't this the whole point of parents, that they shouldn't give you a false account of the world, but should be able to explain it to you properly?

My mother doesn't understand me, thought Madeleine sadly, nor how much I want a baby. Perhaps we all of us have only a fixed amount of mothering inside us and now hers is all used up? Or perhaps it is that she can only imagine the generation that she's made and not the one beyond it?' Madeleine loved her mother. Sometimes, if you looked at Madeleine carefully, you could see several different Madeleines imperfectly superimposed and behind Madeleine the fighter was Madeleine the academic's daughter, a good girl really who worked hard to pass her exams and please her mother.

Madeleine's mother stood in the middle of the kitchen with one hand on the back of her hip. Lately she had started to look old. Lines were now running vertically from her eyes to the corners of her mouth, making the flesh hang down in folds, like curtains.

'Are you all right, Mum?' asked Madeleine.

'I have a pain,' she said, 'here.'

'Have you been to see a doctor?' asked Madeleine in a panic.

'I don't like doctors,' said her mother in a vague but stubborn voice – just like her daughter's.

Madeleine shook her head. 'Please, Mum,' she said, and awkwardly she leant across and kissed her on the forehead.

9

It was August and the days were hot and desultory, blowsy and past their best, when Madeleine went back into the clinic to have her eggs removed by laparoscopy.

They gave her a room on the third floor, taking her up by a lift and leading her down long corridors past open doors where she looked in and saw women reclined on beds, some of them so bedecked in jewellery that they flashed as if lightning were embracing them. To Madeleine these women seemed like another species: idle wives, beautiful mistresses, women frail and sexy, women who lay in bed all day, eating chocolates and dishing out their come-to-bed-with-me eyes. Not Madeleine's kind of woman at all.

Her room had walls the colour of old paper, a cream-coloured duvet on the bed, a deep green carpet on the floor and white, plastic Venetian blinds at the windows, beyond which there was a view of the gardens. A pot of tall, white, funereal lilies stood on the bedside table. They were flushed green at the base of their hungry throats, nodding towards her. A picture of the Madonna and Child in sepia tones hung on the wall above the bed, the woman's neck bent in a manner reminiscent of Martin. 'Uggh.' said Madeleine.

She laid out her few possessions on top of the chest of drawers – some books and papers to mark; a few sticks of make-up in a carrier bag (for lack of a proper make-up bag) and a change of clothes laid out across the bedside table for the morning. It was a meagre-looking handful. Over the years she'd had neither the time nor the talent to amass more. Even her beloved clothes seemed no more than a collection of glad rags – a leather jacket, a ruffled shirt, a pair of Dolce and Gabbana shoes. These shoes were very fine with suede as smooth and deep as cream on their thick heels and a ribbon tied in a bow across the top of each; and yet, although gaudy enough, they made no riotous impression against the sterility of the room.

She went across to the mirror and saw a boyish figure, not tall – although this was peculiar, because surely she used to be? – and very straight-up-and-down, the lineaments touched with solitude, the chin up, Joan-of-Arc defiant; the face with thin lips sprung apart and eyes dark and hollow and solitary. How's he going to make a baby out of all this singleness and aloneness? thought Madeleine. She no longer believed that the process was scientific, let alone natural. She thought that it was magic and that Mr Kalotheou was a magician. That's how they get to you, thought Madeleine.

She lay down on the bed for a while until she heard the sounds of voices and laughter outside the door as if there was a party going on out there. Then she got up and putting on her leather jacket in order to comfort herself – it was the one she had bought to frighten her professor – she went out into the corridor.

She saw a knot of men, tanned and affable-looking, dressed in shorts and open-necked shirts. They had spilled out of the bedroom next door and were now standing in the corridor, smoking – although it was against the rules – and smiling at the nurses. Madeleine saw fleshy lips and flowing locks, deep, coffee-coloured tans that come from foreign holidays and those baggy shorts which say, 'We're little boys really, and all you women are our glorious mamas'. Further on, against another wall, a couple of women were talking to a man. The women had long legs and red lipstick and dark glasses and extravagant tresses. One of them wore a baby-doll outfit, shorts and a top combined, in blue spotted silk, cut high at the sides to show a glimpse of curving brown buttock. The man was dressed in a suit as if he'd come straight from work. He wasn't as tall as them. He had neat, pretty features and maybe the women were teasing him because he was blushing and smiling, but only a little as if it were beneath him to do more. A type, thought Madeleine, with no individual angles, nothing about him to say 'I am a Person and so not like anyone else'.

On the floor at the women's feet were playing three or four children, rolling around and screaming and kicking out with their strong legs. The grown-ups paid them not one scrap of attention.

As Madeleine walked past, the boy-men in their shorts smiled at her whilst further up the corridor the man in the suit turned his opaque eyes in her direction and the women stared with their sightless, black discs. Don't worry, thought Madeleine, you can keep him. I wouldn't be interested in a man like that. The children stopped playing and watched her with frank curiosity. They were plump, rosy-cheeked creatures. Their flesh was laid down lavishly upon their bodies, cream-like in its smoothness and its density. Their clothes were much frilled and flounced and worked-upon to signify expensiveness. A little girl in a country-style dress and waistcoat looked at Madeleine and called out 'mama,' pressing her lips together to make the soft, cushion-like sound.

All these people seemed to embody an extravagant world, lavish in words and flesh and jewellery and tresses. What do they all do? thought Madeleine. Or rather, what do the men all do? (the women being clearly idle). Some kind of meedja-world, thought Madeleine, probably porn films with some cocaine dealing on the side. She walked on round the block, past the nurses' rest room and the kitchens. As she came back from the other direction the children turned their heads and stared at her again.

Madeleine went into her room and lay down on her bed. She tried to picture a child of hers, lying on the bed beside her, but although she could imagine the head and the brains inside it she couldn't imagine the body at all. Recently a small child, bidden by its parents to kiss Madeleine, had come up to her and had offered up her mouth in a kiss which was without love or lust or kindness but was simply itself. Baby kisses, thought Madeleine – sweet but also embarrassing. Will my child know that I'm embarrassed to kiss her? When Madeleine imagined her child she imagined a head but never a body, except that it would be skinny and twiglike, a heap of bones all higgledy-piggledy, just as she was. But how she would love it.

Half an hour later when she went out again she saw that some of the guests had gone and that others had taken their places.

The pretty man in the suit was now standing in the doorway to the next room, talking to a woman who was dressed in a nightgown with a blue wrap on top. She had long dark hair and a beautiful brown bosom and her nightdress was more thickly flowered than the most expensive garden. Tresses of her hair curled across her front, adding a blossoming touch to the flowers upon her nightgown. A man sat on a chair a little way down the corridor. He was dressed in a denim jacket and he was leaning forward with his elbows on his knees and a glass of wine at one foot. He was watching the woman in the doorway – he loves her, thought Madeleine – but the moment he saw Madeleine he jumped and then his eyes followed her instead. Salt after sugar, thought Madeleine with satisfaction. One up on the beautiful women.

Round the corner she stopped by a window which looked out onto the darkening garden. She heard footsteps behind her and knew that the man in the denim jacket had come to join her.

He was not very tall and although his hair was grey it grew long over the collar of his jacket, giving him a boy-ish air. His eyes were light and bright, his manner cheerful, raffish and calculating. He even hummed a little. He didn't look as prosperous as the other men but his expression said, 'I too can sleep with other men's wives, just like the big boys do.'

'It's a funny old world, isn't it?' he said, standing beside her and looking out onto the garden also. 'Here are all you ladies trying to get pregnant, and here am I, trying to get away from my kids for a couple of minutes to smoke a fag in peace. You don't mind if I smoke, do you?'

'No,' said Madeleine, 'I don't mind.'

He drew a cigarette out of the box between thumb and forefinger.

'Do you want one?' he asked.

'No,' said Madeleine.

He tapped the cigarette smartly on the box, lit it, drew upon it for a moment and then said, 'Do you know Gina? George's wife. She's the one who's in here trying to get pregnant. She's an absolute riot of femininity. You'd never think that anyone so feminine would find it hard to have a baby. But there you are.'

'Femininity's got nothing to do with it,' said Madeleine, but he wasn't listening.

'The beautiful Gina,' he said, musingly, and now Madeleine could put a name to the woman in the doorway in the blue wrap: Gina.

'She was an actress,' said the denim-jacketed man, 'or pretending to be, when George met her. Once upon a time I would have offered her my help but in these days of the Child Support Agency you can't be too careful.'

'What makes you think that sperm are the problem?' asked Madeleine incredulously, but he still wasn't listening. 'She was always too beautiful for her own good,' he said. 'I'm off beautiful women at the moment. They always hold back on you.'

'Why, thanks,' said Madeleine.

'What?' he said.

'Nothing,' she said, and now at last he seemed to notice her and fixing her with his light blue eyes he said, 'Are you sure you want a child? I could give you quite a good time if you didn't.'

'Quite sure,' said Madeleine, 'Thank you.'

There came a thud behind them. A little boy was running down the corridor, throwing a football in front of him. 'What's that?' he asked, stopping short and pointing to the cigarette.

'A cigarette,' said the man, 'Don't tell your mother. I'm trying to kill myself.'

'What?'

'Never mind.' His father took the football between his feet. 'Hey, hey,' he said, feinting to left and right, 'Football hero,' and he took the little boy by the hand and dribbled away down the corridor.

So that's what a father is, thought Madeleine. But I can play football also.

When she went back to her room Madeleine saw that the party was over. Only the beautiful Gina was left, standing in the corridor, talking to the man in the suit. That must be George, thought Madeleine. When they saw her coming they fell silent, but it was clear from their mutinous expressions that they were barely suppressing a quarrel. Now that they were standing side by side you could see that Gina was the taller of the two, but she swayed on her feet whilst George held himself quite still. His hands were in his pockets and at first Madeleine thought it was because he was trying to stop himself from hitting Gina. But as she came up closer she noticed his inturned expression and the way his body drooped as if it required self-consciousness and his hands down at his side to keep it upright; and she thought that it was as if – released for a moment from his quarrel with Gina – his mind was drifting off into a world of its own. Poor Gina, thought Madeleine. It was the vagueness of a man who wants to keep the inside of his head private and hidden from his wife.

No sooner had she stepped into her room, leaving the door ajar, than she heard them resume their quarrelling.

'How would you like it if it was you having a laparoscopy?' Gina shouted.

'You've got a night in a five-star hotel and more bottles of champagne than you can count. What more do you fucking want?'

'A fucking baby.'

'That's what I'm trying to fucking give you,' George shouted.

'Well, the fucking isn't any fucking good, is it?' Gina shouted back.

Nineteenth-century woman, thought Madeleine as she sat down on the bed, a woman way back in the harem. But still, what an amazing bosom. It was a bosom that men would once have written sonnets to. With breasts like that why would you ever get out of bed in the morning?

Madeleine fell asleep but she hadn't been asleep for long when she heard a cracking, smacking sound. It reached her muffled by sleepiness and wrapped around with gasps, both male and female. As she swam upwards towards consciousness she held tight to the sound and as the seconds passed the sound grew sharper and more splintered in her memory. First it was an aggressive sound but after a minute it stopped being aggressive and became coquettish instead – a lipstick and nail varnish sound, thought Madeleine, who was now entirely awake and who now knew for sure that Gina had just slapped George across the face. They must be out in the corridor, thought Madeleine. Maybe he wanted sex? Or maybe it was she who wanted it? But what kind of girl slaps her boyfriend anyway? A bad girl and a flirt of course, but an old-fashioned girl as well.

10

When Madeleine woke again it was four o'clock in the morning. She opened her weary eyes and saw the purple darkness which comes just before the dawn and which is so discomforting to those who haven't slept. Tiredness lay like an iron bar, down the back of her head and through her neck and into her shoulders and the top of her back. So much for the well-rested mother, thought Madeleine. She had a headache. Something had gripped her by the throat and was making her want to cry.

I need a coffee, thought Madeleine, but where in this wilderness of rich women with obstetric problems was she going to find one? She should have brought a kettle and a cafetière with her. She never thought of that. She got out of bed and straight away felt better. Activity helped. It always did. Perhaps there was a coffee machine somewhere in the building?

She stepped across to the door and peered out. The corridor was lit but very dimly so, filled with a yellowish gloom of a dense and unvarying nature. To her left, round a corner, was the nurses' station. They'll take one look at me, thought Madeleine, and haul me back to bed and dose me up with valium. She turned right instead and set off down the gloomy corridor. She felt like a child running away. She stopped and listened and beyond the hum of air conditioning and the electric lights she heard the sounds of breathing and coughing and someone crying out, a sleep-cry; and then faint, but quite distinct if you were listening for it, the sobbing, uneven breathing of a couple screwing. Where was it coming from? Was it the nurses or the patients at it? Probably hospitals were full of sex, thought Madeleine, everyone being half undressed and sex combined with frailty having a charm of its own.

She began to look at the doors as she passed them. She came to a door marked 'Kitchen'. She stopped and looked around her, then she pushed open the door and went into a small room, furnished only with a table, a counter round the walls, a single stool and a fridge in one corner. Presumably it was the nurses' kitchen. This will do, thought Madeleine, and she put on a kettle and found a mug and a tin half full of instant coffee.

The door opened. Madeleine jumped. She turned. There stood the beautiful Gina, not three feet away, in her long, blue dressing gown.

'Christ,' said Madeleine, 'You made me jump.'

'*You* made *me* jump,' said Gina.

'I couldn't sleep.'

'Nor me,' said Gina. 'Aren't you the girl in the room next door?'

'That's right,' said Madeleine, and she added plaintively, 'I want a cup of coffee.'

'So do I,' said Gina, sitting down on the stool. She said, 'Is that milk over there? I expect it's the nurses' but don't worry about them. They're terrible cows anyway. I suppose you're in here to make a baby like the rest of us?'

'That's right,' said Madeleine.

'I've been trying for three years. I can't believe how bloody difficult it is. Are you with Mr Kalotheou or Professor Williams?'

'Mr Kalotheou.'

'He's nice, isn't he?'

'He's all right, if you like sexist men who get their kicks out of messing around with women's insides,' said Madeleine.

Gina stared. She didn't understand. 'All my girlfriends love him,' she said.

'What? Are they all infertile?'

There was a pause. 'No,' said Gina with dignity. 'No, they're not. One of them had to have a partial hysterectomy and after that she found she couldn't have a baby.'

'I'm sorry,' said Madeleine. How rude I am, she thought, but perhaps it's the privilege of women who earn money and have to work to support themselves?

'Do you want a boy or a girl?' she asked, trying to be more kind.

'A girl,' said Gina.

'So do I,' said Madeleine.

The kettle boiled and Madeleine poured out the water. She was aware of Gina's beautiful face and body sitting very close to her, the broad forehead, the wide mouth, the wide-set eyes – features arranged to classical proportions – and the tawny hair and the bare feet with coral-painted toenails and the speckled, freckled, tawny bosom, a warm, brown bosom the colour of a warm, brown, boiled egg. A classical beauty, thought Madeleine, and although quite soon it would turn blowsy and frowsy because it tended to plumpness, yet for now it was still beautiful enough to point up Madeleine's shortcomings uncomfortably.

Gina sighed. 'It's hot, isn't it?' she said.

'Do you think any of the windows open?' Madeleine asked.

'I shouldn't think so. In case we ran away. It's like a boarding school here, isn't it?'

'I don't know,' said Madeleine, 'I never went.'

'Lucky you,' said Gina. She had a light casual voice. She said, 'I only have to see this place to know I want to run away. I used to run away from school all the time. I got a real buzz out of it. My mother was living in the south of France with her boyfriend. Le Mans. Tours. Poitiers. Angoulême. I still know the route by heart. From Angoulême you had to hitch. One year a lorry driver picked me up and we played music all the way. It was wonderful. I love the south of France. All those fields of yellow sunflowers. One year I went via Paris. When I got to the Gare du Nord half of Paris descended on me. I was only fifteen and still in my school uniform. My God, I must have looked amazing.'

'I'm sure you did,' said Madeleine drily.

'I got picked up by some middle-aged man but luckily he was impotent. And then I ran away and got on the first train that I could and found myself in a suburb of Paris. Some young men took me home. They were quite kind to me but at the same time they were shit-scared about something. They said they were in trouble with the police. They left me outside a police station and the police rang my mother and put me on a train to her. She burst into tears when she saw me but that didn't stop her sending me back the next day. The bitch. She had a new lover and she didn't want me disturbing things. And then after that I got expelled anyway.'

'What for?'

'Drugs, of course. What else? Well, it could have been sex, I suppose, but in the event it was drugs. The day after I got back we all took a tab of acid. So there I was, straight back at my mother's house only a week later.'

She held her chin in one hand and with the other was pushing some grains of sugar across the table. Although her voice was casual it lay, as it were, upon a solid bed of graciousness, a ripe maturity of body, an unthinking assumption of superiority because her face and body were beautiful and her boyfriend was wealthy. 'Let's take our coffees back to my room,' said Gina.

She had left the light on beside the bed. By its yellowy glow Madeleine saw underwear and shoes strewn across the floor, a couple of silk shirts and a jacket draped across the chair, a litter of make-up on the bedside table: enamelled pots and porcelain jars, with used tissues, lipsticks without their tops, perfume bottles and a hairbrush on whose back was a painting of a Victorian child, all eyes and curls and a wide, submissive forehead and a mouth like a bow – a child who resembled Gina.

'God, what a slut I am,' said Gina, sweeping clothes off the chair so that Madeleine could sit down. She cleared a space for herself on the bed. She leant forward into the light from the lamp and began to rummage around on the bedside table until she found a tiny, heart-shaped, enamelled case. She pressed a spring and the lid flew open to reveal a cluster of little pills. 'Would you like one?' she asked.

'What are they?'

'They make you feel better.'

'They'll show up in your blood test tomorrow morning.'

Gina shrugged. 'Mr Kalotheou knows what I'm like. You'll find that half the women here are out of their heads on something. Rich women usually are.'

She tipped a couple of pills into the palm of her hand. She poured herself a glass of mineral water and swallowed the pills down in one go. Leaning forward, as she was, into the light, Madeleine could see how lively and discontent was her face and

yet how underneath the discontent was a kind of placid voluptu-
ousness which sometimes comes with a surfeit of orgasms. A life
defined by your body, thought Madeleine, glimpsing fragments
of Gina's body – a swelling forearm, the curve of a breast under
one arm, the tuck at the end of the mouth. And a life defined
by shopping, thought Madeleine, surveying the litter of pots and
potions and jewellery and make-up scattered across the bedside
table. Sex and pills and femininity. Sappho, Madame Bovary,
Jean Rhys, thought Madeleine, who couldn't see anything without thinking of the literary character who represented it.

'Was that man you were talking to last night when I walked
by your partner?' Madeleine asked.

'You mean the randy-looking one?' said Gina. 'Yes. Husband
though. Not partner. Husband. His name's George. What's your
husband like? Or aren't you married?'

'Neither. I don't have a man.'

'So how are you going to get pregnant then?'

'Magic,' said Madeleine shortly.

'I like getting pregnant the old-fashioned way. I don't like all
this high-tech stuff. Fucking would do me just fine. Not that
there's a lot of it around these days. I think the situation's
beginning to get to George, having to wank into a bottle and
all that. He's definitely been off me lately.'

'What does George do?' asked Madeleine curiously.

'He's a film producer. Do you know any film producers?'

'No.'

'We don't seem to know anyone else but. They're all the same,
are film producers. They like flash cars and beautiful women.
George is a typical film producer. And they're always either
rolling in it or totally broke. We've had the bailiffs in more
times than I can remember. The first time they came I didn't
know what to do so I rang George at the office. "Why haven't
you given them a drink?" he said. "Give them some champagne
out of the fridge. And don't let them take the double bed. They
can have the sideboard in the dining room instead." "But that's
my mother's sideboard," I said. "So?" he said, "You know you've
always hated it." That's what film producers are like. Casual.
They just don't take things seriously. And of course my mother
thought that he was wonderful.'

'Even after they took the sideboard?' asked Madeleine.

'Even after they took the sideboard,' said Gina.

'One of your friends chatted me up last night,' said Madeleine after a while.

'I know,' said Gina, 'Philip.'

'Is that his name?'

'The little man with the blue denim jacket and the hair over his collar.'

'He's in love with you,' said Madeleine.

'I know,' said Gina. 'He has been for years. It drives George demented. I expect that's why he does it. Philip's a scriptwriter and he earns less than George and that drives Philip demented. Men hate earning less than other men. It makes them want to take revenge. Oh God,' said Gina, 'I don't think these pills are working. I need a cigarette.'

'I can give you a cigarette,' said Madeleine, reaching into the pocket of her leather jacket.

Gina looked at the jacket. Madeleine saw her working out its price. 'So what do you do?' asked Gina, 'You work, don't you?'

'I teach English literature.'

'In a school?'

'No, at London University.'

'So you're clever?'

'Clever enough,' said Madeleine.

Gina said, 'None of my friends really work but they all pretend to have careers because careers are fashionable. The work ethic is in these days. But I don't think that work is that superior and I don't see the point in pretending. I'm an idle cow and that's the end of it.' She frowned. 'How do you get to be the kind of woman who teaches in a university?'

'I expect it's because my mother does,' said Madeleine.

Gina's eyes opened wide. 'You know,' she said and she leant forward and her voice became confiding, 'I have this theory that daughters are just like their mothers – I'm just like my mother really – I like sex and I like money – just as she does—'

'I like sex too,' said Madeleine sadly.

Gina peered at her. There was kindness in her eyes. 'Do you really not have a man?' she asked.

'I did, but he ran off with someone else.'

'God. Who?'

'Just some girl of twenty.'

'What bad luck.'

'Oh, I don't care,' said Madeleine, and at that Gina looked at her with pity.

'Men are bastards, aren't they? I've told George that if he gets himself a girlfriend I'll shoot her with my gun.'

'I'd rather shoot Martin.'

'But then you can't get him back, can you? I'd want George back, all guilty and loving. So how are you going to get a baby without a man?'

'Donor sperm?'

'You mean, the sperm of some strange man you've never met before?'

'That's right. I haven't dared tell my mother about that bit. She wouldn't approve at all.'

'Doesn't she want grandchildren?'

'Not at any price, no. She's a good person. She'd think of the grandchild first and then herself.' Madeleine felt tears starting up in her eyes, childishly, absurdly.

'But do you really have to use donor sperm? I'm sure I can find you dozens of men who would give you a baby?'

'Thank you,' said Madeleine, 'That's sweet of you. But I suspect you don't know as many as you think. Lots of men are put off by the idea of having a baby.'

'George isn't. He's longing to have children. All our friends have got them now. We're the only ones left out.'

'Anyway,' said Madeleine, 'No amount of men are going to help me since my tubes are blocked. I'm going to have to have in vitro fertilisation.'

'So am I,' said Gina, 'What are you in for now? I mean, what are they going to do to you next?'

'A laparoscopy.'

'Me too. Have you had one before?'

'Yes. Once. This is my second attempt at IVF.'

'It's my first,' said Gina. 'Does a laparoscopy hurt?'

'No,' said Madeleine, and now her voice was tender because a small amount of liking for Gina had crept up on her, although whether it was really for Gina or for this kind of female friendship, so rooted in the body, she didn't know. She was feeling for Gina what she sometimes felt for her students – that she was older than them, and could be tender towards them and could impart to them her wisdom. 'No, it doesn't hurt at all. You have an anaesthetic so you don't feel a thing.'

'They make a cut just here, don't they?' said Gina, pointing. 'I told him to be careful of my navel. I told him it was an erogenous zone. I told him it was where I keep my jewellery.' She lay back on the bed. 'Oh God,' she said, and sighed. 'Tell me something else,' she said. 'You know our eggs. Is every one of them different?'

'How do you mean?'

'I mean, does each one represent a different person?'

'Why, yes.'

'So if there are half a dozen eggs inside me now, half might be like George and half like me, and it's simply chance which one gets fertilised?'

'Yes.'

'And put back in the womb?'

'Yes.'

'Then I'm going to pray that the baby that gets through is one that's like George. George is a much nicer person than me.'

'Is he? Are you sure?' asked Madeleine.

'Quite sure,' said Gina. 'What time is it?'

'Quarter to five.'

'They're coming for us at six. Which one of us do you think they'll do first?'

'I don't know,' said Madeleine.

She leant forward. Beside the hairbrush on the bedside table there was a novel. She picked it up. Edith Wharton. Gina watched through half-closed eyes. 'You see,' she said, 'You're not the only one who reads good books.'

'Of course not,' said Madeleine. 'It is good, isn't it? She's one of my favourite writers.'

A pair of earrings lay upon the table, solid silver with a black stone in each.

'These are very pretty,' Madeleine said.

'Have them,' said Gina.

'I couldn't,' said Madeleine, 'they look terribly expensive.'

Gina shrugged. 'Have them,' she said. 'A girlfriend of mine runs a jewellery shop. There's lots more where they come from.'

'Are you sure?' Madeleine picked them up.

Gina shut her eyes. 'They're supposed to bring good luck,' she said, 'and God knows we need it.'

It was Madeleine who went in first. They took her to the theatre where they gave her an anaesthetic and then Mr Kalotheou made a cut near her navel through which he inserted a small, thin telescope to look at her ovaries and to guide a hollow probe which would suck up all her eggs. In this way he got half a dozen of them which he put into an incubator, each in its own test tube. He then took some donor sperm which he first diluted and then put into each of the tubes. Twenty-four hours later when he examined the eggs under a microscope he saw to his delight that two of them had been fertilised. Twenty-four hours after that he found that two more had joined the process of splitting and dividing. He rang Madeleine at college in the middle of the week, his voice shaking with triumph. He wanted her to come in at once and see what he had created. If all went well he intended to put them back in her womb the next morning.

'I'll come at once,' said Madeleine and she jumped up and went off down the corridor to tell the departmental secretary that she wouldn't be in for the eleven o'clock meeting. Professor Atkins was working in his study with the door open. He looked up and caught a glimpse of her smooth, intent, unseeing expression as she rushed past. For a moment he was puzzled as to where he had seen that expression before and then the penny dropped and he remembered his wife's face thirty years ago. You're pregnant, he thought at once, and he surprised himself with the vengefulness of his response. Don't think you're going to get any help from me with maternity benefits, he thought.

Mr Kalotheou met her in the reception area, in amongst the low leather armchairs. 'Dr Kingdom,' he said – he always remembered her title – and as they set off down the corridor he shortened his long step so that she could keep up in the way that grown-ups shorten their steps for children.

He led her down a corridor and into a room where a great metal cylinder was fuming coldly. 'Our frozen embryos,' he said jovially, and he added, as if he knew what she was thinking, 'I know, steaming and smoking like something out of a science fiction movie.' Beyond this room there was another where a technician had set up a microscope over a slide. When Madeleine looked into it she saw four blobs floating in a colourless liquid, each blob appearing to have been drawn with a black pen. 'Absolutely perfect,' said Mr Kalotheou leaning over her shoulder, 'not a hint of a defect in any of them.' But Madeleine didn't hear him, because she was staring in wonder at the fertilised embryos. The last time she'd tried in vitro fertilisation she hadn't even got this far. Now she was moved, despite herself, to see how her children floated in the eye of the microscope and to know that now they were fertilised they had moved away from that parallel universe where previously they had existed and closer to her own universe where they might grow up into real human beings. Heavens, thought Madeleine, feeling an unfamiliar sweetness inside herself, if I have one of these babies perhaps I shall turn out as sweet as a pound of sugar.

'Well,' said Mr Kalotheou after a while, placing a paternal hand upon her shoulder – as if he thought she needed a father – but he's wrong, thought Madeleine, he's wrong – 'if you come with me to the desk I think we should make that appointment for tomorrow morning. Mrs Husselein,' he said to the receptionist, 'will you book Dr Kingdom in tomorrow morning for embryo transfer. Goodbye' – he was smiling now – 'and remember that we like to see our mothers relaxed and smiling on the day if that is possible.' And so saying he turned away, an elegant magician in a fancy jacket.

He and his partner, Professor Williams, had made nearly fifty in vitro babies. If Madeleine conceived hers would be the fiftieth. In all his career Mr Kalotheou made only a handful of mistakes – and they were the easiest ones in the world.

12

The next morning Madeleine went back to the clinic again to have the fertilised eggs put back inside her. George and Gina were also waiting in the reception area, George talking on his mobile phone and Gina standing beside him looking nervous, dressed in a black, linen shift dress, tight around the bosom, and leopard-skin slingback shoes with five-inch heels. Her mass of hair was piled up on top of her head. Her arms and legs were heavily tanned and although it was cool and shady in the clinic her tan gave her a heated look as if she had been baked by the sun and had not yet cooled down again. But those shoes! Manolo Blahnik, thought Madeleine, who was something of a connoisseur of fancy footwear. The heels were as long as stakes to hammer through your heart and poised upon them Gina looked magnificent, but unstable.

A man stood beside them, middle-aged, with silvered hair and a heavy, gold signet ring and a tropical-coloured tan. One of George's friends? thought Madeleine, or a boyfriend of Gina's? Either way it was clear that he was there to provide an audience for a weary marriage.

She sidled a bit closer to hear what they were saying. No sooner did George stop talking on the phone than it rang again. Gina said sharply, 'Can't you turn that bloody thing off?'

George said nothing. The silver-haired man said, 'It's how he makes his dosh for you, Gina darling.'

George said despairingly, 'I was supposed to bring her in all calm and relaxed. But how the hell can I make Gina calm and relaxed?'

'Well, sex is out of the question,' said Gina loudly, 'I've had stomach cramps ever since that laparoscopy.'

'Spend some money on her, George,' said the silver-haired man, 'that always calms them down.'

Madeleine remembered the intimacies of Sunday night. She wanted to ask Gina, 'So did your eggs take? Have you seen them? Is that why you're back here today?' but Gina's eyes kept passing over her distractedly, as if she vaguely – but only vaguely – recognised her confidante of four nights before. So that's that, thought Madeleine sadly, she's back in the ghetto of the rich and feminine. Well, I never approved of her anyway, thought Madeleine.

When Madeleine's turn came, they took her to a small room where they laid her out on a couch. Whilst Mr Kalotheou talked to her in would-be-soothing tones they inserted a fine piece of plastic tubing into her vagina, then through her cervix and into her womb. A syringe was fixed to the other end and two of her eggs were propelled down the tube. 'Only two?' asked Madeleine. 'Only two,' said Mr Kalotheou firmly. He wouldn't transfer more for fear of multiple births; nor did he approve of aborting the extra foetuses as some clinics would. How proud he was of his virtue! Madeleine thought he all but boasted of it.

Afterwards she lay still on the couch as instructed and listened to the hospital's noises. Outside in the corridor she heard the nurses changing shifts. A tall, pretty Chinese girl, about as skinny as you could imagine, came into the room and leant over Madeleine with a huddle of thin shoulders as she took her blood pressure and her temperature. As she went out Madeleine saw that she wore a gold chain around one ankle. 'Am I all right?' Madeleine asked. Suddenly she wanted this baby very, very much. Madeleine thought that this Chinese nurse wouldn't have half her 'O' levels or her 'A' levels. But that's how it went. Out beyond the walls of academe other people had the knowledge and you had to bow to them. The nurse stopped, halfway out of the door. 'What?' she said in an absent voice, 'Oh yes, yes, you're fine.'

She left the door ajar so that Madeleine could hear the banter between the departing nurses – women's voices and laughter, making Madeleine think of girls' schools, hairdressers, harems.

'Well, girls,' the Chinese girl was calling out in her heavily accented voice, 'no sleeping in the gutters tonight. Remember you've got to work tomorrow.' Madeleine thought of all the men with whom she had competed for jobs and drunk with, pint for pint, because she was as good as them. But once you had babies, thought Madeleine, you entered a world of women – nurses, midwives, childminders, nannies, playground leaders, and then of course the primary school teachers, most of whom were women. I shall miss the men, thought Madeleine. How strange and how dreadful, thought Madeleine the feminist, to have to spend your life with women.

Loss began to chime inside Madeleine, one loss striking against another until they touched on the loss of her father and then all the losses of her life, like wind chimes, were striking and ringing together. It was years since she'd had nothing to do but lie in bed like this. It had a dreadful, melancholy Victorian feel about it. If she didn't do something soon her sadness would turn to panic, at being alone, at being perhaps childless, at counting for nothing, at being blown hither and thither helplessly by life. It's idleness that's the trouble, Madeleine thought. List six poems of loss. What literary work best expresses your predicament? But all she could think of was Mary Shelley's *Frankenstein*.

13

After the eggs had been put back inside her Mr Kalotheou sent her home with instructions to do as little as possible for a couple of days. She lay on her bed in the borrowed flat in Mornington Crescent and thought of the blobs floating in the blackness inside her. She pictured them like solitary astronauts floating in space and she prayed that they would implant themselves.

When the afternoon turned into evening there came a knock at the door. It was Martin with another document that he wanted her to sign. It was the first time he'd visited her in the flat. 'Are you all right?' he asked. 'Just a headache,' she said, lying back on the bed and lying through her teeth. She didn't want him to know what she'd been doing. And besides it was none of his business – she'd used donor sperm and the father was thus unknown, un-named, anonymous, and nothing to do with Martin. But still she felt bad because she knew what he would say: You bloody fool, how the hell are you going to look after a baby? Why on earth couldn't you wait until you'd found somebody else? But suppose I don't? thought Madeleine. Why should you take away from me my chance to have a baby, Martin Jenkins, just because you fancied some French au pair girl? And you can't rewrite history, she thought with satisfaction, even the would-have-been, should-have-been father will have his place in this. When she pictured the baby she might have, she saw it with Martin's features.

'This document,' he said, 'it's from the bank, terminating our joint account. I need your signature here and here,' and then he went out onto the balcony and leant against the railings. It was a fine, clear evening and from every window music was curling up like smoke. Below him an old man in a vest stood out on a balcony watering a thicket of roses whilst further down again a gang of children were sitting out on a walkway, smoking and talking. If you listened carefully you could just make out the faint babble in the air of human voices, from dozens of open-air gatherings, but all made hushed and languorous by the summer's night.

Madeleine lay on the bed and watched his back. Having lived with him for seven years she considered that she could still read the messages of his body. Now his back was saying to her, I don't understand why you came to live here, because of course, thought Madeleine, he was embarrassed that his wife, albeit his ex-wife, should be living in such dreary circumstances. On some nearby balcony a party was underway. A man's voice was singing, 'If you're going to San Francisco'. Madeleine saw Martin's face turn towards the revellers so that his nose and his glasses were visible. His nose said, 'You think these magical nights will last for ever. Well, I've got news for you. They won't. They'll finish when the weather turns, on the first day that it rains.'

It was the end of August and more than four months since he'd met Angelina and nearly six weeks since the house had been sold. Oh, you pompous, middle-aged snob, thought Madeleine.

She had wanted to believe that she had forgotten him, that he now meant nothing to her, that he couldn't touch her now because she was way beyond his reach. But that night Madeleine woke at one in the morning and a terrible panic overwhelmed her – the first really bad one since his defection – because he had left her and she couldn't get used to it. The room was hot and stuffy so she got up and went out onto the balcony, but that was worse, because here was all of London laid out before her and the dense black night overhead was both huge and claustrophobic, and said to her that she was a nothing, an insignificance, an abandoned woman whom no man wanted and who counted for nothing. The memory of Martin's ironic, worldly manner, his huge fund of knowledge, his I-earn-£50,000-a-year grandeur were all lumped together at this moment to make a stone that weighed down on her windpipe and ground and squeezed her lungs so that she gasped for breath.

But it was curious that she should remember the money because – although when they had lived together they had been like masters of the universe – going out three times a week and going on holiday four times a year and seeing all the new films and trying out all the new restaurants, at the time the money hadn't seemed to matter. It was only now that she remembered it, as a symptom of his grandeur. He had left her, taking with him his worldliness and his money and abandoning her like a scrap of litter. Oh, that bastard, Madeleine thought.

14

The morning that she went to have her eggs put back inside her – embryo transfer Mr Kalotheou called it – Gina was so nervous it took her an hour and a half to get dressed. She tried on half a dozen outfits and half a dozen pairs of shoes before she settled on the black linen shift dress and the leopard-skin, slingback sandals.

Gina loved these shoes. She only had to look at them to feel her skin prickle and a scratching and a tweaking of desire in her cunt. She had bought them three years before at a lucky time in her marriage, when George had been making a lot of money. He worked in the London office of a big American film company which made children's films of the violent, exciting kind that middle-class parents love to hate. Three years ago he had negotiated a good deal on a children's feature which was going to be very profitable. 'You can spend now,' he had said to Gina, and so she did, filling up the wardrobe with clothes that were so magnificent that you half-expected them, like wild animals, to get up and stroll around. It had been a wonderful spending spree, reviving in her an addiction that had begun when she was fifteen and her mother had taken her to an expensive shop in Knightsbridge – an addiction to the swooning sensation that comes from shopping in a rich man's world where nothing agitates by its poverty and everything soothes with its velvety expensiveness.

She had gone into Harvey Nicks and had slid her credit card across the counter and with this luxurious gesture had carried off the shoes in triumph and had laughed her way round the store with a girlfriend for sheer pleasure in the sexiness of shopping.

And afterwards she had taken the shoes home and had stripped off and had put them on whilst standing in front of the mirror in the studio. She and George lived in a flat in St John's Wood which was part of a house which had once belonged to the painter Augustus John. In the flat was a studio where the painter had alternately worked and screwed his mistresses, a beautiful room although also large and draughty, with a glass vaulted roof and a fireplace in one corner.

Here Gina had stood, brushing out her long hair and looking at herself wearing nothing else but the leopard-skin shoes and lipstick, when George had come into the room. He had come up behind her, a pretty man with grey eyes and tidy features, but with a certain steady hardness in his eyes and his mouth that saved him from being too pretty, too edible, too good enough to eat. He had pushed his head like a baby under the mass of her hair. 'You've been spending my money,' he had whispered into her ear and Gina had said to the mirror, 'Are you complaining?' But of course he wasn't, not really. It was just that it was sexy to reproach her whilst with one hand he held her round the waist and with the other undid the belt of his trousers. 'Here,' he had said, 'look what I've got for you,' and he had reached into his pocket and had drawn out a little white square of paper inside which was a small amount of a white powder. Because this was something they had lately got into, a line of cocaine – like a pinch of snuff – before they had sex, to give it added zest.

George was a taciturn, ambitious man, always brooding over who was getting the upper hand in the office or who was bad-mouthing him behind his back. He liked all the strong male pleasures – cards, drink, clubs, money, drugs and women – and was as self-contained and masculine and sexy, as Gina, with her breasts and flowing hair, was feminine. He liked to come home to her femininity – for him it was like a ball – although too much of it and he would start to yearn to be back amongst the men. It suited both George and Gina that the distance between the genders should be as big as possible.

After sex the day that Gina bought the leopard-skin sandals, George rolled on top of her and spread out her hair across the floor, parting her legs – 'She lies there in disarray,' said the script – marvelling at how easily and effortlessly, with her chin thrown back and all that neck and cheekbone showing, she could be turned into a raped beauty on the floor. But Gina shivered and said, 'This room's cold. Why don't we pull it down?' to which George responded, 'are you kidding?' because he liked to have her here on this floor where Augustus John had been before him, George being a sexy film man with an eye for a story (as well as for a deal and for a leading lady).

In Gina's marriage the pleasures of sex came round again and again, usually hand in hand with money, giving her the optimistic feeling that in a marriage nothing need ever die but simply returns again in a different guise, although each time the sex was more knowing and less innocent than before. This was sex the way that Gina liked it, with make-up and fancy dress, the clothes being props and accessories, but no less delightful for all that: leather jackets and flying jackets and satin trousers and boots with lips that you could lace up with a flip and a tug of your fingers and velvet great-coats and shoes to die for with heels like knives and jewellery worn on naked skin with painted nipples and shaven pubic hair, because that was another craze of theirs . . .

Gina's orgasms were operatic and extravagant. George received them all like bouquets tossed upon a stage. He would come in from work and he would say 'Dress up', and then he would lie down on the bed, still wearing his work clothes – a jacket, a shirt and a tie – and smoking a cigarette. And then Gina would stand in front of the mirrors that lined the room and would pull on her long boots and paint her nipples, even shave her pubic hair for him there and then, watching herself in the mirror, ripe-looking above and below the waist but with the waist itself still bendable, as if you could fuck her equally from in front and from behind. And then George would finish his cigarette and a whole company of him, reflected in the mirrors, would come strolling across – not quite as tall as her when you saw them side by side, with a spare, minimal, slightly gangsterish look about him, and his jacket very sexy against her naked skin. My man and his prick, my man and his prick, thought Gina complacently, because she liked the sound of these words. He was her man who earned her money by day and who screwed her by night and she loved him with her head and her heart and her cunt.

She'd always been good at sex. She'd discovered its pleasures early, easily the first girl in her year at school to have an orgasm, recognising that pleasure when it slayed her as the pleasure that she'd be good at – both at giving and having orgasms – as well as at drinking and dressing and undressing again. But it was a skill that brought her a reputation as a bad girl. She was expelled from her first school for dancing naked behind the tennis courts at midnight and afterwards she turned into the school absconder, running away from her next school four times in all and always in the same direction, to her mother's house in the south of France.

The first time she ran away she went with a girlfriend who was heading for her grandmother's flat in one of those grand, turn-of-the-century seaside resorts on the coast of Normandy – Deauville, perhaps, or Houlgate. Gina spent the night with her but the next day she went on south, because that was the pull, to pass through those familiar northern cities – Caen, Alençon, Le Mans – through a landscape of meadows and poplars and river valleys until, south of Tours, on the road to Poitier and Angoulême, the landscape grows wilder, the sun higher in the sky, the roadside stops dustier and more foreign, the forests full of hunting rifles, the toilets mere holes in the ground, the men's eyes dishing you up their rapist stares as they serve you thimblefuls of steaming espresso.

And then, in Angoulême, the blocks of flats – flat-roofed, of yellow concrete – which made you think of Africa; and south of Angoulême, the yellow sunflowers which grew taller than the car and the rivers which were so green and the sea, a blue memory to come. Oh, the pleasures of running away! It was as good as sex, it was better than drugs. The grown-ups didn't understand. They thought you ran away to frighten them, to sleep with strange men, because you were unhappy. But it was none of these things. The year she ran away she stopped sleeping with men altogether. There was a song which she particularly associated with those days and which could still bring it all back, in a sweet and twisty way.

After the fourth time, they took away her passport and her savings books and after that she went back to sex – not just with boys but with men of twenty-five or thirty, who hung around the school gates and upset the teachers. And after sex she discovered 'Drugs', as her teachers would say in tones of awe and fear – although it was never much more than dope and acid and the girls took it mostly for the camaraderie, which was important to them, since who else did they have but each other, so far away from home, in this boarding school? Finally, one night, she took some acid and took it in the boys' dormitory and was expelled and afterwards her mother and her mother's boyfriend sent her to a finishing school in Switzerland, but by then it was too late because the habits of a bad girl were tattooed upon her; and of ignorance as well, so that when she came back to London at eighteen and started to mess around, trying to be an actress or a model, she was beautiful but entirely uneducated, unable to do long division or to name the planets or to tell you anything about Augustus John.

But she always read a lot of novels, especially the feminine ones – Jean Rhys, Edith Wharton, Rosamund Lehmann – so she knew the feminine life and the feminine fate, which is usually a bad one, but how glorious it is along the way. And knowing these things, she knew how to mix a cocktail and where to touch a man to make him come and how to put on her make-up to best advantage and where to buy an evening dress and how to make and keep female friends, of whom she had dozens. All the women she knew were married to film producers and record company executives or lawyers who worked in television. None of these women really worked, but lived off their men and spent their days in health clubs and restaurants and hairdressers and beauty salons, all these places, but especially the hairdressers and beauty salons, being full of bits of women's bodies – heads wrapped up in white towel turbans, nails splayed out to dry, lips raised ceiling-wards to be painted, cheekbones shiny with cream laid back on pillows – and strong lights and assistants honey-voiced but firm – 'Now, Mrs Kaufman, you must stay still for another five minutes' – and an atmosphere both medical and luxurious.

But Gina wasn't stupid and she knew that beyond the circle of her friends there were other women who lived plainer, more hard-working lives than her, who worked and were even proud of it, and who under the guise of feminism would despise her for being beautiful and rich and idle. Gina was curious about these other women, curious but also tolerant and good-natured unless she felt herself despised, which she often did because they were a self-righteous lot, thought Gina, promoting work as if it were a greater virtue than any other – in which case she would despise them back for being sour and self-righteous and chippy about men.

There was one other thing that Gina knew, had known in fact for years, not even in her head but in her gut and her heart and her backbone, that she was, appearances notwithstanding, the maternal type and that one day she would want to have children.

She wanted a baby on every level, from the most frivolous – that she wanted to go where her girlfriends went, to children's parties and children's shops – to the most fundamental, waking in the night in a terrible panic, that she wasn't real, she wasn't human unless she had a baby. There she was, a riot of femininity, with her breasts and her swirling hair as she sucked George off, and one minute naked with a foot up on a chair lacing up her boots and the next minute on the ground, all bum, for George to screw her from behind – such a riot of first dominant and then passive femininity – and yet she couldn't make a baby. It was such a small thing, just a blending of egg and sperm together, and yet it kept eluding her. When she looked in the mirror she could see her phantom baby with absolute clarity, its fleshy, full-lipped looks – because of course it would look like her, the eyelids so heavy that they seemed to divide the eyes in two lengthways. And she could *feel* the phantom baby, even tracing its outlines as it sat upon her lap. But she simply couldn't make it, couldn't bring it to reality, couldn't flip it over from that universe to this, although of all bodies hers was surely the right one to make a baby?

One day George took her to visit a writer whose story he wanted to buy. This writer lived beyond Colchester on the coast of Essex so George took the Ferrari and Gina as well, because what is a Ferrari without a mass of hair and dark glasses to adorn it? But the writer proved tricky and wouldn't sell his story, and afterwards when George and Gina tried to buy a decent meal in the suburbs of Colchester all they could find were restaurants serving frozen scampi. George began to curse and in his temper lost his way and once lost it couldn't find it again; and meanwhile the road they were on grew steadily narrower and the light ahead of them whiter and more dazzling which could only mean that they were heading east towards the sea, but what did either of them know about the points of the compass?

At last the road gave up on a small, sandy clifftop, maybe ten or twenty feet high, with a caravan site behind them and a tussocky beach below. Gina climbed out of the Ferrari and stood there, clutching in the wind at her strands of hair. George sat in the driver's seat, examining a map and swearing. Gina tottered forwards on her stiletto heels to where the clifftop ended in tussocky mounds and hummocks. She saw a few children playing on the beach below, and a family asleep upon a blanket, mother and father at either edge like bookends, two children in between. A small boy looked up at the shiny green Ferrari on the clifftop.

George got out of the car and came up behind her. He put his arms around her waist. 'How about it?' he asked, but Gina shrugged him off because something had caught her eye in the family group below. The smallest child had sat upright on the blanket and still asleep had started to cry. The mother rolled over with a fluid movement – although she was a great whale of a woman and you wouldn't have thought she had one smooth, sleek movement in her – and taking the child between her legs she laid its head upon her stomach at which the child went out as swiftly and completely as if under an anaesthetic. That movement captured Gina. Again and again she saw the mother roll. Again and again she saw her haul the baby up onto her stomach. Again and again she saw the baby's consciousness obliterated like a point of light quenched by deep, dark water. But my stomach could do that, Gina thought. My body could work that magic on a baby.

It was soon after this that Mr Kalotheou discovered that Gina's tubes were blocked and recommended that she and George try in vitro fertilisation. Much as she complained, Gina enjoyed this first IVF experience. She liked the good-looking doctors and the pretty nurses fussing over her, because she always liked everyone to be good-looking. And she liked her girlfriends visiting her and calling out their sympathy and her menfriends coming up to her privately, one by one, and telling her that they were absolutely sure that their sperm – and nobody else's – could do the trick and give her what she wanted.

Philip the scriptwriter was one of those men who offered to give her a baby. He came up to her one day at a party which was being held in a house beside the Regents Canal. She was out in the garden beside the water, talking to a girlfriend. She wore a scarlet, strapless dress with a full, flounced skirt. It was not the kind of dress that she normally wore, but it suited her. The evening was grey and quiet. The water shone like tinfoil. The women leant against the garden railings, flower-like in their dresses, looking at the water and laughing with each other. When Philip came up to them the other woman said, 'Gina's bewailing all those years she spent worrying about contraception.' 'That was a waste of time,' said Gina. 'I'll give you a baby if George won't,' said Philip slyly. 'Go and get Marion pregnant if you want another baby, Philip,' said Gina. 'Marion says she's had enough. She wants a career. She's not like you,' said Philip. 'Now what does that mean?' asked the other woman. 'That I'm too idle,' said Gina. 'Or too beautiful,' said the other woman, and Gina laughed.

She should have been insulted on George's behalf but she found it difficult to get angry with Philip. Duncan Zahoun, on the other hand, was always annoying her. He was the man with the tropical tan, an accountant and a partner of George's in the film company that George had recently started. He had a plump and placid appearance, his mouth for ever open as if he were about to impart a secret. But although he accompanied them everywhere Gina had the feeling that it was George he was interested in, not her. She told George so and he laughed. 'So you think Duncan and I are having an affair, do you?' he said. It was like George to reduce what she said to absurdity the better to laugh at it.

Gina was always curious about the way other women lived and so she liked to cast her eyes over the other women in the clinic and to fall into conversation with them and discover the stories of their lives. She was much struck by the skinny, dark-haired girl who was a university teacher, although she

found Madeleine alarmingly spare and bleak in her manner –
as if she were the reverse of the King Midas story, as if everything
she touched would turn to iron, not gold. Even her femininity
had a painted-on feel about it, as if the feminine style were a
fancy-dress, just one of many that you could don. With those
looks, thought Gina, casting a professional eye over Madeleine,
she could never be pretty but she could be sexy; and yet of course
she wasn't and never would be, because the mind couldn't light
up the body in a sexy way. So how, thought Gina, do you get to
be the Madeleine-kind of woman, and not me?

The truth was that just as Madeleine condescended to Gina
for her lack of academic achievements so Gina pitied Madeleine
because her face and body were comparatively plain and because
she didn't drive a Ferrari and because she had no father for her
baby. Poor baby, thought Gina, to be brought up by a single
parent; although even as she thought this she was doubting
that Madeleine would ever get pregnant because her body was
so skinny and so unfeminine that Gina couldn't see how she
could ever make and hold a baby.

15

But Gina got Madeleine wrong, just as Martin did before her, because Madeleine got pregnant at her second attempt at IVF, and soon was one, two, three, four, five months so, with a swelling belly and arms and legs like sticks poked out on either side. It was no longer summer but cold, damp February and her face was blotched with strange patches of brown pigment that resembled a five o'clock shadow, whilst her back hurt from carrying her huge stomach and her nipples were the size of saucers and her feet were spread out into platters. Out in the streets she'd grown invisible. In the newsagent's the man behind the counter who had once fancied her now didn't even see her. On his shelves beneath the glossy magazines were the cheap magazines for mothers. It seemed that once you had a baby you were demoted from expensive women's fashions to cheap recipes for children.

Madeleine's money had come through from the sale of the house. She bought a flat in the heart of Camden Town. It was a tiny place, consisting only of a living room with a pair of sash windows, a fireplace, a cornice and a dado; one bedroom at the back with more of the same; and a kitchen and bathroom on the half landing. The rooms at the back looked out onto grey tiles and chimney pots and outhouses with barred windows and blackened glass and buddleias springing forth from their flat roofs. The room at the front looked out over a narrow chasm, between tall buildings, to more roofs and flashing signs and here and there a prettified roof garden, with pots and overflowing greenery, where a design consultancy had decided to posh up the property. From the very bottom of the chasm

– even through the glass – you could hear the steady roar of traffic.

Madeleine's mother came to see it. 'But where will the baby sleep?' she asked. 'In here with me,' said Madeleine shortly. She was cross with her mother who had lately begun to suggest that after all maybe children should have fathers. *Her*! *Of all people*! thought Madeleine indignantly, and when her mother said, 'Wouldn't it be better to buy a bigger flat in a less fashionable area?' Madeleine shrugged and said she liked it just fine where she was.

Down below was a minicab company. To the left and right were restaurants and bistros. All day long traffic roared past underneath the windows and when the summer came the sunlight would work upon these traffic fumes to cook them up into a fine stew of noxious pollution. But in the winter, on blue and rainy days when night came early and the lights in the bistro went on at four o'clock, the crowded streets had a kind of fug about them which was comforting. When Madeleine stood outside and looked up and down the street with half-closed eyes she could imagine that this wasn't London at all but some foreign city.

At night, grief and unhappiness floated upwards from the minicab company's premises: footsteps running to and fro, voices raised in protest and then sinking back down in entreaty; couples fighting; couples parting; voices angry, loving, weeping. One evening her mother came to see her and when it was time for her to go Madeleine took her downstairs to find a minicab. Her mother stepped down the stairs behind her with a crane-like delicacy. As they turned the corner two men appeared on the landing below, rolling over and over with a sudden clatter of aggression, each with his hands behind the other's head and beating it against the stairs whenever he was uppermost. Over and over they went, down and down, to shouts and screams from the onlookers and grunts and gasps from themselves. At last all went quiet. 'It doesn't seem a very suitable place to bring up a child,' said Madeleine's mother but Madeleine said stoutly, 'It's not far from college and there's a bookshop round the corner and the baby and I can have breakfast together in the bistro on a Saturday morning.'

Mercedes-Sally was right. With motherhood there came a certain mushiness of spirit, both inside and out. Madeleine was eating constantly. Her thighs were soft and squashy, her face as round as a baby's. And all the time she was thinking of sex which she never used to do, soft and squashy sex, sex from behind, victim-sex, sex on your hands and knees like an animal whilst faceless men with pricks like columns lined up to screw you. She bought herself a copy of *L'Histoire d'O* and went to bed to read it. She thought, if I am going to read pornography let it be pornography of the classy, literary kind. She couldn't find her old, brittle, hard-edged self at all. She felt as soft as a confectioner's trifle. Sometimes on a Saturday morning she lay in bed in a daze with her fingers between her legs, chasing orgasm after orgasm, as if, thought Madeleine, I were chasing heroin visions.

Another time she was passing Fenwick's when she thought she'd go inside and buy herself some knickers. (The pair she was wearing were plain white and came from Woolworths.) She stepped in through the doors. She steamed and stamped on the carpet, smelly in her wet winter wool jacket, like an animal. She went through the make-up hall and under an arch and no sooner had she stepped through than she fell, as if into bed, into such an array of silk and satin and lace and frills and leaves and roses – French knickers, camiknickers, camisoles, bustiers, all in straw and snow and rose and apricot and cappuccino – that she started to feel dizzy and pleasure began to creep upwards from her groin and to tickle her tummy and to fill up her throat. If she could she would have lain down there and then upon the carpet, so slain was she by sexual pleasure in Fenwick's lingerie department.

What am I going to do? thought Madeleine. I'm an academic. I have to live by my brains but here they are, all soft and mushy.

And pregnancy brought other feelings too, sharper and more bitter. One afternoon in February she went shopping in the fruit market in Camden Town. It was one of those grey, winter days when the wind is so sharp that the eyes of all the passers-by seem to glitter with tears; when the sky weeps and the bare black trees are drawn with pencil and the brick façades of Arlington Road are furred and blurred by poverty and decay. She stood where the market stalls peter out into orange peel and rotten cabbages and looking up she saw a parapet and that's what got her. Because Martin had been an architectural correspondent and so it was a glimpse of a house, a view, a parapet, a silhouette against the sky, an angle that he might or did admire that ruined her.

And another time it was the rear view of a big man dressed in a camel-coloured overcoat and a tiny, slender woman beside him, going into M & S. Martin had always liked small women. The size of the man and the slenderness of the woman were welded together to make a sharp knife that cut her. Oh Martin, Martin, thought Madeleine. She was still astounded that he could discard her so easily, that he could leave her without a backward glance, that he could live so flourishingly without her.

It was about this time that she fell out with Mercedes-Sally who had been her best friend through all the childless years. She and Mercedes-Sally had arranged to meet one night in the bistro downstairs from Madeleine's flat but Madeleine was late because she couldn't find anything to wear. When she stepped into the bistro she saw that all the women were dressed in shades of brown – tan, molasses, honey, cinnamon – with a look of sugared sweetness about their hair and faces, as if they had been dipped head down into candyfloss. Was it their youth or the candlelight which gave this impression? Already Madeleine felt as if she didn't belong in this world. 'I see that brown is in this year,' said Madeleine. All that she'd been able to find was an unfashionable shade of pink.

Mercedes-Sally wanted to talk about her new job but Madeleine was too distracted to listen. She had just realised to her horror that on £20,000 a year and with a large mortgage to pay she could scarcely afford childcare. 'But what will happen to me if I don't work?' she said. 'I don't understand you,' said Mercedes-Sally. 'If you're going to have a baby why are you talking the whole time about finding someone else to bring it up? If you've done something as conventional as getting pregnant why don't you bring it up yourself? My mother brought me up. Come to think of it, maybe I believe in that.' Madeleine was hurt. 'You wouldn't stay at home and bring up a child,' she said. 'I wouldn't get pregnant in the first place,' said Mercedes-Sally brutally and Madeleine could have cried, Mercedes-Sally made her feel so lonely.

Now that she was heavily pregnant she only went to college on two days a week whilst the rest of the time she worked from home. She didn't go to antenatal classes because she didn't want to meet other mothers. At the hospital she sat side by side with them and listened to what they said. Many of them had one or more children already. These children scrambled all over their mothers, turning them into many-armed and many-legged mountains. The mothers gave off a whiff of self-sacrifice and martyrdom which alarmed Madeleine mightily.

One day Madeleine sat next to a good-looking, weary young woman dressed in a long, blue, wool cape which draped across her stomach and fell between her legs. She was reading a novel by Virginia Woolf. A little boy played at her feet and she kept pushing him away with distracted, automatic movements. The little boy wore a thick jacket with a fur-lined hood and soft, suede boots laced up above his slender ankles. When she got up to go to the desk he ran after her with a swagger of his narrow hips, calling out, 'You forgot me, you forgot me,' in a voice both princely and reproachful. When she sat down again he tripped over Madeleine's outstretched foot.

'Jonathan,' his mother reproached him in a remote and weary voice.

'It's all right,' said Madeleine.

Jonathan began to cry. His mother took him on her lap and comforted him. At last he stopped crying. 'I want some chocolate,' he said.

'Well, fancy that,' she said, and her voice had a sweet-sharp resignation about it. 'Is this your first?' she asked, nodding at Madeleine's stomach.

'Yes.'

'It's my third,' she said, 'The oldest one's at school.'

'Three!' said Madeleine.

'I know! I must be mad. You're not going to get any less tired, my husband says. But in the long run it makes sense, because then they can all play together.'

She wants to be friends, thought Madeleine, who now that she'd fallen out with Mercedes-Sally needed another friend. And yet she wasn't ready to have anything to do with the sweet-sharp resignation of motherhood. 'Do you work?' asked Madeleine. 'I work at bringing up my children,' said the woman, roused to defiance by Madeleine's scornful tone. So that was the end of that.

The truth was that Madeleine was afraid. Scarcely a day passed but that she thought of something else that frightened her. She was afraid of the dowdiness and intensity and the martyrdom of motherhood. She was afraid for the loss of her body and its good straight lines. She was afraid of the mushiness of pregnancy, and how feelings flooded down between her legs where the baby was going to come and flooded over her throat. And she was afraid of the domesticity of motherhood, because only now did she realise that once you have a baby you not only have to cook for it but you have to clean the toilets and wash the sheets and hoover the carpets as well. Madeleine couldn't cook. She didn't know how to clean. Up until now she'd always preferred a room full of dust and books and take-aways.

All those months ago when she'd lain awake in the clinic she had assumed that it would be she, not Martin, who kept their friends. But it wasn't true. One by one they had gone with Martin, preferring no doubt his good nature and his easy chairs and his comfortable cooking. So now she sat alone in the clinic listening to the talk of nappies and bottles and routines, and whilst dimly she could see that there has to be an inarticulacy about motherhood because at the heart of it lies something which cannot be said – even so she was depressed by all this talk of domesticity. It's the Dead Mother's Club, thought Madeleine, and the next time her mother said that her flat was unsuitable for children Madeleine said, 'But you don't understand. I'm not going to be a mother in the way that other women are.'

16

Ella was born late one evening in April, to screams of admiration from the midwives – 'But she's so beautiful,' they cried, as she sprang out, fully-formed already, into a nervy, bad-tempered, large-eyed beauty whom they put into Madeleine's arms. There she lay, crop-haired, heavy-lidded and long-lashed, with a bee-stung lower lip and an intent and dreaming expression.

But an hour later she started to cry and all that first night she cried without stopping. It was a terrible, rending cry that yanked at Madeleine's extremities, at her toes, at her fingers, at her nose, at the roots of her hair each time she drifted off to sleep, until Madeleine felt herself pulled in every direction. Once, twice, three times the nurses came in. In the darkness they took Ella out of Madeleine's arms and carried her down the ward, rocking her and whispering, 'You naughty child, you naughty child.' They put her at Madeleine's breast. They hurried off and came back with bottles of milk. They took her to the nursery because she was waking up the other mothers. They even called the doctor to examine her.

At last when it was nearly morning Ella fell asleep through sheer exhaustion with her fists beside her head and her knees folded out on either side to form a diamond. Thus composed at last they brought her back to Madeleine and Madeleine looked at her and knew that the different parts of her love for her baby were fixed already: the blind, maternal love of course; but also an anger and a puzzlement that she should be so wilful; an astonishment at her beauty; and a feeling of protectiveness – this very strong – because it seemed that everyone but Madeleine disapproved of this child.

Right from the start when Madeleine looked at Ella the words were wrung out of her – 'I love that child, I love that child' – with a kind of painful pleasure. And it was Ella's beauty in particular that clutched at Madeleine's heart, although this was peculiar because previously Madeleine hadn't cared at all about women's beauty – brains and ambition and achievements being everything.

When Ella was four months old Madeleine left her three days a week with a childminder so she could teach at a summer school. The childminder was a cool, brisk young woman with two children of her own. She had a plain but polished appearance and each of her movements was definite and a touch complacent, as if to say, 'We do things like this round here. I think you'll find that children like a routine, you know. You simply have to lay it down for them.'

When she opened the door to Madeleine on the first day Ella was crying as usual. 'Yes, yes,' said the childminder, picking Ella out of her basket, 'but you know that we get nothing by screaming, do we?' and she began to straighten the baby's clothing and to rub down her little stomach. The other children were tugging at her skirt but the woman was as cool as marble and quite as impervious, so that try as you might, thought Madeleine, to scramble up her slippery sides you would always slide down again. I should have known it wouldn't work, thought Madeleine afterwards, but at the time she'd been tired and distracted and she'd needed to work and so she'd turned away from the door in hope.

Three days later the childminder rang Madeleine in the middle of a lecture. 'I'm sorry,' she said, 'but I've got to cancel our arrangement. I've never known a baby cry like this. There must be something wrong with her. She's upsetting my children. When can you come and fetch her?' Self-righteous cow, thought Madeleine, but when she took Ella back the baby stopped her screaming and lay quietly looking up at her.

It was Nicola of all people who saved Madeleine's life on that occasion. Nicola was the woman who had been reading Virginia Woolf in the antenatal clinic and whose friendship Madeleine had spurned. But Nicola had turned up again – this time in the park – a pretty woman, married to a financial journalist with three children, the youngest of whom was a baby like Ella, and a handbag full of novels. This time Madeleine did not rebuff her.

Nicola made Madeleine think of old-fashioned quilts – pretty rather than sexy, classy but domestic – with a sweet, sharp, cynical, humorous and despairing way of talking. Nicola didn't believe in feminism. Instead, behind her and looking over her shoulder, stood Mrs Beeton and Benjamin Spock and Emily Lennox, Duchess of Leinster, who in the eighteenth century bore her beloved husbands twenty-one children. Nicola liked history and heritage and old buildings and Victoriana, her interests chiming in with her nature, which was sadly to accept her own half-realised hopes and the compromises that she'd made. Nicola was so humorous and despairing that you could tell her anything. 'Sometimes I think having children is like a death,' Madeleine would say, or 'The trouble with having babies is that you leave the twentieth century behind and enter a nineteenth-bloody-century moral scheme in which hopes are dashed and ambitions curbed and individualism punished, as if they were something disgraceful.' And to all this Nicola would smile and shrug with a weary acceptance.

It was an awkward friendship. Half the time she and Madeleine were loving and the rest of the time they eyed each other up, and Madeleine thought, how terrible to be her, so domestic and good because she lives in that other country, that country of married women; whilst Nicola looked at Madeleine and thought, how could she land herself in this situation, with a child and no father and having to work all the hours of the day and night just to make ends meet?

But when Ella was expelled from the childminder Madeleine understood at last why it was that mothers stuck together. For whom else could they turn to in the crises that continually beset them? Diffidently she rang up Nicola. 'Could you have Ella?' she asked, 'just for tomorrow. The agency will have found me someone by Thursday.'

'Oh God,' said Nicola, 'and of course she would ring in the middle of a lecture. Isn't it all a nightmare? Shall I come in the morning and take Ella up to my house?'

'She'll cry,' said Madeleine sadly.

'I expect she will,' said Nicola, 'but since she's not my child I shan't worry too much.' And she came the next day, dressed in a long frock and a hat, and scooped up Ella, calling out, 'Isn't she beautiful? But doesn't she cry. Oh, you dreadful child,' she said to Ella – but really quite affectionately – as she paced the room with her.

How kind she is, thought Madeleine in surprise – as kind to real people as she is unkind to ideas, to the ideas of Feminism, and Career Women who Go out to Work and Leave their Children, and Hippies and Drug-takers, all of which ideas alarmed Nicola mightily.

17

When Ella was five months old Madeleine went back to work full-time. But quite soon she realised that her boss, Professor Atkins, was trying to ease her out of the English department. Her access to the computer had been reduced. Memos concerning meetings had started to go astray. She was told at a staff meeting that because of the closer ties they were forming with linguistics her office was going to be moved to a room at the end of a parallel corridor – a smaller room of course – although this wasn't said – and hard to find, where she would be cut off from the mainstream of gossip and conversation that flowed up and down the main corridor where the rest of the English department was situated. Finally she heard from a colleague that it had been proposed, at a Friday meeting which she hadn't attended because Ella had been ill, that her course on post-Second World War literature was going to be dropped. 'To put a greater emphasis on traditionals, you know,' the professor had said. 'We need our solid core, Wordsworth, Chaucer, Shakespeare. These things are important.'

Madeleine was dumbstruck. The realisation that he was trying to get rid of her shot through her so quickly she thought she was going to be sick. She was amazed that it had taken her this long to notice. What's more, since he hated overt opposition, he must have sounded out all kinds of people before venturing out this far against her – and yet not one whisper had reached her ears. She saw him in the corridor half an hour later. The whole bulk of him from his great, square face to his dainty little feet loomed up and past her and he blushed round the edges of his jowly face, the blush mingling with his usual look of bewilderment and telling her that he felt guilty and a little frightened of her, but smugly pleased as well.

That night she couldn't sleep. She turned over and over on the bed. She was furious with herself for being so blind, terrified at the prospect of losing the career she had so carefully nurtured, of herself and Ella being cast out penniless into the streets. She conjured up a picture of the professor – of his grey hair and his eyes that drooped with sadness at the corners and his dainty feet and his toes turned out and his gliding walk. Now, too late, she realised that when you reproached him it was rage that suffused his face with smiles and blushes; realised too that once he had fancied her – or rather, that his dislike of her had made him want to screw her – but now, since she'd got pregnant, he didn't fancy her any more but simply disliked her; and so her hold on him was weakened.

She got out of bed. She went across to the bookshelf and pulled down one of his books. She read the blurb and tried to work out what his age would be. About fifty-seven or fifty-eight, she thought. Soon he would be an old man, with an old man's vanity and secret hates and fears about mortality and wails of where's-my-dinner? and why-have-you-all-left-me? King Lear, thought Madeleine. What do I know about an old man's mind, except through books? And would I have known more if I had ever had a father? Probably, thought Madeleine.

She looked at herself in the mirror and saw a bleak, plain, middle-aged reflection. The flounced skirts, the painted nails, the shoes with flowers and bows, all these had gone, and yet although the transformation was sad, it also seemed to Madeleine to be sadly natural. Her days were as regimented as a nun's. She got up at half past five and worked for an hour until the baby woke. Between half past six and half past eight she played with Ella, washed her, fed her and dressed her, washed and dressed herself, put on her make-up, cleared away the breakfast things and got herself ready to leave. She was at work by nine and worked straight through the lunch hour – lecturing, tutoring, marking and attending meetings. She got home by six, played with Ella, fed her, bathed her, read to her and put her to bed by nine if she was lucky. Then she cleared up and after that she worked for a couple more hours, and went to bed at eleven thirty. These days it seemed that there was not one of her but three – Ella, herself and the childcare – and that her qualities had been accordingly redistributed, and Ella was Youth and the childcare was Femininity but she was Finance and Efficiency.

Madeleine put on a suit, lipstick and high-heeled shoes and went to see her professor. She leant against his desk and, smiling down at him, she asked after his research and wondered if he'd like to read a paper that she'd written. She wasn't used to this role – she felt awkward and angular – whilst he looked fearful, his upturned face tense as if expecting a blow. She realised then that in the months since Ella had been born she had frightened him by affording him a glimpse beneath the feminine surface to a terrible maternity. And yet it wasn't hard to soothe him. His expression was opening out already, blossoming into smiles. She didn't like her new, placating role – it smacked of the underdog – and yet what else could she do? She didn't expect to save her post-war literature course but she thought she could stop any further encroachments.

After the demise of the childminder with sides as smooth as marble, Madeleine, who couldn't afford a trained nanny, got in a series of girls by advertising on the backs of magazines. Years later when she looked back on these times she couldn't remember the names or the faces of these girls. What remained was a cumulative impression of women's bodies – hair and breasts and legs; shoes left in corners and handbags left open on chairs so that they spilled out make-up and perfume and address books and deodorant; complex ties of love and need – the boyfriends that the nannies adored, the children they had left behind in far-off countries for lack of passports, the mothers they loved and who were dying: an impression of youthful, dreadful, masochistic femininity.

Only one of them did Madeleine remember well, and that was Lisa who, with her riotous femininity and her manipulativeness, seemed to Madeleine to be all the girls writ large.

She was a tiny Philippino girl, young and slender and not much more than four foot eleven. She laughed a lot and at her interview she squatted down in front of Ella with a supple movement and ringing of her jewellery. She had long, black, shiny hair and when she picked up Ella the child's legs hung down past her knees as far as her long hair hung down her back, whilst Ella's face poked over her shoulder like a bright and shiny coin. She might do, Madeleine thought, for she was way beyond disapproving of so much conventional femininity. And besides, Lisa being so pretty herself might appreciate Ella's beauty and that might make up for the fact that Ella was always crying.

In fact, of all her nannies Ella liked Lisa best. In the evenings when Lisa gave Ella back the child smelt of Lisa's perfume. One day Lisa said to Madeleine, 'My friends – they all say how beautiful she is – they ask me, "Who does she look like, her father or her mother?" and I say, "She looks like me,"' and Lisa laughed uproariously. And another time in the morning when she came in through the door she said to Ella, 'Come to me, my little one, and let me steal you.'

Now, too late, Madeleine learnt that Lisa had a little boy whom she had left at home in the far-off tropics to be brought up by her older sister. 'My sister was jealous of me,' said Lisa, 'because I was pretty and she was ugly. When I was fifteen all the men wanted to marry me so my sister went to our father and said, "You can't let Lisa marry until you've found me a husband,"' and Lisa smiled complacently.

One February afternoon Madeleine came home early from work. The street outside the flat was deep in shadows and only a scrap of bright sky showed over the tops of the roofs. The sun was going down in chilly scarlet and the air was so cold that it grabbed your throat and sat painfully inside your lungs. Lisa was standing outside the minicab company's premises, talking to one of the drivers whilst Ella sat beside her in her buggy. What's my child doing outside in this cold? thought Madeleine, and then – with a flash of the telepathy that Lisa sometimes afforded her – I bet she fancies minicab company drivers, the kind who do a little armed robbery on the side and who sleep with shotguns by their beds.

It was terrible to be afforded these glimpses of Lisa's mind. Lisa came to her in tears one day. She was pregnant, possibly three months so, but the father of the baby was married and what was she to do? Madeleine suspected one of the minicab company drivers downstairs. She began to wonder just when Lisa had got pregnant, and what she and Ella did all day? Lisa had a stubborn streak. If you recommended playgroups and parks to her a mulish look came into her eyes. Madeleine wanted to advise an abortion – anything else was madness – but with a dreadful intuition she knew that if she did Lisa would blame her afterwards for doing away with her baby.

Madeleine was tired of rampant femininity and how perceptive she had grown about it. Sometimes she thought longingly of the world of men, of men tied, jacketed and be-suited, of men as cool as cucumbers, sitting in pubs with their briefcases by their sides, talking about work. She missed the world of men – not sex, she hadn't thought about that for years – but the company of men. When Lisa said she had something to tell her Madeleine knew, even before she opened her mouth, that she was taking her unborn baby home to make a present of it to her family. Madeleine rang an agency and spent some of her savings on a nanny with qualifications called Carol. The day that Lisa left Madeleine became convinced that she was planning to take Ella with her. All the way home from work she sat on the bus with a feeling of grim resignation, the weary knowledge that she would never see her child again. When she stepped into the flat and saw Lisa with Ella in her arms she had the feeling that she was being tested, the layers of hard experience being laid down – like when she and Ella made papier mâché, building up the strips of paper and glue to make a steely structure – but for what? wondered Madeleine.

When Carol came to work on Monday morning Ella cried at the sight of her whilst Carol looked around and began to complain about Madeleine's poor flat and the fact that she was not as rich as her friends' employers. But Madeleine didn't care. It was enough that Carol was efficient and not at all feminine and all that spilled out of her handbag were packets of Polos.

By the time that Ella was two she had turned into a skinny child with so little flesh to spare that when she fell ill she quickly acquired a death-like skinniness. She had a huge range of nervy fads and fancies. For instance, when leaving the house she would only turn left and never right, and any attempt to push the buggy in the opposite direction would bring about a fit of screaming. She would wear only one pair of trousers and that with a pair of shorts on top. She would eat only avocados, wouldn't sleep in her cot but only on the sofa – and then only from half past ten to six o'clock, wouldn't leave Madeleine's lap, screamed for an hour and a half when she saw a spider, would smile only if she chose to and refused ever to kiss or be kissed.

Every day she did something that baffled Madeleine. She's my child, thought Madeleine, and I don't understand her. She began to think about the unknown father and to wonder what he might have contributed to Ella's personality. She even speculated that she might track him down and find out what he was like – simply in order to understand Ella better – although Mr Kalotheou had made it clear that the father was beyond her reach and even beyond Ella's, at least until Ella was eighteen.

And meanwhile it seemed to Madeleine that everyone disapproved of her. When Ella had been a baby, old ladies in the park had come up to her and had said, 'You pick that baby up too often. You should leave her to cry. They need their crying time, you know.' And, now that Ella was two and was having temper tantrums, other mothers shook their heads and said, 'Just ignore her, Madeleine. She'll soon stop crying if you take no notice.'

Even Madeleine's mother disapproved. One day Madeleine

took Ella home. Ella sat on Madeleine's lap. She had a mop of blonde hair which hid her face and which Madeleine kept pushing back, as if to show to her mother that at least Ella was beautiful; which indeed she was, for the lines of her cheekbones, her brow, her mouth and her chin all had a bell-like purity about them, reminding Madeleine that it was Ella's nervy beauty, her terrible skinniness, her strangeness and her crying which had moulded Madeleine's love for her into such an awkward painful shape.

But Madeleine's mother gave Ella a from-a-great-distance look as if really this baby had nothing to do with her, and said, 'Perhaps you need to say "no" to her more often.'

'You mean she's spoilt,' snapped Madeleine.

'Well, they do say that children are happier with clear boundaries,' said Madeleine's mother in her mild voice.

'Well then, you leave her to cry,' said Madeleine crossly, 'You sit and listen to her crying for hours on end.'

'She wouldn't cry for more than half an hour.'

'That's not true,' said Madeleine more crossly than ever.

She was angry with her mother who behaved as if having a grandchild was a pleasure but no obligation at all, although – to be truthful – it seemed to Madeleine no more possible to leave Ella in her mother's charge than to leave her with the blackbird at the end of the garden.

One Saturday morning Ella disappeared. Madeleine had taken her to Kenwood. It was a mild winter's morning and they were sitting out in the café garden whilst Ella watched the pigeons and Madeleine drank a cup of coffee.

One minute Ella was standing beside her, the next minute when she looked round Ella was gone. Madeleine got to her feet. She began to search, slowly at first, under tables, behind chairs, inside the café proper. No Ella. She began to look more quickly – behind family groups, inside the café again, as far as the edge of the garden, across the forecourt and up the steps to where the path began. Still no Ella. Panic began to shift, to stir, to rise, to press. She remembered what she'd read about child abductions, that the first minutes are crucial. Panic was now rushing up the middle of her like steam up a chimney but the fringes of her mind stayed calm and with these she observed herself stepping up to the tea and coffee counter where stood a Mediterranean-looking young man in a white apron.

'Excuse me,' she said, 'I can't find my child.' He stared at her and wiped his hands on his apron. 'Excuse me,' she said more loudly, 'I've lost my child,' and now two old ladies at the table next to her looked up over their crocodile handbags and she noticed with satisfaction that she'd set loose a whisper of anxiety amongst them. 'My child,' she said, her voice rising, 'My child is lost,' but all the time looking over her shoulder in case – please God! – Ella should reappear. But the café and the garden remained empty of Ella, and now the whisper of anxiety was spreading along the tables and people were looking up until at last – but terribly slowly – the Mediterranean-looking boy said something to the older man behind him and wiping his hands on his apron he raised the counter and stepped out. 'Where?' he said, and it was like a signal for all to push back their chairs and get up. 'Where have you looked, love?' an old woman asked, and so it began.

They searched the garden and the toilets and the dustbins and the stairs leading up to the path and the flowerbeds towards the exit and the path which led beside the house and round to the ornamental garden and the rhododendrons and the shrubbery. It seemed that all the old women who had haunted Ella's babyhood with their words of advice for Madeleine, now reappeared. One old woman with ancient flame-coloured hair piled high into a beehive said, 'Children are a terrible grief, you know,' whilst the two old women with the crocodile handbags said, 'You shouldn't let them out of your sight, love, not for one minute;' and all the while families kept parading past her, just as if nothing had happened, strolling along the dinky paths which ran towards the eighteenth-century bridge which shone placidly in the winter sunlight.

At last the young man in the white apron went to ring the police whilst Madeleine, still frantically searching, began to cast her mind far into the future and to say to herself, 'If you never see her again you must keep calm, you must keep it under control, you mustn't let it eat you up,' when all of a sudden there stood Ella, blinking, on the path where all was black and white because of the winter sunshine and the shadows of the shrubbery. Her eyes were full of sunlight. She looked bewildered. She was crying and hiccuping like a drunkard, because she'd only gone looking for pigeons and she didn't know where she was. Her tears were huge. She thrust a finger up into one of them and Madeleine saw the fingertip underwater, magnified hugely.

But when she saw Madeleine she ran up to her and sank her new white teeth deep into her mother's hand as punishment for leaving her, and for a month after this she cried bitterly whenever she remembered how once she had been lost. Again Madeleine had the feeling that she was being tested, that each painful bout of love, each sharp pang of loss, was felt in order to make her stronger. But against what? For what eventuality was she being prepared?

19

George and Gina tried IVF five times before they called it a day. At their first attempt five of Gina's eggs had been fertilised. Proudly Mr Kalotheou had rung her up and asked her to come and see them. She had stood over her test tube and peered down the microscope and seen the embryos divided into eight, like fragments of a blackberry, drawn with pen and ink. Gina had been touched to see that these little bits of her body's essence, which for years had met and mated in darkness and in secrecy, could and would perform for her in public. But even so she had thought that they deserved better. 'Couldn't you at least turn the lights down?' Gina had said to Mr Kalotheou. 'How would you like it, fucking with the spotlight on you?' and she had been satisfied to see him richly blush.

But this first attempt, which began so promisingly, had nonetheless been a failure. On their second and third attempts the eggs didn't fertilise at all. On their fourth attempt four eggs were fertilised and Gina felt that this time she really might get pregnant, but after a couple of weeks she began to bleed and this so demoralised her that she didn't care at all when the fifth attempt was a failure. After this, she told George that she wouldn't try again, that she was fed up, that she wanted a holiday in the Caribbean and could she have the £3,000 that each attempt had cost them and spend it on cocaine and jewellery instead?

But although Gina thought she didn't care about babies any longer, for a long time after this she was distraught. She didn't know what to do with herself. All her friends had babies and just the shopping for their clothes seemed enough to keep them occupied. There was no point in her trying to work because there was nothing she could do out there. She thought of entertaining George's clients at home, but George had long ago got used to taking them to restaurants and now had come to prefer it. She tried charity work and for a while it gave her a smooth, sweet feeling of virtue but she wasn't very organised and quickly got bored and besides George didn't take it seriously. So after that there was nothing but drink and drugs and sex to get her through the day; and even sex, in too large quantities, palled, because it was like eating cake all day.

And if it was hard to live in the here and now without a baby then the future without a child seemed even more intolerable. One evening at a drinks party Gina was struck by the sight of a man and his wife, clients of George's, the man, middle-aged, running to fat, expensively tanned and blinking in a lazy, bemused kind of way whilst his wife with a champagne glass between her fingers was chatting animatedly to a pretty boy. The boy wore a black jacket and winkle-picker boots. The wife smiled and leant towards him as if really it were the pretty boy that she wanted to run between her fingers. To Gina it seemed that both husband and wife had the same look, as if something had arrested their development, as if they had put out shoots but just before the moment of blossoming their growth had been cut off.

There was something they wanted that they didn't get, thought Gina. That's how you grow old when the one thing that you hankered after wasn't granted to you. Is that how I'll grow old? and she thought bitterly that mothers have it easy, that anyone can live in tune with their instincts, that what's so difficult is to try to cross them.

Another day Gina took her credit cards and went shopping in South Molton Street. Afterwards she went to the bank on the corner of Oxford Street to get herself some cash but she and George had reached their overdraft limit and the bank would give her nothing, so Gina took a bus home up the Edgware Road with her last one pound coin – something which she'd scarcely ever done before.

As she waited at the bus stop her eyes settled on a young man waiting for the bus. He was tall and plump with a fat, sensual face and large brown eyes. His dark hair curled down over his shoulders. He wore a long, black overcoat with white socks just visible underneath and expensive-looking moccasins that were downtrodden at the back. His hair was dark and richly curled and he looked to Gina like a chocolate cake with thick cream and dark and milk chocolate icing on the top. But what really caught her eye was the bundle that he carried, a baby wrapped up so thickly in a blue nylon sleepsuit that it lay flat out in his arms as stiff as a board. From time to time he patted vaguely in the direction of its bottom.

Gina sidled up to him to see what the baby looked like, but the young man was tall as well as large and he held the baby high. The bus came and Gina let the man get on first so that when he sat down she could sit down beside him. 'How nice,' she said, nodding in the direction of the baby. 'Can I see?' He stared at her in puzzlement and she realised that he probably spoke no English. Even so he must have understood enough because he tilted the baby down in her direction. 'Oh,' went Gina, because the baby was very young, hardly more than three weeks old, and asleep with that look that tiny babies have – inturned, composed, as if still dreaming of its previous existence. It had a thick black fringe the colour of dark chocolate and its lips were cherry-red. Reposed in its sleeping suit it looked like a chocolate figure in cellophane wrapping. Gina thought that at the slightest movement it would rustle.

'Oh,' went Gina again, her breath coming out with difficulty and something clutching at her stomach and making her want to pee. A woman in the seat in front turned round. She was the maternal-looking type, big-bosomed with a look as if a hundred babies had marched across that way. She smiled at Gina. She smiled at the baby. 'Isn't it sweet?' she said. Gina shrugged and looked away. The maternal type wouldn't stop her cooing. Gina gave her a cold look. She thought, I wonder if that baby really belongs to him? Something in the way the man was holding it made her think that perhaps it wasn't his. But then again, maybe she was only attributing to him her own stealing fantasies?

She cast another look at the baby – and, Oh God, it had opened its eyes and had started to munch its mouth like a little old man. I'd like to hold it, thought Gina, but what had seemed to her simply a light thought became suddenly alarming, because there were her fingers, of their own accord twitching and itching in the direction of the baby, even getting so far as to touch the slippery nylon, whilst her breath froze in her chest and her mouth curved in a shape somewhere between a smile and a cry. I want it, she thought, I want it.

She stood up hurriedly on her tottery high heels, with her shopping clutched against her and with one last cold look at the maternal type and one look of yearning at the baby she got off the bus. She waited by the bus stop until she felt calmer, until she was able lightly and humorously to think, if things go on like this I shall be quite a danger to other people's babies.

And George also was beside himself. He kept staring at other people's children in the street and watching the children of their friends. It was hopeless to ask him why he wanted children – 'why' questions never interested him. Perhaps he only wanted them because other people had them, which would make it an ordinary ambition but nonetheless a powerful one and not to be dismissed, because probably everything he had done had been because other people did it. He had girlfriends of course, and that was bad enough, but suppose one day one of them gave him a baby?

These girlfriends. Gina knew about them in various ways. She knew about them because of the looks that George gave women at parties and because of the looks that women gave George. And she knew about them because her friend Charlie warned her, murmuring in her ear as she strolled past, 'Your replacement's here, darling,' because Charlie and Gina had an agreement, to keep an eye out on each other's behalf, for thus at least the loyalty of your friends could be a consolation. And she knew when George had a girlfriend because he was laughing and distracted and spent hours grooming himself in the mirror and at night slept with his back to her, his shoulders hunched as if thus he could exclude her.

It seemed to Gina that George never thought about their marriage, although Gina did. Like many people without children she valued her marriage precisely because that was all she had. In the evenings when George was still at work she used to lie in the unmade, luxurious bed, flipping through women's magazines and novels and trying out the pills that she got hold of from her girlfriends. These pills, it seemed to Gina, cast a slantwise but truthful illumination on her marriage. They caused odd images to pop into her head and under their influence she found she could spin out sentence after sentence to explain her life. 'Marriage,' said Gina, lying between the satin sheets and rather out to lunch on a couple of dove-grey sweeties, 'Marriage,' said Gina, having not bothered to dial the number and so talking to an imaginary friend down the telephone, 'Marriage is like the Tardis, hugely bigger on the inside than the out.' In fact, on the inside it was like a continent where you can find every kind of terrain from intense love to intense hate and all gradations in between – 'and where,' said Gina sadly, 'you think at the beginning that you will walk hand in hand with your partner, but afterwards you discover that each person walks alone . . .'

Gina tried to hold the knowledge of George's unreliableness at a great distance. The existence of his girlfriends was dreadful and if they couldn't be wished away they were best acknowledged with only the most superficial parts of her mind, because it was no use being sad, it simply didn't go with her luxurious lifestyle. But sometimes, in fact quite often, although she tried hard to hold herself back, she would start up a quarrel. Perhaps George would come in at midnight, long after she'd gone to bed, and she would call out from underneath the duvet, 'You shit,' catching herself off-guard and George as well. 'What?' he would say. 'You shit,' she would say again and then he would answer coldly, 'What do you think I have been doing? Wining and dining my mistress?' 'Don't be fucking stupid,' she would say, although that of course was exactly what she thought. He would sit down on the bed and pull back the duvet. 'So you think I'm not sexy enough to have a mistress?' he would ask, and then she would reach up to smack him round the face but he would catch her wrist and roll on top of her and then she would start to laugh as well as to cry, because sex like this, mixed up with tears and slaps, was glorious.

George didn't take these emotions seriously. For George it was as if all Gina's emotions were very close to hand, as if she could, and would, lay her hands in an instant on lust and anger and sadness and happiness – whatever the occasion demanded – and the more easily she reached for these feelings the less seriously he took them.

20

It was at this time that Gina began to rely more than ever on her girlfriends. She loved her female friends. She felt warmed and consoled by her love for them. For Gina having female friends was as good as shopping for clothes and drinking champagne, and nearly as good as going to bed with a man. And of all her friends Charlie was the best, a big, tall girl with a swooping smile the size of a melon slice and a shrewd and cheerful nature. She and Gina shared a taste for drama and strong stories and were always coming home with extraordinary stories overheard at the hairdressers or the beauty clinic: stories of girls who fell hopelessly in love with long-lost half-brothers and ran off and had babies with them, or girls seduced away from behind the perfume counter at Harrods to go abroad with Arab princes. 'For God's sake,' George would say, 'you don't believe that story, do you?' He was a taciturn man, always mocking his wife's enthusiasm for words. But Gina did believe these stories, and what's more, suspected that George believed them too; or if not believed them at least enjoyed them, because of course he liked a good story.

And Gina and Charlie also shared a taste for palm reading and tarot cards and horoscopes and other, more obscure ways of telling the future. It was Charlie who put Gina on to the fortune tellers. 'And they're not only fortune tellers, darling,' she said, 'they're healers as well,' and she told Gina how a friend of hers had a lump on her breast which the consultant said was cancerous, but one of the fortune tellers healed her with his hands so that when they took the lump out they found it was benign. 'But I don't have a lump on my breast,' said Gina. 'No,' said Charlie, 'but you have a tragedy and maybe they can help you. Just find out the time of your birth. It's one of the things they have to know.'

Gina rang her mother in the south of France to find out her time of birth but although she rang at ten in the morning her mother was drunk as usual and after long and careful thought said, quite definitely, 'Half past three in the afternoon,' but then she began to ramble on and after that she changed her mind and said no, she thought it was more likely eight in the evening. Gina thought that the first time was probably the right one, but that it was like her mother not to know.

The fortune tellers worked from a chapel in the back streets of Camden Town. It was a little, low building with a billboard out the front on which was written 'God is truth and truth is love'. The front doors were locked and the walls were window-deep in weeds. Gina went round the side and let herself into a vestibule and from there went through double doors into a gloomy waiting room, the walls of which were painted a dark brown and lined with chairs. Two dozen people were sitting there. They were Gina's first surprise. Because in Gina's world very few people at all were old – except for the parents of her friends and most of them lived in Miami or in Florida – so that the people who sat in this waiting room, who were not only old but poor as well, struck Gina for one moment like ghosts, and she, in her scarlet suede jacket and her white jodhpurs, like the only living person here.

She paid one pound fifty to an old man sitting at a table and after twenty minutes or so of fidgeting in silence she was ushered through a pair of doors into the chapel itself. The light came in through stained-glass windows. On the walls and ceiling there were moons and suns and stars, desert sands and Egyptian temples and the faces of the gods, all depicted in blues and pinks and golds. Chairs had been pushed back from the centre of the room where there had been erected half a dozen high couches, each one reached by a little flight of steps. An old man stepped forward and this was her next surprise, because he was such an old little man with a pale, papery face and blue eyes and hair of sugar whiteness; and not only was he very old but he had a curiously silvery look about him as if there was a halo on his head. In fact he was altogether silvery: his hair and his light, low voice and the way he stood and watched her take off her jacket. A little, old man and terribly ordinary and poor-looking to Gina who was used all the time to wealth and youth, but with this silvery presence.

Gina climbed up onto the couch and after a moment or two he laid his hands upon her – or rather, not quite on her, but an inch or two above – and though they never touched her, his fingers had a radiant feel. He began to talk in a soft and reassuring voice, telling her that everything was changing, not only for her but for everyone, that the planets were on the move again, sliding away from their unlucky configurations, that she'd made many sacrifices but quite soon she would see that the planets were ushering in a time of luck and happiness. And so soft and reassuring was his voice that she felt an embarrassing sensation as if her hard heart had started to melt and she began to sniff and to snivel and quite soon was telling him the story of her life, although she'd promised herself she wouldn't, the better to test his skills . . .

He listened to her gravely and when she stopped for breath he asked her the time of her birth. Then he stared into thin air – just as Charlie said he would – but what she hadn't expected was that he would start to grow spooky so that by the time he began to speak again she was shivering and his voice was prickling on her skin. This is what he said: that peculiar things would happen to her; that what she wanted so badly she would get but not at all at a time nor in a way that she might have expected, and then only after a terrible fight between good and evil, although good this time would triumph. It was all hocus-pocus of course – 'Hocus-pocus,' said Gina, tripping out of the chapel and into the narrow streets where the sun was going down already. She looked around for a taxi to take her back to St John's Wood. 'Hocus-pocus,' said Gina again, but even so she felt how her mind, which normally looped along in a slack kind of way because it had nothing much to occupy it, now grew tight with excitement and anticipation. Gina was a great believer in luck and destiny and fate and fortune-telling. For a while she even managed to forget that she was infertile, although only with the upper part of her mind, whilst deep down inside her she kept an eye out for the unexpected circumstances that would eventually – as he had promised – give her a baby.

21

It was astonishing to Madeleine how you never got what you expected. It was almost a rule in life. By the time Ella was three she began to grow a little plumper and more solid, and her fearful rages no longer merged one into another but were separated out by periods of contentment, so that it was easier now to see what had caused the rage in the first place – usually a kind of nervy panic at some imminent change. Panic made the child obnoxious. Perhaps it would always do so? Not good in a crisis, thought Madeleine, unlike herself and her mother, both of whom in a crisis were bleakly capable.

And then, in between her rages, Ella began to reveal her character: a steady gaze, an unsparing criticism – 'But why did you do that, Mummy? Why?'– a brutal regard for the truth – 'But it's true, Mummy' – and at the other extreme, and seeming to come from some deeper part of herself, a certain luxuriousness of mind and body. It was the way she snuggled down in the bed beside you. It was the way she reclined on the sofa when watching television and how every night she came into Madeleine's bed and every morning woke early and began to talk in her shrill, high voice, but lightly and luxuriously reclined in the depths of the double bed as if rocking to and fro in a hammock. When she knelt on the back of her heels in the bath you could see how she had developed hips and a bum, the water magnifying the curves and making them almost extravagant. Her blonde hair now had an auburn tinge that made her look worldly and glamorous. 'Mummy,' she said, when Madeleine tried to avert her eyes from the child's beauty, 'Mummy' – knitting the ties between mother and child stronger and stronger. When Ella got into bed with her Madeleine held her only very lightly. Ella was three but Madeleine was still shy of kissing her. They related to each other like two heads which had no bodies.

Ella's luxuriousness was almost as surprising as her rages. Where did it come from? Not from Madeleine, who was straight-up-and-down skinny like a twig on a tree. Madeleine thought perhaps it came from her father? Dimly she could remember a man dressing himself in her childhood – holding out an arm, and exposing the softness of the inner wrist as he did up a button; using one hand to divide the sock between the toes and make it more comfortable; wiping down the jacket smooth; digging his hands deep into his pockets to stretch out his arms and his back and his neck. Did he luxuriate, as Ella did, when he made these movements? My mother took away my father but my daughter brought him back. The very idea filled Madeleine with astonishment and gratitude.

And Ella was showing herself to be bright, which also pleased Madeleine enormously. At two she began to talk in long sentences. At three she began to use words like 'could' and 'should'. At four she wanted to play chess and was peering at words on the page, trying to understand them. She could sit quite still and listen to long and complicated stories. She's going to love books, thought Madeleine, she's going to be like me – and she boasted of this to her mother and was pleased when her mother dropped at last her apparent indifference and admitted it, that her granddaughter was exceptional.

When Ella was four she went down the road to the local infants' school and from that moment on the system embraced them both. On her second day there Madeleine quarrelled with the headmistress. The school had a policy that at the beginning of the year children in the reception class should go home at lunch time. But for Madeleine who was always hugely busy in September and who had only with great difficulty found a childminder to take Ella after school, this policy was inconvenient and exasperating. She went straight in and told the headmistress so. 'Mrs Kingdom' – 'Dr Kingdom,' said Madeleine – 'Dr Kingdom,' said the headmistress, 'these arrangements are put in place for the good of the children and if' – her voice rising to cap Madeleine's objections – 'if you can find childcare for Ella after school I am sure you can do the same for a month or so over the lunch time period.' She was immovable; the whole place was. It was a good little school but it looked upon the parents as no more than bit-part players in the child's drama.

The following spring Madeleine saw Martin again. All these years she had been reading his architecture column and fantasising that somehow she'd got the better of him – had become richer or more famous or simply happier than him and could flaunt her good fortune in front of him and rub his nose in it. And then one day she saw him in the flesh. The college had employed a fashionable architect to build an extension to the library and when it was finished had invited to the opening, amongst others, the architectural press. There he stood in a knot of people and the first thing that struck her – no, it more than struck her, it burnt into her vision – was the absolute daisy-freshness of his appearance, of the youth and shining happiness of his face, of the mint-freshness of his clothes; whilst the second thing she saw was that he hadn't changed one iota, that he still blushed and ducked his head when talking, still clutched in one large ham of a hand the slender neck of his glass, still wore his clothes with a tentative air, as if he were afraid that too sudden a movement would tear them.

'Oh, the bastard,' she thought. 'Oh, the bastard,' because he looked so well and because in all her dreams she had been hoping and expecting the reverse. Was he still with Angelina? Had he ever had children? How could he look so well, so untouched by life? I should have brought a gun with me and shot him dead, thought Madeleine. That would do something for his daisy-freshness. This, it seemed, was the difference between men's and women's lives, that women's lives lent themselves to the plots of novels, precisely because of the terrible journeys of self-discovery that they were sent upon, as if their lives were a female *Pilgrim's Progress* – but this was a novel she had always hated! – whilst men's lives didn't change at all and so they could live on, untouched by suffering, in perpetual youth.

That night she went to bed, sad and angry and disconcerted

by the sight of him, but the next morning she had a sudden change of heart. It happened as she was sitting at the dressing table, putting on her face cream. Ella came in and climbed onto her lap. Madeleine felt the sudden weight, the curve of the small back fitting itself into her body, the feathery head pushed up against her chin, the small hands placed on the larger hands sweeping back the face creams to make a space for the chess board. She laid out the pieces, white to the left and black to the right. When she put one in the wrong place Madeleine set her right. 'I'll start,' said Ella and she moved a pawn. Madeleine did the same. Ella moved another pawn and Madeleine did the same again. 'You're copying me,' said Ella complacently, and she moved a bishop, then kept her finger on the bishop's head. Madeleine saw the child's eyes track across the board, following the path that the bishop would take, and her gaze was so transparent in its intentions that it seemed to leave a shiny train behind it like a snail's trail – and this made Madeleine laugh, so that suddenly she thought, gleefully and pleasurably, with both a light pleasure and a deep pleasure, Oh, that bastard, that bastard, because in the end it was she who would have the last laugh, because Ella was hers, because she was Ella's mother.

22

And then it happened.

Gina saw the piece as she and Charlie were sitting in the hairdresser's having their highlights done together. First they had greeted each other – laughing and kissing and calling out their admiration for each other's shoes and for their late tans, because it was already the beginning of October. And then, when their hair had been wrapped up in twists of silver foil so that they looked like a couple of rag dolls, they had sat down on the sofa together to gossip and to flip through the newspapers and the magazines and to examine each other's jewellery – Charlie's earrings, Gina's pearl bracelet – the ducking of the head to show off the earlobes, the wrist held in light fingers as the pearls were examined – and all the while the jokes called out to the girls who did their hair.

The piece was on an inside page of *The Times* under the heading 'Fertility Clinic in Egg Swap Scandal'.

'A well-known North London fertility clinic is facing legal action over allegations that it implanted the wrong eggs into three of its women patients. The alleged scandal came to light when a baby boy born at the clinic developed cystic fibrosis. Doctors who ran tests on the boy have established that he cannot be his parents' child. Since then two more babies born at the clinic have been shown to have come from eggs wrongly implanted. The clinic was one of the pioneers of in vitro fertilisation. All the families involved are threatening legal action.'

'Have you seen this? What do you think it means?' Gina asked

Charlie and she passed the piece across. Charlie read it. 'Maybe some other woman's got your eggs?' she said, and then the girl who did their hair wanted to see the piece as well and when she'd read it she said, 'But would you mind? I mean, you didn't give away the child, you gave away the eggs.'

'Mind?' said Gina, 'Of course I'd bloody mind. And anyway, if it happened, I didn't give my eggs away – they were stolen.' Gina thought, this girl doesn't even have any children, so what does she know?

Charlie said, 'Maybe he sold your eggs, Gina? Maybe he's got a business on the side, selling women's eggs?'

'Can you sell eggs?' asked Gina.

'Of course,' said Charlie, 'There's a huge demand for them because there's not enough egg donors so although they're not supposed to sell them I expect they probably do.'

'I don't think Mr Kalotheou would do something like that,' said Gina.

'It'll be an amazing story if it's true,' said Charlie, her eyes alight for gossip.

'This is my life, Charlie,' said Gina bleakly, and then Charlie said, 'I once heard of a clinic that implanted a monkey foetus into a woman by mistake,' and at that everyone shrieked in horror, except for Gina who was sitting quietly staring at the page of the newspaper.

After her hair was done Gina went straight home. She rang George at the office, trying to keep her voice light and casual-sounding. She had a wife's habit of wanting her husband's opinion, the more so because she was only a stay-at-home wife whereas he worked in the outside world and thus knew more than her. But she caught him at a bad moment. He sounded off-hand and uninterested – she could all but hear him shrug – so then she felt deflated. The excitement of it all had given her a headache. She went to bed with some pills and a glass of wine in the unmade, luxurious bed, with her image reflected in all the mirrors that lined the wall, making a harem of herselves to keep her company.

The pills helped her think. She wanted to get her mind round the idea of some other woman having one of her eggs. First she subtracted the pregnancy and the birth and the feeding of the child and the holding of the child, until she thought there was nothing left, that an egg was only an egg, that it was nothing more than that. But then she remembered what the egg carried, all the inheritance, the thousands of genes which gave the child its characteristics, which were yours and your husband's and your mother's and father's characteristics, and then all of a sudden the egg became something important again, it became the child, it was the child, because – more or less – there was nothing else.

Thus the egg first shrank then grew then shrank then grew in significance until Gina felt giddy. At last it settled itself into being significant and Gina began to think that all her calmness about being infertile was a sham, that she wasn't and never could be calm about it, that she had to have a baby, that she had a right to have a baby, that the need for a baby was like the need for food and drink and sex; and that if it were true that a little Gina had been born out there, *her* child, a fragment of *her* genetic material, with *her* eyes and nose and mouth – but holding the hand of some other woman – then she wanted her back because she, Gina, was the real, the biological mother. She'd once heard of a surrogate baby whose adopted parents couldn't stop it crying, and whom only the real mother could soothe, because the biological tie was that important. And then another thought occurred to her. That if an egg of hers had been given to some other woman, whose sperm would have fertilised it? A strange man's? Or George's? Because if it was George's sperm that had been used, then what had been created was what she and George had been struggling to achieve for all these years, a baby that was part her, part him, a baby that genuinely belonged to both of them. And at this a wave of pity came over Gina – for her child who was lost in the wrong life, with the wrong parents – and a hunger to get it back, although when she examined the feeling it was not so much like a hunger as like a sexual feeling, like wanting to go to bed with a man.

She began to fall asleep. The pills were giving her peculiar dreams. She dreamt that she had a dozen children, every one of them about six months old and the size of a large doll; although they were also seven or eight and, dressed in shorts and T-shirts, they were racing round her, shooting at each other with their guns. When they saw that she was awake they turned their guns on her. They were fearsome in their unfamiliarity. But then she looked more closely and saw that they had her fleshy looks, her rounded wrists and ankles, although when she looked for a third time she realised that they weren't children at all but were the cherubs in all four corners of her gilt-painted dressing-table mirror.

And then she woke to see George, who had come home early, creeping into bed beside her. He caught her before she was fully awake and drew an orgasm out of her ever so sweetly, so sweetly in fact that she started to cry, although George didn't notice. He went across to the mirror, naked from the waist downwards but from the waist up still dressed in his work clothing. From the bed to the mirror the floor was strewn with the bedspread and her underwear and her best silk jackets and a new pair of shoes, so that with every step he took he trod on money.

He stood in front of the mirror, digging his fingers into the knot of his tie to loosen it. 'What was his name?' he asked. 'Who?' asked Gina. She had stopped crying. The orgasm had given her a dewy, rapt expression which made her look very young. She was thinking that she liked to see a man in a bedroom, that men filled up a room in a way that women couldn't. 'Mr Kalotheou,' said George, 'That was it. He fancied you. If he's screwed up I'll sue him for millions.'

'He fancied you,' said George but what George really meant was, 'You fancied him.'

23

George had never liked Mr Kalotheou. He used to refer to him as the Greek Love God and, when Mr Kalotheou emerged from his room and walked across the waiting area in his courteous, stooping, patrician way, George would mutter to himself, 'Watch him walk. Jesus. On his tippy toes.' Gina took no notice. She had grown accustomed, as beautiful women do, to hearing one man jeer about another in her presence.

But it was true, as George had feared, that Gina had always rather fancied the consultant because of his kindly and paternal manner. Long ago, when she was eleven, her father had died and although she didn't remember missing him his death still had an effect on her, giving her a weakness for men in authority and a heightened pleasure in very male men – men like George who were taciturn and sexy – and for all the accoutrements of maleness: for ties and cufflinks and suits hanging in a wardrobe and shoes, size 11, and keys and wallets and cigarettes and whisky.

The next day George went away to Scotland for a week to shoot a film. He left early whilst Gina was still asleep. He kissed her perfunctorily, running his hands absent-mindedly over her body.

'What about Mr Kalotheou?' she asked.

'I'll see to it,' he said. 'I'll ring Oliver Hewitt this morning. Let the lawyers deal with it,' and with that he left her, his kept wife, in her silk pyjamas in the big double bed.

She lay there for a while thinking about Mr Kalotheou and what possible motive he could have for so bungling matters. She couldn't believe that money was the cause – he hadn't seemed the type – although presumably the system was open to abuse. How could it be otherwise? Indeed, if he'd wanted to, what was to stop him mixing his sperm with every egg in the clinic and fathering himself an army? But she couldn't believe he was either corrupt or vain. Surely he'd been too high-minded to be either? She lay there on the bed conjuring up a memory of Mr Kalotheou, that knight of gravity and self-possession, the grey at his finely-bred temples and his long fingers which he liked to steeple before him in his classy way. But the more she remembered his grandeur the more angry she felt, because, for all his superiority, he had failed to give her a baby. And then quite suddenly the knowledge of what she was going to do popped into her head like a letter into a letter box. At this minute she didn't really believe that there was a baby but still she was going to go and see Mr Kalotheou because he had let her down, because the years had passed and he hadn't made her pregnant. He had failed her and she was glad that he was in trouble and now she was going to go and see him again, to add to his agitation and to punish him for his failure.

She wasn't used to doing things without asking George first. The idea of it gave her a feeling of boldness, of temerity, but also of nakedness – because she was exposing the extent of her desires. When she drove into the clinic car park she saw that nothing had changed. It was still the same clinic, the gardens still flowering although it was so late in the year, as if in defiance of nature; the same foreign-looking beauties going in and out with eyes as large as window-panes; the same receptionist behind the counter; the same Mr Kalotheou glimpsed rushing into his room – had he seen her? was he trying to escape?

Now, too late, she realised that she didn't have an appointment. She hesitated. For one moment she didn't know what to do and then the answer came to her. It was easy. She stepped up to the reception desk. She asked for Mr Kalotheou. When they blocked her she let her voice begin to rise hysterically and she banged on the counter. She started to talk about lawyers and newspaper reports. She felt her voice carry across the waiting area, knew that she was planting the seeds of hysteria in this well-ordered and opulent setting. And in about two minutes flat Mr Kalotheou loomed up beside her, his voice still like honey, the set of his mouth still delightful; but was that tension beneath the light touch of his fingers on her shoulders as he steered her in the direction of his room?

For one moment she thought – part panicking, part pleased – that perhaps he was going to hit her? And yet at the same time she didn't really care what he did, because the truth was that she was older and that age had brought a certain bleakness with it – it was alarming but it couldn't be denied – and she no longer felt so soft nor saw the world so softly. And she didn't fancy Mr Kalotheou any longer and couldn't imagine how she had ever done so. To her eyes he now looked staid and dull and nineteen-fortyish and absurdly pompous. All she cared about was the screw-up he might have made over her baby.

She sat down in front of him. She came straight to the point. 'I've been reading all about you in the papers,' she said, waving around the article from *The Times*. 'How can you convince me that some other woman didn't get my eggs?'

He took the article from her and read it carefully before he answered, because he was too clever to be bounced into saying anything unnecessary. 'Mrs Kaufman,' he said, and his voice was as courteous as ever, although weary-sounding, and he gave Gina a look, if she could but recognise it, which men who work will sometimes give to women who don't, a so-how-could-you-understand-what-it's-like-to-see-your-career-destroyed look. 'Mrs Kaufman,' he said, 'we are carrying out an investigation in conjunction with the Human Fertilisation and Embryo Authority. The investigation will be very wide-ranging. As soon as there's anything to tell you, I promise you will be told,' and she saw that he meant to block her in every which way and to tell her nothing.

So she began to run on – 'Do you know how much money we spent, trying to have a baby? Twenty thousand pounds. Do you know what it's like to want a baby and not be able to have one? No, of course you don't because you're only a man' – but with each passing minute she could hear her voice growing less convincing, because he knew and she knew that he was allowing her to shout on because every other way was blocked.

And then the intercom buzzed on his desk. For one moment

a look of relief came over his face. He knew that intercom was going to go, thought Gina. A woman's voice spoke out – what she said was inaudible to Gina – but Mr Kalotheou listened and then switched it off. He rose from behind his desk. Relief put back the sweetness into his voice. 'I'm wanted in the theatre,' he said, 'but Sister's coming in. I've suggested to her that she explains our procedures to you. I think you'll find that helpful and reassuring. Don't worry, Mrs Kaufman' – and so great was his confidence now that he came round the desk, smiling at her – 'We're all very confident that this matter will be sorted out.'

Sister was a beautiful Asian woman with a cherry-red mouth and black eyebrows thickly drawn as if with charcoal. 'This is Mrs Kaufman,' said Mr Kalotheou and Sister nodded. Gina noticed that between the two of them – as she took over, sitting down in his chair and rifling through his notes and as he closed the door behind him – there was a faint flurry of embarrassment. Sister raised her beautiful eyes to Gina and suddenly Gina understood the embarrassment, that Mr Kalotheou had been sleeping with her and now there was resentment on her part and embarrassment on his. This gave Gina an idea. 'Let me tell you how things work here,' Sister began, but as she did so Gina got to her feet.

'Wait a minute,' she said and she stepped across to the desk. She reached into her bag and drew out her wallet from which she extracted two £50 notes, each clean and crisp and starched-looking. 'That's my file there, isn't it?' she said. 'Listen, all you have to do is go to the bathroom, shutting this door behind you, and leave me for five minutes. When you come back you can have these' – tapping the notes with one finger – 'and I'll go without a murmur, I promise you.'

She was dumbstruck by her own audacity. She hardly dared raise her eyes. But when she did she knew that she was right, that Mr Kalotheou was not corrupt – he hadn't been selling eggs – but he was incompetent and too charming for his own good and prone to sleeping with the staff. What's more this woman needed the money. You could feel how her eyes hung upon the notes. Because for some people, thought Gina with amazement, one hundred pounds was a lot of money. 'Go on,' said Gina. 'Go on. I promise you, I only need five minutes,' and Sister was gone.

Gina pressed some keys on the word processor and her name and her details came up on the screen. She pressed a few more keys but the screen didn't change any more so then she opened the file in front of her and began to go through it. The letter was near the bottom. It was from the Human Fertilisation and Embryo Authority. She read it very fast: 'We are concerned about the cases of Mrs Gina Kaufman and Dr Madeleine Kingdom . . . the same laboratory assistant . . . from July to October 1990 . . . standards of procedure were well below what is required . . . one possibility which must be considered is that Mrs Kaufman's eggs were implanted into Dr Kingdom.'

She put the letter into her bag. As she stepped towards the door it opened and in came the beautiful Sister. 'Thank you,' said Gina gratefully and she put the two £50 notes into the woman's hand. On her way home she stopped the car and taking out the letter she read it again and again. On the third re-reading she remembered who Mrs Kingdom was – it was a name that stuck in the mind. She was the girl who had sat in her bedroom talking, the morning that both of them had had a laparoscopy – a lecturer in English at London University. 'So it was you who got my child, was it?' thought Gina.

As soon as she got home she rang Charlie. 'Charlie?' she said, 'maybe I have a child.'

'What?' said Charlie, 'you're crazy.'

'No, really,' she said, 'Listen.'

When she'd finished Charlie said, 'But even if your egg was put into another woman you don't know if it took, you don't know that that other woman got pregnant.'

'No,' said Gina, 'but she might have done.'

'And you don't know who the father was, it needn't necessarily have been George?'

'No,' said Gina, 'but it might have been.'

'So, who is this other woman?' Charlie asked.

'I met her in the clinic,' said Gina. 'We were in at the same time. I suppose that's how the mistake might have happened. I remember her. She was a single parent. She taught English at London University.'

'It wouldn't be easy to get a child back,' said Charlie. 'It would have grown used to loving this other woman.'

'It could grow used to loving me,' said Gina.

'You'd have to go to court,' said Charlie.

'That's all right,' said Gina.

'Poor bloody other woman,' said Charlie. 'Can you imagine loving a child and then losing it like that?'

24

Charlie's words made Gina feel guilty. Round and round the flat she paced and she who wasn't used to guilt felt it now in her body, like a headache and a stomachache, and in her mind like a discontent and a sadness and a nervous desire to chew on her nails and to pick at the skin on her feet. Moral dilemmas confused her. She opened a bottle of wine and after a glass or two she began to feel an understanding of her situation was flitting past her and bits of it she could understand and bits of it she couldn't. But this much she did know, that Charlie's words made her feel like a thief, that it was like being accused of wanting another woman's husband, only that was a commonplace amongst her friends and this was far, far worse, because in her heart every woman knows that the loss of a child is far worse than the loss of a man. But anyway it's not the same, thought Gina, because I don't want to take something that belongs to someone else but to get back something that was mine all along. It was as if she were a child again, having to prise some other child's fingers off her doll, because – and this was the difficult thing – life had now put her at the disadvantage of power, because she was no longer the innocent victim of infertility, but with the power to make another woman unhappy.

She couldn't bring herself to ring up George because she knew what he would say: 'Don't be stupid. If there's a child and if it's ours then we're getting it back and that's the end of it.' George's ruthlessness, which previously she'd found sexy, now gave her a chill, uncomfortable feeling. For the first time she realised that she and George could differ on a moral issue.

The next morning, she rang Charlie back. She was crying by

now. 'Listen,' she said through her tears, 'It's all very well for you – this talk of "poor bloody woman" – but you've had your two children. What about me? Don't I have rights too?'

'I didn't mean you shouldn't try to get it back,' said Charlie, confused and defensive, 'I only said, "poor woman".'

'There you go again,' said Gina, crying louder than ever, and she put the phone down.

That morning Gina went to have a facial in a beauty clinic just off Oxford Street. As she lay there she began to listen to a conversation going on beside her. A woman was having a face mask applied. All you could see of her was the tip of her nose, her chin, a length of neck and her mouth enunciating words. She was saying, 'Well, he came from somewhere in Eastern Europe and after communism collapsed he went back and claimed his family lands and she married him and went with him. They had twins first of all and then a little boy with some kind of handicap – he couldn't walk properly. Quite soon the marriage started going wrong – she was terribly lonely out there – and in the end she left him – well, really he drove her to it – but when she said she wouldn't go without the children he said, "All right, you can have the handicapped one." "What do you mean?" she asked and he said, "It's your own fault, you smoked in pregnancy." And that's what he did, threw her and the little boy out, although he was semi-paralysed.

'At first she didn't even have his medicine. She had to hammer on the door and then he didn't bring it out himself but sent it with the housekeeper. But that housekeeper liked her and brought her out her handbag with some money in it and that's why, although she had to walk to the nearest town with the little boy in her arms, she could then catch a train to some city where she rang her parents who sent her out some money. In the end she came back by train, halfway across Europe, with only the clothes she was standing up in – she said it was nothing but forests of fir trees for days on end – and she was crying all the time because although she had the little boy she was going further and further away from her two other children . . . Well, she's been back a few times but he won't let her see them – he's got a lot of clout locally and people daren't cross him – even the taxi drivers won't drive her out to the house. It's an unbelievable situation but I did warn her when she married him. I said there are some countries where a woman's children are not her own, in the end they belong to the father. But she won't give up. She'll fight him in the courts. She's already spent all her savings and taken out another mortgage and persuaded her parents to do the same. And I know how she feels. I'd do the same if I were her.'

Gina thought, the stories you heard in these places. Some of them were so fantastic you couldn't believe that they were true – and indeed they probably weren't because she herself from time to time made up stories if she were somewhere where she thought nobody knew her – although her stories were quite gentle and believable – about her three children and the life they led together. Poppy, Clara and Amelia were the names of her three children – three little girls, because George had wanted a boy and so they'd kept on trying but the truth was, she, Gina, wasn't sorry to have three girls and such pretty ones . . .

Gina hoisted herself up onto her elbow. She knew the girl who was putting on the face mask.

'I think she'll bankrupt her parents to get those children back,' said the woman behind the mask, 'and of course the husband has told his lawyers that the children are settled with him and it wouldn't be in their interests to disturb them. But I don't think he understands that women in the west won't accept that kind of talk any longer. These days women are strong and they know what they want and they'll fight to get it.'

Women are strong and they'll fight for their rights. Even in Gina's circle these sentiments were common. Gina hadn't registered them before but she heard them now and thought that these were sweet, heady words, that they could give you a buzz. 'We will survive, you and I,' goes the song, 'we are the survivors.'

'The truth is,' said the woman behind the mask, 'a woman will fight for her children in every which way she has to. I know I would. I've got two children and they're more important to me than anything.'

'I know an even more terrible situation,' said Gina bleakly and because exchanging stories was a part of the currency of these places she said, 'A friend of mine was having fertility treatment for years at an IVF clinic, but although they spent thousands on it she never got pregnant. And now she's heard that the clinic made some mistakes, that a couple of times they implanted the wrong egg into the wrong woman so that several women gave birth to other women's babies. Well, my friend went back to the clinic and discovered that her case is one of the cases under review, that they suspect that one of her eggs may well have been implanted into another woman who was in the clinic, in the next room, at the same time. So what's she going to do? Because whilst she's still child-less this other woman may have given birth to what is, in effect – I mean biologically-speaking – her and her husband's child. My friend keeps thinking of this child out there who's in the wrong life with the wrong parents, and she doesn't want to ruin another woman's life but really can she just let it go?'

The women thought about it. 'But perhaps,' said the girl who did the face mask, 'there was something in that other woman's body that made the pregnancy possible, so that if it hadn't been for her there wouldn't have been a baby at all. Doesn't that give her some rights to the child?'

'Perhaps,' said Gina. 'But perhaps equally that was a good embryo, the embryo that was always going to survive, but the wrong woman got it.'

'I wouldn't let it go,' said the woman in the mask, 'not if it was me, not if I hadn't had a baby, if I were still childless. Women want babies. Infertility is a dreadful thing.'

'But suppose the other woman loves it,' said the girl who did the masks. 'What about her? How is she going to feel?'

'You know what I think?' said the woman in the mask. 'If it's not her child she'll know it. I mean, it will feel like a stranger even if she gave birth to it.'

It was a comforting thought. The whole conversation was comforting – or perhaps not so much comforting as uplifting, thought Gina – for afterwards she had a sense of the strong events that overtake women, of the dramas and the tragedies of their lives, of how strong they have to be to survive, and how glorious it is to be a surviving woman. And it was because she was elated by the upward rush of these feelings that Gina went to see Madeleine, not to say, 'Look, I want that child back', but rather to say, 'Look what has befallen us – or may have done – this strange situation, because you can't discount me, because here I am with you, in the very middle of it.'

25

She came one rainy, blue-black night at the beginning of November when Ella, who was now six and a half, had gone to sleep, and Madeleine was standing in the living room looking out of the window. Madeleine was holding up her face very close against the glass so that she could see beyond her own reflection to the navy darkness and the splodges of red and yellow lights and the endless rain that fell within the compass of these lights, so finely and so steadily that it didn't seem to move or fall at all. She was standing there because she had that feeling that mothers have when the children are in bed and there's no chance of a babysitter, the feeling that the world is hopelessly shut out and that you are hopelessly shut in, till morning. But it wasn't true, because then the doorbell went.

A woman stood on Madeleine's threshold. She was wearing what looked like a man's smoking jacket, but long, down to the knees and made of brown, embroidered velvet with black at the cuffs and the collar. Underneath this she wore brown velvet trousers and ankle boots, whose leather was scarcely stained by the rain – because, of course, thought Madeleine, whose eyes had been travelling down her, she must have come by car or taxi. Her hair lay in a mass across her shoulders and this and the sunglasses perched on top of her head gave her a theatrical look, as if she were not just a rich woman but one who liked fancy dress as well. She had a beautiful face but there were lines appearing on it, marking the ends of her wide mouth and staining her smooth forehead, lines which both enhanced her beauty and destroyed it, making her look peculiarly old, as only beautiful women can.

'You don't remember me, do you?' she said and when Madeleine looked blank she said, 'Gina Kaufman. We met at the fertility clinic. We were both trying to have a baby,' and then recognition dawned on Madeleine, and Gina said, 'Can I come in?' and Madeleine stood to one side and in stepped Gina, running one hand through her hair as she did so, and away she swung up the stairs in the direction that Madeleine indicated. It seemed to Madeleine, as she followed, that from the hem of Gina's glorious, embroidered coat there were trailing intimations of the outside world that both excited and disturbed – the night-life and the parties and the roaring traffic and the street lamps that smeared their yellow lights into the blue-black puddles. But perhaps it only seemed like this to Madeleine, because she went out so little?

She sat down on Madeleine's sofa. Madeleine saw that she had all the nervy mannerisms of beautiful, neurotic women: the strained look in the line of her mouth, the swallowing of the throat, the playing with her earrings, the tugging at the tips of her fingers – mannerisms which were part preening, part anxiety. There was a ripe, even louche look about her which she hadn't had seven years before – too much sex, thought Madeleine sourly – but at the same time the ripeness had a frozen look, as if she were some extravagant, ice cream confection. She made Madeleine feel uncomfortable. Everything about her suggested another world.

She began to look around Madeleine's room and the first thing she clapped eyes upon was a picture of Ella that stood on the mantelpiece. She turned as white as paper. So she never had that baby, Madeleine thought. 'Do you mind if I smoke?' she asked and when Madeleine shrugged she took out a cigarette and lit it and then lifted it up to her face to take the end of it with a curious twist of her neck and a flutter of her nostrils.

'Well,' said Gina, 'do you remember the clinic? I remember how hot it was and how you came into my bedroom and we talked.'

'I remember,' said Madeleine. 'You told me how you used to run away to your mother's house in the south of France.'

'Did I? Yeah. Well. That was true. What else do you remember?'

'That you had a good-looking boyfriend but that he was always getting into trouble and the bailiffs were always at the door.' Gina smiled bitterly. 'That was a long time ago,' she said, 'Six years. George is now stinking rich. I suppose I should be grateful for small mercies. You got that baby, didn't you?'

'Yes.'

'Is that her?' nodding at the picture.

'Yes,' and though it was on the tip of Madeleine's tongue to complete this scrap of conversation by saying, 'but you never got yours, did you?' the words remained unspoken in the air.

Gina asked, 'So where is she?'

'She's asleep. Through there.'

'And this is where you live. It's not very big, is it?'

'It's big enough,' said Madeleine in surprise.

'Where does she go to school?'

'Down the road,' said Madeleine, more surprised and stiff than ever.

'What's her name?'

'Ella,' said Madeleine.

Gina nodded. 'That's nice,' she said.

Gina took another puff on her cigarette. She took a deep breath.

'Have you heard from the clinic?' she asked.

'No. Why should I?'

'You will,' she said, and when Madeleine looked enquiring she said, 'It was in the papers. Don't you read them? There's been a mix-up over eggs. Two – no, three – women were implanted with another woman's eggs. It came to light because one child developed some disease and when they did a test on him they discovered that he couldn't be his parents' child.'

'So?'

'So I went to see Mr Kalotheou. Remember him? Handsome Mr Kalotheou. I said, "Prove to me that some other woman didn't get my eggs." He was very smooth and reassuring, just as you'd expect – he always did have an amazing bedside manner – but then he passed me across to some nurse and I got a chance to have a look at my notes and right at the bottom of the file I found a letter from the Human Fertilisation and . . .'

'Human Fertilisation and Embryo Authority,' said Madeleine.

'That's right. Saying that in their view there was a good chance that my and George's egg had been implanted into a certain Dr Madeleine Kingdom. That's you, isn't it?'

'So what are you trying to say?'

'That I think that your little girl – what's she called, Ella? – is mine and George's daughter.'

There was a silence. Madeleine swallowed. 'You're mad,' she said at last.

'No, I'm not. It's perfectly possible. It happened to other women in the clinic. They're investigating us now. Sweet Mr Kalotheou was simply incompetent.'

'No,' said Madeleine, 'the point is that you never conceived and now you've come here to steal my baby.'

'It's not your baby . . .'

'What proof have you got of that? You're talking complete rubbish.'

'No, I'm not. I've got a letter from the Human Fertilisation and Embryo Authority, saying that yours and mine is one of the cases being looked into.'

'I don't believe it,' said Madeleine. 'You want a baby and you can't have one and it's driving you bonkers.'

'Is it? Look at that photograph. Who does she remind you of? She doesn't look in the remotest bit like you. She's mine and George's daughter.'

Madeleine began to get angry. 'Get out,' she said, 'and don't come back here again, talking such crap in my house.'

'It's not crap,' said Gina, jumping to her feet, her voice rising also. 'You think you're so clever, but I'm not stupid. Look at her. Look at her face. She doesn't look in the least bit like you. She's mine and George's. Biologically speaking, there's not one scrap of you inside her.'

Madeleine stared. A terrible idea had occurred to her. 'You've been spying on us, haven't you?' she said. 'You've been following her and seeing what she's like? How did you get my address? No, I don't want to know. Out,' she said and she was suddenly very cold and brisk. 'Out,' she said again, and she took hold of Gina's arm and ushered her towards the door. 'Out,' she said, as if shooing out a cat as she pushed Gina down the stairs. 'Down,' she said, 'and don't come back. I'm not interested in your stupid stories.'

Gina began to wail. A wordless cry rose up from out of her, so intense that for one moment Madeleine paused in her shooing motion. Then she whisked her down the stairs even faster, reaching round her to open the door and to push her through. Gina permitted herself to be bundled out but as she went she called out, 'You can't just deny it. We can force you to have tests done and they will prove it one way or the other. And if we are the biological parents, then we have rights as well,' and then Madeleine slammed the door and after that there was silence. She stood there for a while staring at the panelled door through which had come such a disturbing idea and then she went upstairs to the living room. Her hands were trembling from the shock. She began to search around until she found a bottle of brandy and poured herself a glass. She took a gulp or two and the spirits, burning in her stomach, both strengthened and weakened her so that she started to cry. She went into the bedroom where Ella lay asleep on the bed. She lay down beside her. She kept swallowing as if there was something huge in her throat that she had to contend with. After a while she slid one arm under Ella's body and raised herself on one elbow and looked down at Ella's face. The child slept with a pure expression, face lifted heavenwards, the eyelids and the nostrils fluttering, each of her features reposed in purity – the wide mouth, the high forehead, the classical proportions.

26 ∫

She had looked up Madeleine Kingdom in the phone book and had found one of them in NW1, plus a couple of M. Kingdoms in places like Wembley and Battersea. She had looked up the NW1 address in the *A-Z* and had found that it was in Camden Town and remembered an association between Madeleine and that part of London.

She had parked her car beside the market and walked through the rainy streets. Across Parkway and along Arlington Road groups of men had stared after her because in her long, velvet jacket and her high-heeled boots and her mass of hair she didn't look the kind of woman you normally see walking in the streets, but rather the kind who is snapped by photographers alighting from Bentleys outside nightclubs.

She had rung Madeleine's doorbell. She had recognised Madeleine even after all these years, although the other woman looked twenty years older and with a mother's bent and weary-looking figure. She had gone up Madeleine's stairs feeling very calm and good and it was only when she saw the photograph on the mantelpiece – the child's face floating within it, the wide mouth, the large eyes, the high forehead, a familiar face, one she knew, one which set up echoes of familiarity – it was only then that she felt her calmness falter, fall victim to a rush of indignation, because the likeness was so obvious there could be only one conclusion, that this woman had her child.

She had looked around her and had felt unfamiliar maternal thoughts like, 'Is this flat a suitable place for my child to be brought up in?' and 'what school is she being sent to?' And then just as she was trying to keep a hold of herself, Madeleine had begun to accuse her of being stupid and neurotic and of inventing stories, and at that point she had lost her temper and had begun to feel as George often did, a cold determination that no one else was going to get something over her, that no one was going to walk off with something that didn't belong to them. I hate mothers, thought Gina, so complacent, so pleased with their fertility.

Afterwards she rang George in Scotland and told him what she'd done. 'You bloody fool,' he said, 'you just couldn't wait, could you? You had to jump straight in without thinking?'

She asked him, 'Don't you care that some other woman may have our child?'

'Care?' he said. 'Of course I care, but these things have to be done through lawyers.'

'But I did learn something,' she said, 'I learnt that it's a girl and that her name's Ella and how much she looks like you and me. I really think that she might be our child, George,' said Gina.

'I've been in touch with Oliver Hewitt,' said George. 'You and I are going to see him on Friday.'

'Did he understand?' asked Gina.

'Not at first he didn't,' said George. 'I had to explain to him about eggs and sperm. I asked him, "Where did you learn the facts of life, Oliver?" and he said, "Behind the bicycle shed at school but it was never like this in those days." Anyway, when he understood what I was saying he said that if we could prove our case we could sue the clinic for a fortune.'

'But what about the child?' said Gina, 'will we get her back?'

'Well,' said George, 'at first he thought we were just after the money. I had to repeat several times that it was the child we were interested in. And then he stopped talking and thought about it and he said, "Well, there's no precedent for it," and I said, "So? Create a precedent," and then he said, "Well, it'll cost you an arm and a leg," and I said, "So? Are you complaining?" and then he said, "How much evidence do you actually have that the child might be yours?' and I told him and he said, "We could take a flyer, test out the water a little, write a letter to the other side, saying that we were after pre-action discovery.' 'What's that?' I said, and he said, 'Under Section 33 of the something-or-other if you think you've got a case you can compel the other side to reveal all the medical evidence relevant to that case, and that could include DNA samples on the child. Because we need to have that anyway for the case against the clinic.'

'But will we get the child back?' asked Gina.

'He doesn't know,' said George. 'He can't give any guarantees. But there are some things in our favour. Such as that we've remained childless so there is a clear loss here. And that you've never had a miscarriage.'

'What's that got to do with it?' asked Gina.

'Well, if you had, the other side could argue that you wouldn't have kept the embryo anyway. And there's one other thing in our favour, and that's the other woman's situation. He asked what kind of family the baby might have gone to, and I said, as far as we knew, a single mother, working, not well off, and he said, "Ah well, nobody loves a single mother."'

27

The letter came ten days later, from a firm of lawyers, Hewitt, Cavendish and Jameson, of Brompton Place, SW3. It was written on behalf of their clients, Mr and Mrs Kaufman and it announced that in the light of reported irregularities at the Fountain Clinic and evidence from the HFEA they would be seeking DNA samples from Ella as part of a pre-action discovery to establish biological parentage.

For some days after the receipt of this letter Madeleine couldn't work. She couldn't think. She could hardly talk. She rang in sick and stayed at home instead, drinking cups of coffee and smoking cigarettes. And if before life had seemed like a tunnel it was nothing to the dreadful, narrow imprisonment of her thoughts in the days that followed the receipt of this letter. Sometimes she was angry. Sometimes, often, she was disbelieving. Sometimes she felt hugely weary at the struggle she would have to go through in order to keep her child. Sometimes, several times, she woke in the night with a feeling of light-headed relief, because the answer had come to her, that all she had to do – it was very simple – was to take Ella and go abroad with her, just simply vanish – but each time she woke again in the morning with a heavy heart, because of course the answer wasn't so simple, that she could go abroad, yes, but what was to stop George and Gina following her? Once, she even woke in the night and thought, well, why don't I give her up? It would hurt for a while but I'd get over it. But then she thought, if anyone comes to take my child away I'll stick a knife in their stomach.

Outside in the streets it snowed, the first snowfall of the winter, and when Madeleine fetched Ella from the childminder's they walked home through a blue snowlight which hovered over the snowy pavements, turning the air and the snow and the naked trees and the tall buildings all to a mournful blue. The lights from the shop windows leapt out and mingled with the street lamps and the lights of cars to form a canopy and under this canopy, in a shrunken world, Ella and Madeleine walked together. The cold got in everywhere. It got down your neck and up your sleeves. It left a bare, desolate touch on the skin. At night the snow reversed the natural order of things so that the earth which was normally darker than the sky became unnaturally white and shining whilst the sky was very black. Ella's patent leather shoes had lost their shine. The lights glittered on the snow piled up in the gutters.

One day as they crossed a road on amber the cars leapt towards them – like dogs who could scarcely be restrained, thought Madeleine. She hurried Ella home. She didn't feel safe outside. She felt that the snow and the cars and the people all were threatening Ella. All these years that with fascinated horror she had been seeking out stories in tabloid newspapers about children who had been abducted by one of their divorcing parents! All the time she had lain awake at night worrying about the different ways in which you can lose a child! And now her single mother's fears were being magnified hugely by what had befallen her.

She began to want to talk to someone, but who was there who would understand the enormity of what had happened? She was afraid to tell her mother because lately, since her mother had started to grow old, she had developed a curious philosophy in which all emotions were dwarfed by the idea that anyway we were going to die and thus that under the eye of eternity the strong emotions – love, anger, jealousy – amounted to nothing. It was a kind of mental longsightedness which meant that she couldn't see what was under her nose and Madeleine hated it. She dreaded hearing Ella dismissed in this way.

In fact, the only person Madeleine could think of who was strong enough for the story – or perhaps it was that the story was strong enough for her? – was Mercedes-Sally. Madeleine had long ago forgiven Mercedes-Sally for betraying her in pregnancy, but now she discovered that Mercedes-Sally had disappeared and all that anyone seemed to know was that she had married a rich old man – a Lord So-and-So, someone big in television, and was working in television herself – but which company? – when she wasn't rattling around a house in Knightsbridge.

Ella made Madeleine take her to Brent Cross. She wanted a sweater with pink patchwork hearts upon it. Her clothes were a constant grief to her. She wanted to be like everybody else. She wanted to be like nobody else. In the shops she drifted along the railings with a dreamy look in her eyes which said, 'If only I could have that I would be different.' But then on Monday morning she saw a girl at the school gates wearing the same sweater and she turned on Madeleine, kicking and punching her. Her face looked terrible. It was like a skull's head, contorted into ugliness by grief. But who else could she blame for her unhappiness, there being no one else but Madeleine in her world? – so that she hardly knew where she herself ended and Madeleine began. 'Spoilt,' whispered all the old women of Ella's babyhood. 'Spoilt,' no doubt Mercedes-Sally would say as well. Madeleine thought that women judged a mother harshly and that men didn't judge at all but that was only because to them a mother was invisible. People should stop judging me, thought Madeleine angrily. She was fighting shadow-enemies, opponents whose faces she couldn't see.

Madeleine went to the university medical library. Within half an hour she had worked out what George and Gina were hoping to do. First, thought Madeleine, they would try to establish parentage by using the new DNA techniques which can show family similarities in DNA sequences. At the same time, presumably, they would approach the clinic to try to compel it to release evidence of its procedures in the years when Gina was a patient there. They would also approach other families to pool evidence of irregularities and the HFEA to compel it to release what evidence it had which pertained to the case. If they could establish Ella's true parentage they would then do two things. They would lodge a suit against the Fountain Clinic for gross injury and damages, and, more importantly, they would start court proceedings against Madeleine to get Ella back, emphasising of course that they could offer the child a stable home with two parents and a mother who didn't work, a nice, old-fashioned set-up.

Next Madeleine went to the newspaper cuttings library in the City where she discovered that there was a case outstanding against a Canadian clinic where at least thirty women were alleged unknowingly to have provided eggs for other women or to have received the wrong eggs themselves. It was as Madeleine was reading this that the realisation came to her that the idea that Ella wasn't hers – which ten days before had seemed preposterous – now seemed quite possible. It was of course Ella's strange beauty which had prepared the ground for this idea, her unfamiliarity which even after all these years had not quite gone away. But what was interesting was that this idea, which was so enormous, in reality changed nothing. It was true that it had the effect of shifting the child slightly away from her grasp, of making her that little bit more a stranger. But no sooner did Ella seem to move away than Madeleine had an impulse to reach forward and snatch her back, because this equally was true, that she didn't care where Ella came from, she could have come from the moon for all that it mattered. All that she could feel was that she had loved and nurtured and toiled for this child and now they were linked together indissolubly.

That evening Madeleine and Ella quarrelled. Madeleine had collected her early from the childminder and now she was cooking fishfingers in the kitchen whilst Ella lay on the sofa in the living room watching television. The table was covered in glue and scissors and bits of paper where Ella had been making a model that morning. 'Ella?' Madeleine called out, 'can you come and clear the table?' No answer. 'Ella?' called Madeleine again, 'can you clear the table?' Still no answer. Madeleine went into the living room. 'Ella,' she said, 'clear the table.' The child didn't move. Her eyes were fixed on the television screen. With her head tilted back against a cushion you could see the bee-stung lower lip, luscious, the colour of raspberries, making a sensual shape, for all the world like Gina's mouth. Madeleine felt herself on fire with rage. She strode across the room. She seized Ella by the shoulder. 'Ow,' shrieked Ella, 'that hurts.' Madeleine held her tighter. 'Well, clear the bloody table then,' she said. 'Ow,' shrieked Ella, 'you're hurting me.' She wriggled free. 'I hate you, mummy,' she said, 'I wish I had a father,' and she burst into noisy crying and ran into the bedroom, slamming the door behind her.

Madeleine sat down on the sofa. She started to cry. All these years of struggle and work and not once had she cried, not even when Martin left her, not even when she was dog-tired when Ella was little and she had no one to talk to. But she was crying now. 'What have I done?' thought Madeleine, angry and despairing. But before long she heard through the wall the sounds of Ella sobbing, and then straightaway her love started up again, as if this love were now her foundation and everything else – anger, irritation, revenge – were just things she had built on top. Would she care less if Ella were less pretty or less bright? Who could say? She had fallen into the habit of worshipping her child.

28

The snow melted in the streets but lingered on the rooftops, picking out the lines of window sills and roof edges and gutters and the upper lines of twigs, turning the world to black and grey and white. Madeleine was tired. The cold made her tired. When she came in from outside her ears roared and her face burned. It was so cold that even the thought of warm weather hurt, in the way that it hurts to dip freezing fingers into warm water. And her insomnia had returned. The late November nights seemed to go on for ever, darkness eating up a huge portion of every day. Ella went to bed in darkness and got up in darkness too. Madeleine was waking at one o'clock, three o'clock, four o'clock. When she drew the curtains the street lamps and the traffic lights looked gloomy and fantastical.

Night after night, Madeleine sat at the living-room table, drinking cups of coffee and she who had once prided herself on the freedom of her mind, now pursued the same thoughts obsessively. She was thinking of the Kaufmans whom, in her mind's eye, she now saw as a rich and powerful couple. Her anger against them was hot, obsessive and tiring. She was exhausted by her own thought processes, by the images that kept jumping up in her mind in the most inappropriate of places – in tutorials or when she was talking to her professor – images of herself turning on George Kaufman and angrily upbraiding him, grabbing his hair and yanking back his head, shouting the truth at him whilst he stood there, open-mouthed. Because whilst she blamed them both, it was George she blamed in particular. Because Gina was only another infertile woman, desperate for a baby, whilst George was the one with the money, worldly enough to go to a lawyer, powerful enough to make the moves. So the question was, why did George want a baby, or rather why did he want a child who might or might not be his, and who anyway was female?

She struggled to recover a memory of a little, pretty, hard-eyed man in an expensive suit, blushing as the women teased him. She tried to picture where George and Gina might live, the cars they would drive – because of course they would have one each – the holidays they would take, the clothes in their wardrobes – there would be plenty of these – the recreational drugs they would take, because of course there would be plenty of these also. She remembered his profession – a film producer – and hers – a beautiful, kept wife. And she remembered how he had stood there in the corridor, drinking champagne, and she thought, I hate him, I'd like to stick a knife into his stomach and watch the drink spurt out. She saw the knife go in. She saw the blood on his fine, new shirt. She felt the pain, a hot, turbulent pain, way down in the pit of the stomach, carried there on the tip of her knife. I could do that, she thought, and her fingers itched for a weapon to spoil the pretty face and the pretty shirt.

Why do men want children, and why does that man want my child in particular? Madeleine thought bitterly.

She went to see a lawyer in an expensive practice in Piccadilly. He was a tall, dark-haired, ruddy-cheeked young man – handsome if you like that hard-edged look – with hands in his pockets and fashionable horn-rimmed glasses. But no sooner did Madeleine clap eyes on him than she felt intimidated. What's wrong with me? she thought, I never used to be overawed by men with power. But the reason of course was Ella, because fear for Ella had made her nervous and nervousness had taken away her confidence, making her too conscious of the fact that men with power, like this man, rate youth and money and beauty, all of which are diminished by a baby.

She had brought with her a cutting about the Canadian case and it was just as well she had because the lawyer seemed to find it hard to grasp what had happened – both what George and Gina alleged had taken place, and the original process of conception by donor sperm – so that Madeleine, who had wanted to ask if she could countersue for upset caused, found herself instead having to explain about donor sperm and in vitro fertilisation.

'So you knew from the start that your husband wasn't the father of this baby? but then who did you think the father was?' asked the lawyer.

'I used donor sperm,' said Madeleine impatiently. 'It's quite common. Anonymous sperm. In effect there isn't a father.'

He fixed her with dark, hollow eyes. 'But you think that there has indeed been some muddling up of the eggs at this clinic?'

'What does it matter?' asked Madeleine sharply. 'That's not the point. The point is that I've loved Ella and looked after her and she's mine, wherever she comes from.'

'Maybe,' said the lawyer, 'but from the legal point of view that's not the whole story. Legally, biological parents have rights as well. Think of surrogacy. Commercial surrogacy is of course against the law. Other forms of surrogacy are allowed, but although the biological parents may be quite happy to give away their child, as far as the law is concerned they remain the parents and retain parental rights and responsibilities. As I say, under the law biological parents can't be discounted.'

Madeleine stared at him. He's only saying that because he doesn't approve of me, she thought. He doesn't approve of single parents. He's probably just started on a family and he wants to believe in family life. This man dismayed her. She thought that for two pins he would hand her child over to the opposition. I'll have to find someone else, she thought.

Ella caught flu. Every afternoon her temperature went up, every night it hovered at a 104° or over, every morning it came down leaving her pale and skinny and exhausted-looking. Madeleine had to give her Calpol every six hours. The last hour of every six was the worst when the temperature was a 104° and rising but it was not yet time for her medicine. Madeleine tried sponging her down but Ella whimpered and fought the sponge. Her skin was rough. Her arms were like wooden spoons. Her teeth, in her skull-like face, were the size of tomb stones. She kept bursting into tears and upbraiding Madeleine bitterly. For three days Madeleine stayed at home and nursed her. They slept in the same bed together.

When Ella rolled against her she burnt her mother with her skin.

After three days Madeleine went back to work for fear of losing her job, and employed a student to come in instead. During Ella's convalescence the child grew very sweet. At the weekend she lay on the sofa listening to story tapes and watching what Madeleine did, and Madeleine who was already stretched and softened by mother-love, now felt herself stretched even further. Ella wouldn't go back to her own bed. Every night she climbed into the double bed where she lay asleep with her chin on Madeleine's breast, just at that place where if she had been a white-haired patriarch Madeleine would have had a beard.

One day Ella was trying to skip with one of Madeleine's scarves. 'It makes quite a good skipping rope,' she said, 'except that I'm rather too tall, which is glad for me to think that I'm too tall for something.' She was small for her age. She was the smallest child in her class. She went back to school looking like a stick of glass.

When Madeleine went into college for her ten o'clock lecture she found her students standing in the forecourt waiting for her. They stamped their feet and chatted and laughed and turned up their collars against the cold as they shared a cigarette, calling out to her, 'Hello, Madeleine'. To Madeleine it seemed that her students were free, that they were not bound, as she was, by a painful love for a child. Their gestures were romantic. A cloak of Hollywood romance covered their relationships. Madeleine loved too, but no one judged there to be anything romantic about loving your child.

She dreamt one night of Martin. In her dream he was skiing across the snow above the French Alpine town where Angelina's family owned a couple of hotels. He looked prosperous and tanned, all dressed in winter-white. Half a dozen children were fanned out behind him, shrieking and shouting, all of them his sons and heirs and every one of them identical. When he saw her he laughed. He said, 'You could have had me if you hadn't kept picking quarrels.' Even in her dream Madeleine could see that family life suited him, that really he was very pleased with it. And then the dream changed and now she was sitting at a table and Martin had cooked a meal for her and was putting it in front of her as he used to do. To be waited on like this had a sensuous feel. In her dream she felt it, like a sudden warmth on an icy day, making a luxury of tears, the lip of a warm wave overflowing her throat and filling her mouth and her eyes, so that her grief for Ella and for herself and for the past was a sudden blow on the head, a shriek, a yell, the turning-on abruptly of the lights.

I've lost my nerve, she thought. I can't go on any longer. I need a man to help me. I need a man to protect me.

29

Ella wanted a father. It was amazing to Madeleine that she had never foreseen this possibility. If a bus driver spoke to Ella, if a shopkeeper smiled at her, so long as they were men, she would blush and smile straight back at them. Since she'd got better and gone back to school she had acquired a tough and matter-of-fact manner. All the girls in her class had it. It was how they survived in the playground. Towards Madeleine she was comradely on a good day and cool on a bad, but in the presence of doctors, bus drivers, teachers, shopkeepers – anyone who was male – she melted. When they passed the open door of the minicab office on the ground floor she hung on Madeleine's hand, holding her mother back and tripping her up, whilst all the while she simpered at the minicab drivers and they smiled back at her their gangster smiles. Like one of those Hollywood movies where the little girl is trying to find a husband for her mother, thought Madeleine in embarrassment. It was as if sugar was being stirred into Ella's vinegar, as if – like any old-fashioned woman – she wanted a man to make sense of her, to reveal to her who she was.

But Madeleine was no better. She had found herself a lawyer, a Mr Paul Chatoo, of Chatoo and Godwin, recommended to her by Nicola's husband William. 'He's compassionate and he likes a tricky case,' said Nicola. So Madeleine wrote a list of questions she wanted to ask him and the strategy she wanted him to adopt, and putting on a little grey suit, she went to see him.

His offices were behind the Inns of Court. Madeleine was early. She was ushered into a large room where the lights gave off an old yellow glow and the walls appeared to be lined with brown paper. There were rows of gold-bound books and computers glowing greenly on every desk and heads huddled over them in subdued conference. Madeleine sat down on a sofa. Before long Mr Chatoo came in. He'd been in court all morning. He was a little man, dressed in a heavy, black overcoat with a woollen scarf folded at the neck. He had a long nose and ruddy cheeks and shiny yellow-brown eyes. He smiled at Madeleine and came across and shook her hand. 'Yes,' he said, 'recommended by William Gale. Yes.' He led her into his office. 'Now, what a story,' he said.

Madeleine began to talk very fast, outlining to him exactly what she wanted him to do. He let her talk for a couple of minutes and then suddenly he asked, 'Do you have a photograph of the child?'

'Why, yes,' said Madeleine in surprise and she drew out of her bag a photograph of Ella.

'Charming,' said Mr Chatoo, 'charming. And does she go to school? Can she read? Can she write? Excellent. Excellent. Now do you have any family?'

'Yes, my mother,' said Madeleine.

'And does she see the child?'

'Why, yes.'

'Good, good. So the child has a loving grandmother. And you? You work, of course.'

'Yes,' said Madeleine

'Hard?'

'Of course,' said Madeleine.

'So, a bright, hard-working woman who has dedicated her life to bringing up her child. I think we can do something with that,' said Mr Chatoo.

'Now,' he said, 'tell me in your own words the story of what has happened to you and – Ella, is it? – yes, Ella.' He sat quiet and listened to her with his hands held tightly on his lap and a look of bird-like alertness in his eyes. As she spoke Madeleine had the feeling that he was folding the events of her life into the shape of a story, as Madeleine sometimes folded paper into origami shapes for Ella, creating a heroine – that was herself – and a couple of villains – they were George and Gina – and a child-victim – that was Ella. 'Good,

good,' he kept saying in a low, cautious voice, but his sombre tone was belied by his smile of relish. He looked at the letters from George's solicitors. 'I'm surprised they've taken on the case,' he said. 'They mostly deal with media matters. But I'm not surprised they'd take a flyer. I expect they'd like the publicity.' He examined the Canadian cuttings. 'There's no precedent,' he muttered in a doubtful voice, but all the while he was smiling as if really the challenge were delightful.

'Now,' he said when the story had been recounted, and Madeleine opened her mouth to speak – but then closed it again because she saw that he would take on her case but only on his terms, not hers. 'Now,' said Mr Chatoo, 'I think we must get in touch with the other side and see if we can find out what evidence they have accumulated.'

'Is it wise to talk to the enemy?' asked Madeleine.

'Sometimes it is necessary,' said Mr Chatoo, and he added, 'you do realise that if they have a case of gross negligence against the clinic then so do you.'

'I'm not interested in that,' said Madeleine, 'I just want to keep my child.' He looked at her in smiling silence. 'I just want to keep my child,' Madeleine repeated because she was begging him to reassure her. At last he said, 'The law in general sets great store by the natural mother which of course is exactly what is in dispute here. On the other hand the Children Act also favours the status quo – which it defines as wherever the child has lived for three years or more – because the welfare of the child is paramount. 'I can't give any definite answers because in this kind of case there are none. All I can say is that I don't believe any judge would take your child away from you.'

The last thing he said to her was, 'This couple – the Kaufmans – what do you know about them?'

'Not a lot,' said Madeleine, 'she was in hospital with me, in the next room. She was – well, she was rich and she didn't work – she was, you know, the kind of woman that the rest of us used rather to despise.' (She was thinking of herself and Mercedes-Sally.) But Mr Chatoo didn't know. It was clear that for him there was no judgement to be made in whether or not a woman worked. All he said, with a smile of relish, was, 'It would be useful to know something more about them.'

Afterwards Madeleine sat in a nearby café and reflected that you could go on for years without thinking of your father and then you met a man of a certain age and it started up again, a weakness for his smile, a tendency – quite uncharacteristic – to do whatever he said, a nineteenth-century female pleasure in saying, 'Yes sir, no sir, three bags full, sir'. It was at the moment that he had started giving her orders that she had gone weak at the knees, with a sweet, sexy, Mills-and-Boon mixing of lover and father, a fantasy last indulged when she was about thirteen, that there was a man out there who would understand her every feeling. 'He's a compassionate man,' Nicola had said. 'Compassionate, compassionate,' Madeleine kept repeating as if compassion had suddenly become a sexy commodity. Afterwards these nineteenth-century feelings of obedience towards him lingered on, reviving whenever she rang him up or wrote to him, and whenever there was a crisis in her life.

Ella had a new childminder, a big, tall woman called Norma with custard-yellow curls and face like a cliff. Norma had spent her life with children, first as a dinner lady, then as a lollipop lady, then as a childminder. It was Norma who discovered that Ella was being teased by two girls who had previously been her friends. When Madeleine discovered this she was almost as upset as she was by the Kaufmans. It seemed to her that everywhere her child had enemies. When Madeleine went to collect Ella from school on Friday afternoons she saw Ella's erstwhile friends coming out of school together, heads as close as two beads on a string, faces shiny-smooth with innocence. And only if you were the mother, only if it was your child who was being teased, would you notice their tiny smiles and the way their eyes slid round to watch you, each of these small movements saying that they knew that you knew that they were bullying Ella. That night in the bath Ella cried because she wanted her old friends back. Madeleine washed Ella with rough, impatient hands. She thought, Ella is grieving for her best friends and I'm grieving on her behalf because of the Kaufmans. This child is nothing but grief. Suddenly she felt very cold. I can't stand this, she thought. She wanted to cry. She wanted to ring up Mr

Chatoo and beg him to help her. She wanted to marry a rich and worldly man like Mr Chatoo because she wanted someone to look after them, to take Ella out of her present school and find her something better.

30

It was Andrew Harvey of all people who gave her the idea. He was one of her third-year students, a pretty boy with a lanky grin who dressed in tartan trousers and a leather jacket. Andrew Harvey had always made a great show out of fancying Madeleine. All through the years when she had loved Ella he had come across to her in the canteen, saying, 'Mind if I join you, Madeleine?' or 'I wish I was in your tutorial group, Madeleine. I feel I can talk to you,' or 'Women like you, Madeleine' – this said admiringly – 'are tough' or 'Do you think I should do a PhD, Madeleine?' Everything she said he seemed to find sharp and knowing and funny. He blinked and smiled in her presence as if she dazzled him. In her tutorials he stretched out his long legs in her direction as if to say, 'All these engaging limbs are yours, darling.'

Madeleine didn't believe that he really fancied her. She thought it was how he consoled himself for her status and authority. Even so she had felt faintly tender towards him, admiring his looks and his nerve in trying to chat her up – though her other feelings had always been stronger: her love for Ella, of course; her love for her mother; even her love for Nicola. But then this situation with the Kaufmans had arisen, since when she had gone off men altogether, so that now when she was with Andrew Harvey she found herself glittering with irritation because – although he was only twenty-two so it was quite unfair – she couldn't help thinking how feeble it was to live a life where all the strong feelings are avoided and all you had to worry about was what trousers to wear in the mornings. It seemed to her that the strong events of her life – first motherhood and now the Kaufmans – had rendered her enormous, and that in her presence Andrew Harvey was a delicate and fiddly thing, whilst she loomed over him with a cartoon grotesqueness.

One lunchtime Madeleine went across the college forecourt looking for him. She went from group to group. She crossed the road to the greasy spoon café and peered in through windows that were misted up and dripping. She saw him drinking a cup of coffee and went in and sat beside him at the table. 'I hear you have a job, Andrew Harvey,' she said. She had heard it on the college grapevine. It was a rule that all term-time jobs had to be cleared by your supervisor.

'I've done your essay, Madeleine,' he said.

'I know you have.'

'Were they asking about my job at the staff meeting?'

'They're always asking about your job. So what is it?'

He blushed. 'You'll never believe it,' he said. 'I'm working for a detective agency.'

'What on earth does that mean?'

'A detective agency. It means that we offer divorce surveillance, that we're undercover specialists and we find missing persons and provide bodyguards and debugging services and adoption enquiries. Although actually most of what I do is answering the telephone and doing the mail-order catalogue,' he added.

'You've been reading too many detective novels,' said Madeleine.

'Well, who's fault is that?' he asked her slyly and he grinned that bedazzled grin of his. 'I wish I was doing more of your lectures this year, Madeleine,' he added.

'Madeleine' he kept calling her. He might just as well have called her 'mother'.

'It sounds like men's games to me,' she said.

'Not at all,' he said earnestly. 'Have you ever thought of getting a personal alarm? Protection against rape, assault, that kind of thing?'

'And that sounds to me like hyping up the market in order to make a sale.' She got to her feet. 'I'll tell them that the job's not a problem. But if your essays start coming in late or not up to scratch it will be a problem. Right?'

He had given her an idea. She woke up in the night thinking about it. It was the kind of idea to make you smile, to make you get out of bed and go into the kitchen and pour yourself a glass of wine, to make you sit at the table at one in the morning smiling to yourself as you thought about it.

She found a detective agency in the *Yellow Pages* and having first of all checked that it wasn't Andrew Harvey's she went to see them. They were situated in a tall, narrow Victorian house in a faded and anonymous part of North London. She stood on their doorstep, ringing their bell and looking down an empty street. She spoke into an intercom, climbed a narrow flight of stairs, past a landing window which looked down on to a courtyard garden, very full of rubbish, and came to a first-floor room where a woman sat at a computer screen showing a lot of leg and two men unpacked a box of equipment. They were dressed in ties and striped shirt sleeves. The older of the two had cropped hair and a bullet head and round, steel-rimmed glasses, but the other one was young and very tall and thin, in dark shades and with long, spidery legs. On one wall was a pinboard with pictures on it of missing women and abducted children. There were advertisements for bullet-proof vests and high-tech guns, and manuals pinned up on how to lose yourself, to fake a suicide and to get false papers. The atmosphere in the room was one of subdued gaiety and excitement – probably, thought Madeleine, who was standing there dressed in old leggings and a shabby donkey jacket, because they were working up that favourite male myth of double agents and subterfuge.

The middle-aged man had hard, cold eyes. It was as if he saw all the bleakness in life and wished that he did not. 'Can I help you,' he asked.

'My name's Madeleine Kingdom,' she said. 'I rang you. I need a private detective.'

He got off his chair. 'If you'll wait a minute,' he said, and he vanished through a door into another room. The other man in shades seemed kinder. The woman at the computer screen called out, 'Paul? Can you help me?' and he went across to her, tucking his dark glasses further up his nose and folding up his spidery legs as he sat down on a chair beside her. 'Well, Sharon? now what?' he asked, peering at the screen, and she giggled.

The middle-aged man reappeared. 'If you come this way,' he said, and he showed her into a back room with a desk, a computer, a couple of chairs, a pinboard with a handful of items on it and a window which, when he raised the blind, looked down onto the same, rubbish-filled courtyard. He switched on his computer and it began to whirr and buzz. He wiped down a chair and pushed it in her direction. Then he leant back in his chair, fixing her with eyes that were like hard, cold pebbles flecked with white. 'Well?' he said.

'There's a man and his wife out there,' she said, 'I want to know everything there is to know about them.'

'And we are talking London here?'

'Yes.'

He nodded.

'I want to know everything he does during the day,' she said, 'and what she does as well, and what they do in the evenings, both separately and together. This isn't about another woman,' she added, 'it's about a child.'

That made him stare. 'Of course,' he said, 'that's the pattern, isn't it? Most of the women who come to us are fighting for their children, not for their men.' He smiled. 'Sad, isn't it? At least it is if you're a man.'

Madeleine shrugged. 'I can't help that,' she said sadly, 'I want to keep my child. And I only pay by results. I need to discredit the man but the truth is all that interests me. Made-up stories won't get me anywhere.'

He didn't like her bullying him. His eyes were sardonic and unfriendly. They said, 'I give back everything I get and give it back tenfold.' 'Do you want to know details of his bank account?' he asked. 'Overdraft. Any bankruptcies. Money owed. That kind of thing?'

'Can you find that out for me?'

'Of course,' he said, 'do you want a week or a fortnight?'

'Can you find out enough in a week?'

'I don't know yet,' he said.

'A week,' she said, thinking of her shrinking budget. 'Start on Monday and ring me Monday week, but for God's sake not at work. Here's my home phone number although if you're half as good as you claim I expect you can find it for yourself.'

All this while he had been tapping fast and light with his thick, sausage fingers into the computer. He smiled. 'I have done already,' he said '*Dr* Madeleine Kingdom.'

Standing there in the detective agency in her old black leggings and her shabby donkey jacket she had felt humiliated by her dowdiness. That afternoon she went shopping. She bought herself a pair of ankle boots, a pair of narrow, black velvet trousers which made her skinniness look blessed, a white, satin shirt with tails and another one with ruffles and a black jacket with a scalloped fringe. The next weekend she went to the hairdressers and had her hair cut short and the tips dyed blonde and then she went to a big, department store where she had the make-up girls darken and enlarge her eyes, put hollows under the cheekbones to suggest a leanness and paint the lips with a pale gloss to give them curves and a hungry look.

As she sat there on the stool with the chequered tiles beneath her feet and the vaulted ceiling overhead and the lights shining on the glass cases and the oval mirror in front of her, the idea, which was so simple, suddenly overwhelmed her, that all these years the gap between what she wanted to happen and what was going to happen, had been growing steadily wider, as it so often does for mothers; but now she saw that it didn't have to be this way, that there didn't have to be a gap at all, that she could be – indeed she would have to be – again what she had been before Ella's birth. She thought that it was better to fight back, that it was no use giving up, no use becoming a soft and loving mother when what she needed were the qualities she used to have, of quarrelsomeness and aggression. But she'd also forgotten what a buzz you could get from defiance, how good it could make you feel. She was feeling it now as she stepped out of the store, because thus armoured and prepared she was going out into the world to fight for her child.

31

The Agency's report on George Kaufman was full of gyms, pubs and wine bars; parties in penthouses and on canal boats; jazz clubs and Chinese take-aways; hotels and blondes in red suits and kisses and cuddles with them on dark pavements; dinners with clients in the Lord Jim, a restaurant on the top floor of the Diplomatic Hotel in Park Lane; and dinners and quarrels with Gina outside fish restaurants in Soho.

Gina's report comprised a list of facials, hairdressers and beauty treatments; restaurants for lunch and afternoon visits to the cinema, mostly in the company of her girlfriends, although on Wednesday after a morning visit to the gym she was observed having lunch with a man in Hampstead.

Madeleine sat in her study reading the reports. The view from her window looked out over Tavistock Square. The snow had gone but it was still cold and the naked trees and buildings all had a harsh and wizened look. She rang the Agency and got through to the younger, kinder of the two men.

'This man that Mrs K had lunch with on Wednesday?' she asked.

'Probably her gym instructor.'

'Do you think she's having an affair with him?'

'Hard to say. She was fairly plastered when she came out of the restaurant and with that amount of alcohol inside her she'd have fallen into anyone's arms. Idle, isn't she?' he added unexpectedly.

'Utterly,' said Madeleine with bitterness.

'Mr K's got quite good taste in jazz.'

'How would you know?' asked Madeleine rudely.

There was a pause. 'I know,' he said. 'Nice kid, is it?' he asked.

'Gorgeous,' said Madeleine. 'Well no,' she added, 'a bit of a brat really but she's mine and I love her. Anyway' – she turned a page of the report – 'The Cavendish Hotel. You say that Mr K visited it for an hour on Saturday morning whilst Mrs K was at the hairdresser. The Cavendish is just round the corner from here. What kind of hotel is it?'

'Large. Modern. A bit down-at-heel. A lot of empty rooms. Mr K probably has a room there which he keeps on a retainer. The hotel won't mind. Times are hard. They'll be glad of the custom.'

'And do you think he was going there to meet a woman?'

'Of course.'

'How do you know?'

'Because the lift man saw them.'

'Which woman?'

'The blonde in the red suit.'

'And the Diplomatic Hotel in Park Lane. What kind of hotel is that?'

'Big. Very expensive. A lot of foreign clientele. It's known for being a good place to pick up a rich man, especially Lord Jim's which is the restaurant at the top. Most hotels operate a strict policy on prostitutes and brass. The Diplomatic has a slightly looser policy.'

'Brass?'

'Women who'll swap sex for money.'

'You mean prostitutes?'

'No. That's putting it too hard. Brass are slightly different. Brass will put time into nurturing clients. Brass think longer term. Brass are sometimes even thinking about marriage. The blonde in the red suit is probably brass. But the thing about brass is that they'll only marry where there's money. And brass are old-fashioned of course. You won't catch brass wearing anything other than perfume and high heels.'

'Well, count me out then,' said Madeleine.

'You don't know anything about men, do you?' said the man. It was his revenge on her for her remark about the jazz.

Madeleine took no notice.

'And this financial report?' she said, turning a few more pages. 'Is their overdraft really £100,000?'

'It is. If you live that kind of lifestyle you soon get there.'

'Jesus!' said Madeleine.

When Madeleine put the phone down and looked out of the window she saw that somewhere to the south the sun must have come out, for the sky, although still grey, was lighter and more radiant, and a sudden, yellow light – the colour of boiling, creamy milk – was spilling across the chilly square. So sudden and so delightful was this yellow sunshine that Madeleine smiled and with the smile the realisation came to her that she was going to use that blonde, that she was going to compile such a dossier on Mr K's behaviour that no judge in his right mind would put him in charge of a goldfish.

She thought she was on her own, that her story was too odd, too strong, too unlucky for anyone else to cope with. But it wasn't true. She rang Nicola that night and told her. 'What a bugger,' said Nicola, and her voice came tossing and swaying down the telephone lines, but not weak, not weak at all. 'What a bugger.'

'I'm going to go to Lord Jim's,' said Madeleine, 'will you come with me? I want to spy on him, and see the kind of people that he mixes with.'

'I don't have anything to wear,' said Nicola, 'I'm a mother now. I don't have those kind of clothes.'

'It doesn't matter,' said Madeleine. 'Come for my sake.'

And so Nicola came, wearing a dress that her mother had bought from Jaeger twenty years before, and which made her look well-bred and all of fifty-seven. But it didn't matter because she gave Madeleine that warm feeling you sometimes get from female friendship, that it is like toast and coffee and fruit and cake and cream to a starving man. Madeleine thought that though it is often bleak the friendships you make in the Dead Mothers' Club are some of the best you will ever have.

32

'Dear God,' said Madeleine. They had ascended by a glass lift, past real trees and vines and bougainvillaeas, with a lift man to press the buttons and to eye them up with a yellowy, jealous, desiring look. They had passed acres of black glass, beyond which there was presumably the glitter of the city; but the brightness inside exceeded that without, and quenched it so that all they could see as the lift slid by was black glass and their own bright reflections in it. When they stepped out at the top their coats were removed and they were taken to a bar and seated at high bar stools with their legs dangling down and bright pink cocktails with rose petals floating on the surface and slices of mango were put before them. There was a Christmas tree, cone-shaped, as no real tree is ever shaped, starred and draped with lights and ribbons and streamers. It was three days before Christmas.

And then Madeleine looked around and saw that in stepping into Lord Jim's they might just as well have stepped into another country. It was not only the glitter and the flowers and the dazzle on the glass. It was not only the myriad blondes of every hue and the glimpses of their underwear. It was not only the bloom of money on hair and eyes and legs, and that muffling sense of wealth beneath the talk and laughter. It was not only the way that the men's bodies were bound into shape by their dark suits whilst the women's bodies seemed to fall apart into their gorgeous bits. It was more than this. It was the suggestion of a world untouched by feminism, a world where men are old-fashioned and women feminine in the way that your mother – or your grandmother – was feminine before you, a world of the senses and of extremes of femininity and masculinity.

'Dear God,' said Madeleine again, 'to think that while I was working they were all partying.'

Nicola complained, 'I don't feel properly dressed.'

'You shouldn't worry,' said Madeleine, lying through her teeth, 'you look absolutely fine to me.' Madeleine was wearing a man's suit but made of some silky, dark blue fabric, self-patterned, and underneath it a white shirt. From a distance she looked like a boy. Only if you peered closely could you see the mother underneath.

The young man who brought them their cocktails was a pretty boy, with eyes the colour of dark red wine in a bottle and a plump, cushiony lower lip the colour of a plum. He moved along the bar towards them, wiping the surfaces as he went, his eyes lingering on Nicola. His smile was sweet. It said both, 'I'll look after you', and 'No, you look after me'. That edible man, thought Madeleine. 'You see,' she said to Nicola when he'd turned away, 'all things are available.'

'William's eaten here a couple of times,' said Nicola, 'I'd no idea.'

'You probably thought he was eating out at the local Indian restaurant,' said Madeleine.

'Do you think they're all prostitutes?' Nicola whispered.

'Brass,' said Madeleine.

'What?'

Madeleine explained. She said, 'The man in the detective agency told me. He's my explainer of the world. Every mother needs one.'

'Why aren't I like these woman?' Nicola asked.

'It's our mothers' fault,' said Madeleine, 'they made us what we are. Women are what their mothers make them.'

'And do you think any of them have children?' Nicola asked.

'They look very young to me,' said Madeleine, 'most of them look about twenty. But I expect they've taken a vow to remain childless.'

Nicola shrugged. She had a mother's contempt for women who choose not to have children in case they ruin the party.

'Where did you meet William?' asked Madeleine after a while.

'At University,' said Nicola, 'we were one of those couples that met in the first week and never got round to parting. Next year will be our twentieth anniversary.

'And who do you love most, your husband or your children?'

'Oh, my children. Doesn't everybody?'

'It hasn't always been like that,' said Madeleine. 'In the fifties if your husband was in the Services and got posted abroad you left your children behind with relatives and went with him.'

'But in those days women loved men the most, whereas nowadays we love the children. Poor bloody men,' said Nicola. 'And poor you,' she added, seeing Madeleine's face.

'Oh, I've got no intention of letting anyone take my child away,' said Madeleine.

'I asked William about your situation. He says he doesn't think any judge would rule against you.'

Madeleine shrugged. She was pursuing her own thoughts. 'Tell me,' she said, 'why do men want children?'

'I don't know,' said Nicola. 'Lots of men don't, but those that do . . . I suppose they want to be king amongst the little ones, to have little ones running after them and looking up to them and admiring them. At any rate, that's how William feels.'

They asked for the menu. They were just beginning to look at the prices and to wonder if they could afford to eat here or whether they should simply share another cocktail, when Madeleine saw him. He was sitting in a group of men. They were the noisiest table in the room. One of them was singing and another was beating time with his fists while half a dozen waitresses were running to and fro, plying them with food and drink, like mother birds feeding a nest of babies. On the other side of them was a table of blondes. One, two, three, four, Madeleine counted. They had turned round and were talking to George's table. One of them had an arm round his neck. She wore a dress of Father Christmas red. She looked like a shiny package waiting to be unwrapped. She was trying to kiss him on his cheek, swaying around as if seeking a particular spot.

'What is it? Is he there?' asked Nicola. Madeleine nodded. She had only seen him once before but the sight of him slotted as perfectly into the remembered image as a snooker ball into its pocket.

'Where?' asked Nicola.

'Don't turn round,' said Madeleine, 'but Mr K himself is over there with a couple of bimbos getting himself smashed.'

'Will he remember you?'

'I shouldn't think so.'

'So what are we going to do?'

'Have another drink and spy on him at our leisure.'

'I can't see him. I want to turn round,' Nicola complained, but Madeleine wasn't listening because now George was standing up, slowly, with difficulty, seeming to have to push down at his companions to ease himself up. He was squeezing himself out from between the blondes. I hate him, thought Madeleine. He was threading his way out between the chairs, looking flushed and dishevelled. I hate him, thought Madeleine. He was coming in their direction, presumably on his way to the toilet. I hate him, thought Madeleine, staring at him with eyes wide; and hatred made her eyes glitter and turned her cheeks to a rosy colour, giving her a look – if you didn't look too closely – of warmth and Christmas good cheer. She didn't bother to hide her hatred. Anonymity made her feel invisible and besides he was so drunk – she could see this now – that he would never even notice her. He was wearing a stone-grey suit with a black polo-neck beneath and black shoes of some faint, sharkskin pattern with gold chains across the top of them. What a naff pair of shoes, thought Madeleine, glaring at him, what kind of man wears shoes like that? And then, just as he was passing, he caught her glare and as if he'd snagged himself upon it he pulled up short and looked her straight in the eye. And, oh shit, thought Madeleine, because of course he thought she fancied him.

On his way back from the toilet he stopped in front of her. He stood there with his hands in his pockets and his head tilted to one side and a bleak look in his eyes because he didn't like to ask a woman anything. 'Don't I know you from somewhere?' he asked. 'No,' said Madeleine, flat and unadorned, and gradually the flatness of her answer filtered into his drunkard's consciousness and he shrugged. 'Oh well,' he said, and he moved on with his head down, back to the table and the blondes.

But he didn't forget her. Several times she saw him look in

her direction and when she got up and went to the toilet he must have followed her, for when she came out she found him standing there, in the middle of the corridor, weaving about a little with a drunkard's concentration.

'Have a cigarette with me,' he said, and they leant side by side against the wall and he lit her a cigarette.

'I'm drunk,' he said.

'Yep,' she said.

'My wife says she prefers me drunk because when I'm drunk I talk. Otherwise, I stay silent. What about you? Do you like to talk? No, clearly not. My wife would like me to be the opposite of whatever I am. You know what wives are like?'

'You created her,' said Madeleine remembering the beautiful, nervy Gina, 'and now you're complaining.'

'How do you know I created her?'

'Didn't you? Don't all married couples create their partners in the image that they want?'

'You're not like my wife,' he said.

'No, I don't suppose I am.'

'You look to me like a puritan.'

'I'm a feminist.'

'Same thing,' he said.

'Smart-arse,' she said. He was so drunk and she was so very angry, she felt she could say anything.

'But you really aren't like the other women here,' he insisted, peering at her more closely, and he added, with alarming prescience, 'you must be here for a reason.' But at that she shrugged and wouldn't answer.

'What do you do?' he asked her.

'This and that. What about you?'

'I produce films.'

'And are they any good?' she jeered.

He said nothing, just looked at her. 'I run a company called Double Vision,' he said. 'We make children's films. The kind with action and excitement and mystery and adventure. A bit slick but it's what the market demands and anyway, I like them like that. Cowboys and Indians, or the modern equivalent. Goodies and baddies. Men and women.'

'A man's got to do what a man's got to do?'

'Why not? There's nothing wrong with that.' He blew out his cigarette smoke. 'We made—' he said, and he named a children's film which had recently been released.

'I saw it,' said Madeleine. 'It was very good, very exciting, but you got the history wrong.'

'We did?'

'The body-snatchers. You didn't make them gruesome enough. They were far more gruesome than that.'

'So you mean we missed a trick?'

'Sure you did.'

He looked at her broodingly, as if now he were prepared to consider what had eluded him before, the charms of a clever woman. Why is it? thought Madeleine, that clever women chase clever men but clever men chase bimbos.

'Let's go somewhere and have a drink,' he said.

'What about my girlfriend?'

'She can come too.'

'I don't think she'd want that. And anyway, won't your friends miss you?'

He looked at her stonily, as if to say, So what do you care if my friends miss me? 'What's your name?' he asked. She said nothing. 'Where can I get hold of you?' Still she said nothing. 'Very well,' he said in an irritated voice, and he pushed himself away from the wall and began to walk away.

Suddenly she saw the possibilities of this situation. 'No, wait a moment,' she called after him. 'You can't have my phone number – I'm – I'm married – but I could have yours.'

He reached into the inner pocket of his jacket and drew out a card. 'George Kaufman' was printed on it. 'I don't know your name,' he said.

'Suzanne.'

'Ring me,' he said.

She watched him as he made his way back to his table. As he squeezed past the blondes, one of them must have said something to him because he started to laugh. He was only a small man, sharply dressed and with boyish features, but that laugh! – with the lips apart and the eyes half-closed and the chin thrown back and the head tilted up as if he were standing under a shower of female admiration – that laugh pierced Madeleine and mingled sharply and painfully with her hate for him.

When they got back to the car Nicola asked, 'But how could you talk to him? I mean, did you tell him who you were?'

'I said my name was Suzanne.'

'*Suzanne*?'

'Why not?'

'Is it really him?' asked Nicola.

'Oh yes. The same name. Both film-makers. Both identical-looking. It's him all right.'

'Why did he give you his card?'

'Because he wants to see me again.'

'And will you?'

'I might.'

'Why?'

'Because I want to understand him. I want to know why a man like him wants children. And I want to know why he wants my child in particular,' said Madeleine who had her eyes shut and was picturing George Kaufman's nature, thinking that although he was dapper he wasn't soft – in fact he was quite the reverse – he was harsh in the way that very masculine men are harsh, their temperaments so hard that they can bruise themselves upon them. She didn't like him. She didn't like him at all, and yet mixed up with her dislike was a hot, excited, even sexy feeling, because to spy upon a man, to hold a secret over him, to know more about him than he knows about you – all this was a sexy feeling, and to steal something sexy from George Kaufman seemed only right and proper, given what he was trying to steal from her.

33

All these years since Ella had been born Madeleine had hardly given a thought to sex, remembering – if she remembered it at all – the sickly-sweet masochism of *L'Histoire d'O* with embarrassment and horror. It was as if something had been switched off inside her so that she could watch nude scenes on television, could read love poetry, could watch men in the street, could even put her fingers between her legs without one flicker of interest.

But not long after the evening at Lord Jim's Madeleine dreamt of sex and woke up clutching a bright fragment of a dream in which George Kaufman had pressed down on top of her, his arms spread-eagled, his hands splayed out against her flattened hands, his mouth, like a baby's, searching for hers. Something in this dream must have satisfied her because she woke up sighing deeply in her chest with contentment, her body very warm and heavy against the mattress and her fingers between her legs . . . George Kaufman, thought Madeleine. Jesus. How embarrassing. Fancy having a sexy dream about the enemy, George Kaufman.

But after this dream her world had sprang suddenly into three dimensions. The hours after Ella went to sleep which previously had been empty were now full again. She tried on make-up. She looked at her clothes. She picked up novels and books on poetry. She looked at herself in the mirror and her body, which for all these years she had ignored, she now regarded with tender curiosity as a possible source of pleasure. The cold made her tired but tiredness in itself was sexy, leaving her weakened and vulnerable and open to thoughts of sex. A procession of vivid images was passing through her mind – images of naked men, shadowy as ghosts, faces hidden, pricks erect; thoughts of the pleasures and the delights of sex – food, whips, fine clothes soon removed, sex from in front, sex from behind, the tracing of fingers and the licking of tongues all over. Unexpected pleasures. Pleasures to astonish you. Pleasures you didn't even know you knew of: Let a stranger have me secretly from behind. Roll me up in chocolate and put a candy on each breast and have me for dessert. And sex whilst others watched, their faces flowering in the darkness into admiration for you, whilst all your lines and wrinkles were smoothed out by the night.

Now that she wanted sex again her mother's asexuality was frightening. It alarmed her to see how her mother prowled around the living room in the evenings as she tidied her books and papers, looking bleak in the electric light, with all the painted femininity worn off her so that she resembled a wolf. At night Madeleine looked in the mirror and saw that pregnancy had filled out her straight lines, making her deep-bosomed, long-legged and narrow-hipped. 'I'm only thirty-six,' thought Madeleine, 'I'm not old, I'm not old at all. There's all my life before me.'

Madeleine and Ella went home to Madeleine's mother's house for Christmas Day. They ate lunch in the morning room beside the frosted-glass partition. The wallpaper on the walls had copper kettles on it. There was a cocktail cabinet in one corner with place mats and glasses and bottles of ancient spirits inside. The curtains were of a hideous orangey-brown and the lampshade was the same. 'Don't you think it's time you did this house up, Mum?' asked Madeleine discontentedly. She thought, I want more than this measured-out existence. I want men and sex and an extravagance of thoughts and feelings and sensations. She looked at herself and her mother, two women without men, and in her eyes they looked like a couple of children.

After lunch Ella fell asleep on the sofa in the living room. Madeleine's mother brought the lunch things through. Madeleine washed up in the scullery at the chipped, white, butler sink and stacked the crockery on the plate dryer. It was the same plate dryer that had been there when she was a child. In Madeleine's mother's world nothing was ever thrown away but was kept until it fell apart. Madeleine began to complain of how tired she felt. 'Perhaps the old way was right, after all, in which two adults brought up a child?' said Madeleine's mother.

'Do you think that if I could find myself a man I wouldn't?' said Madeleine bitterly, and her mother looked surprised, bewildered even. 'Well, I don't know,' she said and then slyly she asked – for she was not above the pleasures of revenge from time to time – 'So have you recanted of your feminist principles then?' Madeleine's mother thought that feminism was necessary in the workplace but dangerous in the home.

'It's not feminism that's failed, it's life,' said Madeleine, crashing around the cups in the sink.

'It's the same thing,' said Madeleine's mother soberly.

'Do you ever wonder if Dad's alive, Mum?' asked Madeleine.

'My father went too, you know.'

'But that was the war. Dying in the war was not unusual.'

'If there's not a war they'll find some other reason. Men vanish and that's just the way of it. He might be out there somewhere. But he knows where I am. I haven't moved.' *My* father too, thought Madeleine, not just your husband but my father too.

As Madeleine dried the crockery she told her mother what had happened with Ella and the clinic. 'Oh God,' said her mother faintly, 'Oh God.' She had once sat on a committee looking into the ethics of IVF and other fertility treatments. 'To think what can happen,' she said. 'We never thought of this, that the eggs once separated from their rightful bodies could find their way into other women's bodies. And of course any mother would rather her child was dead than lost in another woman's life, because so long as the child is alive out there somewhere the maternal itch can never stop. And that, of course, is the trouble with adoption, as we explained to them. Do you have a lawyer?' she asked.

'Yes,' said Madeleine.

'A good one?'

'Yes.'

Her mother looked relieved. Madeleine saw that she would get no strength from this source, that her mother was too old to give out strength and could only rely upon the lawyer, just as Madeleine did.

But what she couldn't give to Madeleine she could give to Ella. The child was still asleep on the sofa. Madeleine's mother placed a coat on top of her. 'What's this?' asked Ella, stirring and opening her eyes and plucking at the coat's fabric. 'Good God, that's Dad's jacket,' said Madeleine stepping forward. A Reefer jacket, double-breasted, of navy wool blurred and softened by age, its lining in shreds. 'Which dad?' asked Ella. 'My dad, your grandfather,' said Madeleine. *My* dad, thought Madeleine again.

After this Madeleine's mother rang up more often to ask to look after Ella. Ella liked going to her grandmother's house. She liked her grandmother's old ladynesses: the long shanks, the stooped shoulders, the stockings instead of tights, the hot-water bottles in their hot-water bottle covers. She was astonished at how ignorant her grandmother was, how she knew nothing about Barbies and Polly Pockets and Tiny Tears, and she was intrigued at how far back in time her grandmother could see, to *her* mother and *her* grandmother, way back to the Victorian period.

34

That winter George and Gina's overdraft went over one hundred thousand pounds, but even so George bought Gina a bracelet of pendant diamonds for Christmas whilst Gina bought George a Calvin Klein dressing gown. George was expecting to hear good news from New York any day now about the distribution of a recent film. The spectre of bankruptcy advanced and then receded and then advanced again. George worried about money whilst spending it freely, whilst Gina neither worried nor forbore to spend. George considered that his worrying made him more responsible than Gina and thus that she was more to blame than him for the size of their overdraft.

Since George was working right up until Christmas Eve, Gina said she'd do the food shop. But Gina got drunk two days in a row with Charlie in a new restaurant near Piccadilly and so the shopping never got done and George came home on Christmas Eve to find the fridges empty, except for three pounds of chocolate truffles and two dozen oysters, rather old. George went down to Selfridges ten minutes before closing time and pushed his way through the exhausted, hysterical crowd, buying what he could find: smoked salmon and brandy butter and whisky, but no bread nor butter and worst of all no coffee. And then, when George got home again, he found that Gina had disconnected the fax in order to plug in her hair dryer so that the long-awaited message from New York which he had hoped to receive before Christmas couldn't get through.

On Boxing Day evening George and Gina went to dinner with a business colleague of George's, a man called Lawrence Hershl who had made millions through property deals and who liked to invest it in films and art. That afternoon George had gone into the office and didn't get back until a quarter past seven. When he did he found the flat steamed up from Gina's bath, the floor strewn with clothes, Gina sitting at the table in her underwear with a glass and bottle beside it, talking on the telephone. 'Us middle-aged lushes,' she was saying. That must be Charlie, thought George, and he pricked up his ears, because he was always curious about Gina's female friends and liked to gather up the details that Gina let slip (he was amazed at how indiscreet women were to their husbands about other women) and weave them into stories.

But the conversation was disappointingly one-sided. 'Yes, yes', was all that Gina was saying, 'yes, yes', so George moved off, none the wiser, and after having showered and changed went to sit in the car and listen to his music.

This car was his pride and his joy. It was a new, dark blue Mercedes Estate, as long as a hearse and shiny enough to reflect a face in it darkly. Inside was a flashing dashboard, deep, comfortable seats and the warm, sealed atmosphere of an aircraft. Sometimes after work George would park outside the flat and there he would sit for half an hour or so, listening to music and enjoying the company of the harem of women who peopled his head: ex-girlfriends; film stars and celebrities that he fancied; women he knew and had always wanted and should have had, had life been fair; and, lately, a newcomer to this harem: the smart-eyed, crop-haired girl with the blonde-tipped hair in the man's suit who had stared at him so knowingly in Lord Jim's.

She hadn't been his usual type – she'd been too sharp and intelligent-looking for that – but even so, there had been something about the way the leg swung on the bar stool and the curve of the hip in the man's trousers, which had fastened itself on to his mind and wouldn't let go . . . Once upon a time, before he'd gone into producing, George had made commercials. He liked the way things looked. He had an eye for line and style and gesture, and so a touch in the way a woman dressed or walked could make her leap into life for him, as a button on a folding chair can make it spring into three dimensions. A dykey sort of woman, George had thought on first sight of Madeleine, but then she had turned into something else: a Hollywood woman, like Lauren Bacall perhaps – because George loved films and was always comparing women hopefully to Hollywood stars.

Gina came down the steps. She was wearing a bright green lace dress slit up the sides to show a lot of thigh. As she got into the car it shifted slightly on its springs and he gave her a quick, sideways look and saw how much weight she had put on lately. George thought it was amazing how you could go for years without noticing how your wife changed, the old self merging imperceptibly into the new self until some small thing drew your attention to it. But to see your wife put on weight was a depressing thing. It was as if her growing larger could make you shrink.

'Is that dress new?' he asked.

'I told you I bought it,' she said defensively, and she gave him a surprised look because lately George had been quite good to her – which meant that although he didn't give up his girlfriends, he didn't, for instance, complain about how much money she spent. However, his feelings fell only just on the positive side. It didn't take much to flip them over into irritation.

'Did you bring the flowers?' he asked, as they drove up the Finchley Road.

'Oh, shit,' she said.

He sighed and looked in the mirror to see if he could turn round. 'Well, you forgot them too,' she said.

'I've been working,' said George, who didn't love Gina much at this minute but was quite stoical about it. That's how it went in marriages, he thought. Some years you loved and some years you didn't.

But, stoical or not, George was jealous of Lawrence Hershl who had everything that a man could want: a big house on the edge of London and another one in Italy; three cars; a boat; a beautiful wife of oriental extraction, five foot nothing and skinny with it; and two little girls, who were racing each other over the thick, pile carpet as George and Gina came in, the little one rocking and swaying, doll-like in her dressing gown, whilst the older one, more lissome and more beautiful, leapt ahead of her. They were racing for a doll. 'Da, da,' called out the little one, plaintive as a seagull, 'Da, da,' and the sight and the sound of it stabbed George painfully as he stood there in the hall.

'Mind you don't trip over your dressing gowns,' he said to them, awkward and avuncular, because George liked little children very much. He liked their dinky looks and their diminutive bodies, though they made him blush and smile and stare after them with a puzzled frown because although he liked them he couldn't understand them. He thought that they were dolls. He couldn't comprehend how they could talk. Lawrence Hershl's children were standing hand in hand, staring at him with long, dark, shiny eyes like lychee stones. They had soft faces, like cakes which have just begun to rise but are not yet firm. 'Jesus, Lawrence, what beautiful children,' said George.

And then the wife came forward to take their coats. She was dressed all in black with hair cropped short like a boy's. The black clothes didn't make her look widowed. On the contrary, they gave her a rosy look. Gina towered over her on her high-heeled shoes. As the wife turned away with the coats over one arm she held out the other soft, vulnerable wrist to check the time against the smells emanating from the kitchen. George saw the gesture. It was the gesture of a child-wife, only she was more than that – she was a graphic artist who worked and earned money, her beauty being filtered, as it were, through intelligence, and so pointing up all the more the slack confusion of George and Gina's life together. At this moment to have a wife who earned money as well as spent it, seemed to George to be a wonderful thing.

Everything about Lawrence's household soothed and scratched at George's equanimity. Would it always be like this? Would Lawrence always be ahead of him as the older child is always ahead of the younger? The two children were going up to bed. George watched them go. He thought that a man wanted children in order to complete the pattern; so that he could be like other men, only better, with better, smarter, more beautiful children; and because without children you had the curious feeling that the future had been chopped away, that there was no solid ground ahead of you, just a nothingness that gave you vertigo. At one time, so that she might console herself, Gina had gone through a phase of reading books on infertility. 'You know what our trouble is,' she said to him, 'we don't have any role models, any hero figures, who've been this way before us, so we have to be pioneers.' At first George was silent, fazed by his wife's unexpected thinking processes, but then he thought, But I don't want to be a pioneer. I'm a conventional man. I want to be like other people.

George and Lawrence talked money during supper. Over the main course the beautiful wife asked Gina, 'Do you work?'

'No', said Gina, and George overheard and gave them a sly, amused look, because he could feel how the beautiful wife was casting around for a topic of conversation – if Gina didn't work and had no children then what *did* she do? Gina was clearly discomforted. The beautiful wife was not only talented but skinny as well, whilst Gina's bosom overflowed in all directions. George wasn't clever but he was often intuitive and at this moment he could feel how uncomfortable Gina was but he didn't much care. His impatience with his wife was making him feel disloyal.

Lawrence brought out a dessert wine to drink with the pudding. It was Lawrence's way to laugh a lot. He had a light touch on life but with this light touch he had made millions. George didn't know whether he wanted to admire him or get his revenge on him. 'You and I should play pool, Lawrence,' he said, because George was a demon on the pool table, and anyway he would cheat if he had to, with all the passionate resentment of a younger child playing against a more powerful older brother. The younger of the two children appeared in the doorway and came padding across to her mother on her quick, bare feet. To see her run across the carpet fuelled George's bitter, powerful longings. I should have a child like that, he thought.

She rang him at the beginning of January when he was back in the office. It was the exhausted, hung-over time of year. His secretary buzzed him. 'It's Suzanne on the line,' she said.

'Suzanne?' he asked. 'Which Suzanne?' and then he remembered and triumph jumped up inside him and punched him gleefully on the throat: the way she stared at me, he thought. I knew she fancied me. I knew it.

'Put her through,' he said, and her voice came on to the line.

'Hi,' she said. 'We met at Lord Jim's just before Christmas. We shared a cigarette together.' It was a bold voice, equable and in control.

'I remember,' he said. 'Did you have a good Christmas?'

'Not bad. And you?'

'All right,' he said, in the polite, remote, guarded way that he reserved for clever women, although the truth was that it had been lousy.

'You ordered me to ring you,' she said, very bold.

'And do you always do what men tell you?' he asked, equally bold.

'It depends on the man,' she said smartly, and in the pause that followed she said, 'How about lunch?'

He thought. 'I'm not around next week. We're filming out at Hillingdon. Except Thursday. Thursday lunch I could do.'

'OK,' she said, 'Thursday it is.'

'Come to my office. Double Vision. 17 Broadwick Street, Soho. Twelve thirty.'

'I'll see you then,' she said, and rang off, and it was only after the silence had settled back on the room that he realised he had forgotten a meeting with the accountant next Thursday at half past twelve in Knightsbridge – so he wouldn't be back until half past one at the earliest and then he ought to be on his way to Hillingdon. He sat there undecided and then he realised that he couldn't ring her because she hadn't left a number. He began to curse her and just at that moment she rang him back.

'Sorry,' she said, 'I can't do Thursday lunch.'

'Nor can I,' he said. 'It's bloody irritating not being able to get hold of you.' He thought her pause was a satisfied one. 'I've a meeting at twelve thirty in Knightsbridge and then I ought to go out to Hillingdon,' he said.

'I thought you were the producer, not the director.'

'I raise the money. I like to know how it's spent.' He had recovered his cool and his poise.

'What kind of film is it?'

'A Victorian vampire movie. For Cable Television.'

'If you're going by car to Hillingdon,' she said, 'you could take me with you. Film shoots interest me.'

'All right,' he said, 'come to my office at a quarter to two and you can come with me.'

35

They drove to Hillingdon in the dark blue Mercedes Estate, whizzing along in it as stealthily as a couple of thieves. Madeleine wore a big sheepskin coat which had once belonged to Martin. It was one of the things she had stolen from him by way of compensation. George wore a camel-coloured overcoat with sharp lapels. Madeleine thought that he looked like Gina, that he looked both young and peculiarly old – as if the coke and the champagne had aged him whilst the health farms and the expensive holidays had had the opposite effect.

After a while he asked, 'So what do you do for a living?'

'I'm a journalist. I also write books.'

'Yeah? What kind of books?'

'Books on feminism.'

He nodded. 'So you're clever,' he said, as once his wife had said before him.

'Sure,' said Madeleine.

'And you're married?' he asked, looking at the wedding ring which Madeleine had thought to slip onto her left hand.

She nodded. 'And you?'

'Yeah,' he said. 'Happily so?' he asked.

'Happily enough. I'm just not very good at it.'

He smiled. 'Me neither,' he said.

This is all very polite and self-controlled, thought Madeleine. It must be because he thinks I'm a good girl. It'll be the bad girls who get the flamboyance.

They went out by the Westway and the M40, and then took a turning just before Uxbridge. They drove between scrubby hedgerows and sodden fields. George looked at nature with uninterest. He put on a cassette. He didn't say any more and nor did he seem to expect Madeleine to speak either. Madeleine thought that all these years she had been using words to impress or persuade, not thinking of those other worlds where people do not talk. But then how do you get your own way in this world? thought Madeleine. By silence? By looks? By money?

They turned right and right again and now they came to a pair of gates, a lodge house, and inside a forecourt and a couple of caterers' vans standing in front of a group of shadowy buildings. George parked the car. He got out without saying a word. He led the way inside, or rather in he went, and she followed, through swing doors and down a brick-lined corridor, and through more swing doors until they came to a door marked 'Fire Escape'. She followed him in and found herself in a huge, barn-like space. Overhead the roof was criss-crossed with steel girders and hung with chains and cables and studded with powerful lights that dazzled in the darkness. Up ahead was a set built of splintery orange wood. Across the floor, wherever there was space, were cables; ladders; trolleys; cameras on tripods; metal boxes; folding chairs with half-eaten ham rolls left sitting on them; and pot-bellied, middle-aged men going to and fro with wide-legged swaggers; and girls with belts hung with keys and gloves and walkie-talkies; tombstones stacked against the set; a coffin; flurries of activity, pools of busyness, and everywhere else, the intent idleness of a film set.

He led her round the set. People stepped to one side to let them go through. It seemed to Madeleine that they were saying, 'So you're the producer's new girlfriend, are you?' Not me, love, not me, thought Madeleine.

At some point he left her behind. She had fetched up beside a group of middle-aged men in sweaters, with beer guts and flesh laid down in slabs. Up ahead of her Madeleine could see that the set was a collection of snapshot images built in wood: a pair of church doors; flights of steps leading up to nowhere; a platform; the doors to a crypt; the façade of a tumble-down house; a couple of twisty alleyways; and here and there a real tree growing bizarrely and luxuriantly in the dusty dazzle of the artificial lights.

George climbed up a flight of steps, up onto a platform where there stood half a dozen lighting and camera men, a boy-actor made up to look filthy and a girl in a dress with a tight bodice and a long skirt, which was flounced and layered and veiled in salmon-pink and fiery red. She had a pale, luminous face and she was wearing a huge hat which spewed out veils and flowers like a Catherine wheel. She had been sitting on a chair. When she saw George she stepped forward, sighing, and George put his arm around her. He looked dapper, fastidious and moneyed. A small man, built like a bull and with a rock-like face, came forward. This presumably was the director. A girl with a clipboard under one arm brought them each a cup of coffee.

The director was talking to the boy. A crowd stood at the foot of the set, looking on like an audience at the Creation. The men with beer bellies watched through narrowed eyes. Madeleine began to feel in her pockets for her cigarettes and the man next to her pulled out a packet and offered her one with his beefy fingers. A man's world, thought Madeleine, a camaraderie, a different kind of camaraderie than in the world of women.

At last things began to happen. The boy and the girl took up their positions. A camera on a crane moved forward. Another one began to whir beside the church doors. The lighting changed. A bell rang. People spoke into walkie-talkies. 'Action,' shouted the director and now the boy and the girl stepped forward, and began to walk in a long, curving sweep up the ramp and round and under a tree and up to the doors of the church. 'Cut,' shouted the director. The boy looked too po-faced. They did it again. 'Cut,' shouted the director. They weren't following the chalk marks on the floor. They tried again – three, four, five times, whilst George looked on from various parts of the set, always smoking, always with an intent expression. The girl in the dress was sighing and protesting. The director shook his head. He had a brutal charm. 'On we go, sweetie,' he said, pushing her back to the set. Sometimes the director called George over for a consultation. Nothing seemed to impress these two. A camera whirled round and a dazzle of light struck across the dusty darkness, piercing the gloom like the light of God, and lighting up the back of George's head so that he seemed to have a halo. The director looked up. 'Do something about that,' he shouted to an assistant. 'If I'd wanted to make a fucking art movie I'd have told you.' And to George he said, 'You look like Jesus Christ.' 'I am,' said George, 'I am.' Madeleine thought that the two of them were loving it all; the darkness, the artificiality, the fiction, the leading ladies. The girl in the long dress began to protest again. 'Siobhan's in a difficult mood,' said one of the men beside Madeleine. She went across to George and to gee her up he smacked her on her ruffled, flounced behind. Like a horse, for God's sake, thought Madeleine sniffily.

'What's the story of this film?' she asked the man beside her. 'The girl's a vampire,' he said. 'The boy doesn't know it yet. He's a vampire-killer. But the audience know what she's up to. She's going to seduce him into bed and then try to suck his blood and he's going to have to kill her.' Jesus, thought Madeleine.

She went outside for some fresh air. A thick, blue twilight filled the courtyard but overhead the sky was pure and bright and puffing out its coldness. The lights of aeroplanes and satellites were traversing it steadily. The ground was starting to freeze. The men with the beer bellies were drinking coffee beside the caterers' van. When they saw the producer's girlfriend they blew out their cigarette smoke and squashed the butts into the earth. Madeleine thought she saw interest in their eyes, because she was such a lean-looking woman and dressed with a flourish, a woman you wouldn't have to hoick around but who could stand on her own two feet.

Back in the barn a girl was looking for her. She was carrying a tray of sandwiches and a glass of wine. 'From Mr Kaufman,' she said, and again Madeleine thought she heard the onlookers say, 'We told you so, the producer's new girlfriend.' As the mobster owns his woman, thought Madeleine, as the patriarch owns his wife. A weasel pleasure. As wicked a pleasure as any that a feminist can feel. I feel both raised up and demeaned, thought Madeleine, when I ought to feel neither.

George stood at the foot of the steps. He was talking to the director. The director said something and George laughed. It was that boyish laugh again – with lips apart and eyes half-closed and the chin thrown back and the head tilted up. The laugh dazzled on Madeleine's eyes. It licked across her senses. For one moment she was all cunt and nothing else. It was years since she had dwelt in this dimension. It was a painful feeling – a mixture of lust and dislike and a pleasure in his boyishness which was even quite maternal – but it was also a zestful, elated feeling, because anger was heavy but fancying someone was light and buoyant.

She made her way to the door. She passed the wardrobe girls. They were dressed in jeans and sleeveless jerkins over heavy sweaters and neat little suede boots which encased their feet. Their eyes were heavily painted and their luxuriant hair was heaped up on their heads to show their chunky earrings. They were flirting with the electricians. One girl was having her shoulders massaged. 'Oh, that's good,' she kept saying, 'just let your fingers do the walking.' Another girl was doing a handstand. She looked too topheavy to turn herself upside down and yet up flew her legs whilst the electricians looked on, grinning. Madeleine thought how huge was the gulf in this world between men and women, a hole between them big enough to fall into. Or to get laid in, thought Madeleine.

36

All week long he had been looking forward to this moment. On the drive down he'd given her covert looks and had felt each bit of him pinprick into life, because although her nose was too narrow to be pretty and her eyes too deepset to be ditto and her cheekbones too sharp to be the same again – yet even so there was something about her that drew the eye. And he had cast more covert looks at her coat – which surely was too big for her? – and had thought that it must belong to her husband, and what kind of man was it who would wear a coat like this? A journalist probably, thought George, just as she was.

All afternoon as he'd worked he'd been thinking about Suzanne the journalist, but on the drive home – and he'd noticed before how typical this was – he started to panic. Panic turned to gloom and gloom turned to despair. It was for a start, he thought, her conversation, which was not so much a conversation as an interrogation. As they left the shoot Bill came out after them to ask if George would be in the editing suite at nine o'clock to view the rushes – but also, of course, because he wanted to cast an appraising eye over this new woman.

Afterwards Madeleine asked, 'What are the rushes?'

'They're the film from the day's shooting. They get developed every night.'

'And how much longer will the shoot go on?'

'Another three or four weeks.'

'And then what?'

'And then it goes to the cutting room.'

'And how long will it be there?'

'Perhaps ten weeks.'

'And then?'

'How do you mean?'

'I mean, when does it get released?'

'I don't know yet,' said George, and to get the upper hand and to stop all these questions he asked her, 'So why did you want to come on a film shoot?'

'Because I was interested,' said Madeleine.

George's gloom deepened. He tried to make conversation but nervousness tripped him up. 'Who did you talk to on the set?' he asked and Madeleine described the two beefy men. 'I know,' he said, 'Tom and Simon. They're quite a duo although in fact they're probably the only men on the set who aren't queer.' She started at the word 'queer' and this made him nervous. 'You're a journalist, aren't you?' he said and he added, 'you must work a lot with young men,' and no sooner had he said it than he wished he hadn't because it sounded as if he were suggesting that she slept with them.

He fell silent. He kept his eyes on the road ahead and tried not to look at her. But even so he was aware of her rubbing a clear patch in the glass as she pursued some line of thought – because of course she was a clever woman who would always be watching, always thinking, always having ideas. Gloomily, he considered the sheer number of books she must have read, the exhibitions she must have been to, the amount of knowledge inside her head, and he pictured the books like a wave so huge that as it came towards him it gave him drowning visions. George had such a pang of yearning for Gina and her familiarity that if she had been here he would have pushed Madeleine straight out of the door and installed Gina in her place instead. His sadness became overwhelming. As they stopped at the lights on Great Western Avenue it jumped the gulf between them and for one moment he put a hand sadly and heavily on one of her knees.

(But Madeleine was thinking, if I were a man he'd talk to me. If I were a man he'd point to that tower block over there and he'd say, 'A friend of mine ran a property company. He built that tower block. They borrowed a hundred million from the bank but they hit problems putting it up and they couldn't repay in time and he ended up killing himself – literally – for that building.' Or he'd point in the other direction and he'd say, 'You see that office building over there? We once shot a film in that building. It was a thriller. But I was working with a director who was nuts. One of the actors died, falling from a window, and all the director said was that the shoot must go on.' Stories from the world of men where the talk is of money and scams and projects they want to make and great ambitions and adventures. But because I'm a woman he'll tell me nothing.)

But then, as the car began to climb by the Westway, George's mood began to change. Perhaps it was the car itself which was rising and swooping and rising again over Notting Hill Gate with a wonderful smoothness? Or perhaps it was the lights of London, which on this frosty night, had a rich and capitalist glitter, like the scattered contents of a money box? Whatever the cause, George began to smile and to tap the steering wheel and when they stopped at the lights on the Euston Road he lit himself a cigarette and lit one for Madeleine too. He saw how she leant forward to take the light as if towards something that she cherished. He saw how the flame flared and burnt against her profile. He put away the lighter. He felt himself emboldened to ruffle the hair on her head. 'I'm hungry,' he said, 'come and have something to eat with me.' She looked at her watch. 'I'd have to make a phone call,' she said. He shrugged. 'That's all right,' he said, and he drew up in silence at the next turning. 'There's a phone box,' he said, and he waited whilst she made the call, then leant across to open the door for her. He assumed she had been making domestic arrangements. He wouldn't deign to ask what she had told her husband.

They ate in a small Italian restaurant not far from the British Museum. It was six o'clock and the restaurant was nearly empty. The food was stodgy and badly heated-up, the conversation stilted, the waiter young and handsome, serving Madeleine with a smile and George with a kind of sulky swank as if he were a rival. When they left the restaurant they walked up past the British Museum. Its columns were lit up by spotlights – they shone out as bright as day – but the whole place had a night-time hush upon it, the brightness and the hush together giving it a stagy look. Overhead the sky was black, painted flat above the museum. You could set a horror movie there, thought George.

She didn't ask where they were going. He was trying to edge

her in the direction of the Cavendish. He took her on a short cut along a concrete precinct between two London University buildings. The night was burning cold. A blue light from somewhere was bathing them from top to toe. There were black shadows and a gateway and a concrete vista beyond. A crescent moon like a lump of marble was hanging heavily in the sky, the line between the shining outer edge and the dark inner edge as hard as if it were carved in stone. From one of the buildings there came the sounds of a kitchen, sharp as breaking glass on this icy night. The cold was enough to murder tramps and dossers. There was not a human face in sight except for theirs.

Oh God, thought George, because although his stomach was full of warm food his teeth were chattering. She was as cold as he was. 'I have to go,' she said. The two of them were almost dancing with the cold. He kept wanting to put his hands inside her coat and up her jumper where he fancied they would be warm. In his head he was feeling a curiosity about her mixed with a discomfort – even a dislike – of her cleverness and her strangeness. But in his fingers he felt simply pleasure and anticipation. 'Come here,' he said – he was determined to warm himself – and he got his hands in and up around her waist and felt the first electric touch of flesh. He closed his eyes and swayed slightly with the pleasure of it. But then she nearly lost it for them both. 'Do you do this often?' she asked. Now how the hell am I to answer that? he wondered. For a clever woman she did ask stupid questions.

He shut his eyes and concentrated on what was before him.

'You're very dictatorial,' she complained.

'I'm the producer,' he said. He had recovered himself. His fingers were growing warmer. He was warming to the task of chatting her up, the words coming more easily now, because George, who usually found words difficult, always grew more fluent when he was chatting up a girl.

'And that's the very tops, is it?' asked Madeleine.

'The very tops,' he said.

'God on earth?' she asked.

'God on earth,' he agreed.

'You could even get the director sacked?'

'Sure I could get the director sacked.'

'Poor Bill,' she said, 'I have to go.'

'Come here,' he said again and he got a kiss in somewhere between the mouth and the neat, white ear. She was as slippery as a fish, she was as warm as melting butter and he was absolutely sure that she fancied him. That husband of hers can't ever give it to her, thought George, and briefly he was sorry for that unknown man who was clearly not as good at sex as he was.

'Come with me. I know of somewhere we could go,' he said.

'You're meant to be in the editing suite at nine.'

'It doesn't matter. That can wait.'

'Where were you thinking of?' she asked, struggling to get free of him.

'The Cavendish. It's just round the corner. It's quite smart,' he said.

'I should think it is,' she said. He had got his hands up her back. He could feel her start to float, the back losing its springy tension and going limp, the eyes floating closed like a baby's at the bottle. 'All right,' she said, opening her eyes again, 'but I hope to hell you've got a condom because otherwise I'm not interested.'

God, he thought, women are so direct these days, but all he said out loud was, 'I expect it could be arranged.'

It was a large, modern hotel with miles of empty, carpeted corridors between the reception desk and his room. When he opened the door for her and switched on the light, she saw a double bed, a drinks cabinet and a television in one corner. The air was dim and golden, lacking all substance, and the temperature was pitched at a steady heat so that it didn't matter that the curtains were thin and that there was nothing but a sheet and blanket and a thin counterpane on the bed. It was a room for walking naked in. In the cupboard behind the door was a hairdryer and a trouser press. In the adjoining bathroom was a stack of neatly folded towels and a multitude of sachets and bottles of lotions, for the skin and the hair and the nails. I must take some of those back for Ella, thought Madeleine. She went to the window and saw that they were at the back of the hotel in one of the disregarded rooms from whence you can catch a glimpse of Tavistock Square. The hotel was turned away from it as if it did not rate at all the square's nineteenth-century glories.

'I'd like a drink,' said Madeleine, looking out of the window and still dressed in her sheepskin coat. Panic was overwhelming her. It was making all her sexual feelings drain away, as if the world which had sprung so dizzyingly into three dimensions was now folding itself back into a flat, plain, two-dimensional world. She was wondering what she was doing here with a man she didn't even like and who was trying to do her down. And she was worrying about Ella, whom she had left with her mother – worrying that her mother wouldn't get her to bed on time so that she, Madeleine, would have to take her to school the next morning, irritable because she was so tired.

George was sitting on the edge of the bed, talking into his mobile phone. 'Bill?' he was saying, 'I'll be late. Yes. No, no, I've been held up.' He put down the phone. 'A drink?' he said, and he went across to the small fridge in the corner from where he took a bottle of champagne. He opened it with a racing driver's flourish and poured a brimming glass for her. He went back to the bed and began to unlace his shoes. 'So what did you think of my film?' he asked.

'Why was the girl dressed up in all those frills and flounces?' asked Madeleine. He paused in his unlacing and stared at her. (He was thinking, how would you start to explain?)

'Because it's sexier like that,' he said at last.

'I thought your film was sexist,' Madeleine said, and he stared at her some more. He said, 'There's nothing very feminist about drinking champagne in a hotel room with a married man,' and now it was her turn to look at him sulkily.

He began flicking through the television channels with the remote control. She took off her coat, sat down awkwardly on the bed beside him.

'There's something I have to see,' he said.

'What?'

'A crappy horror movie on Satellite TV.'

'How do you know it's crappy?'

'Because it was made by a friend of mine.'

She raised her brows.

'The point about Satellite TV,' he said, 'is that they haven't yet realised that Bill and I are the best.'

'Are you the best?'

'Sure.'

'What does being "the best" mean?'

'It means,' he said, and his tone was coldly defiant as if he felt himself amongst enemies, 'that we have the best ideas, that we get the best scripts, that we're the best at raising lots of money fast, that we make the best product and we're the best at selling it.'

'I wish I were a man,' said Madeleine, 'I wish I could talk like that,' and he looked down at her sharply.

They watched the movie in silence for a couple of minutes. Madeleine lay back, stretched out her legs, closed her eyes. Oh God, I'm tired, she thought.

'Christ, this is bad,' said George. 'Are you all right?' he asked.

'Tired,' she said.

'Why?'

'My boss is giving me a hard time.' It was true. Lately Professor Atkins' animosity had started up again. The misplaced memos, the lack of access to a computer, the decisions made behind her back – all had begun again.

'Tell him to fuck off.'

'If I tell him to fuck off I'll lose my job.'

'I'll get you another one,' he said.

That annoyed her. He didn't take her career seriously. 'I don't want another one,' she said, 'I want the one I've got.'

'I bet I could get you one that's better paid.'

'I'm sure you could. But doing what?'

'Whatever you want. You're a clever woman.'

She thought about this. He said, 'But probably the money doesn't mean anything to you anyway, because people like you don't believe in money.'

'Of course I believe in money.'

'No, you don't. You pay lipservice to the idea but the truth is, you'd work for nothing because your job is what matters to you.'

'Well, isn't that true for you as well?'

'No,' he said emphatically, 'I work to make money. I want to be rich.'

'Anyway,' she said, 'what do you mean by people like me?'

'Clever,' he said, 'smart, liberal, intellectual. God, this movie's dreadful.'

He got up from the bed and went across to the shelf and she saw that there were dozens of video cassettes up there. He began to pull them down and look at them.

'You've even got a video,' she marvelled.

'Of course. That way I can claim the room is for work and set it against tax.'

If he puts on a porno film I shall go off him altogether,

Madeleine thought, but when the title came up on the screen she saw that it was *Heat*. A Boys' Own film, thought Madeleine, Men's games, the dreams of the Mister Race. The champagne was making her feel better. 'Do you like Hollywood movies then?' she asked. He just looked at her. She was getting used to his silences. If she asked an obvious question he stared as if to say, 'So why are you asking me when you know the answer already?'

He was wearing a soft, expensive-looking shirt and tobacco-coloured trousers, very sharply and narrowly cut. His shoes, beside the bed, were made of suede.

'I've never slept with a man who dressed so expensively,' she said.

'Haven't you? What do your other friends wear?'

'Cords. Jeans. Jumpers. That kind of thing.'

How dreadful, said his silence. 'Does that mean you're going to sleep with me?' he asked.

'I don't know.' Nervously she got up from the bed and went across to the window. On the far side of the square she could dimly make out the nineteenth-century houses, in one of which she had an office. To think that this other world had always been here, underneath her nose, and she hadn't even known it.

He came across the room. He put his arms around her waist and pressed against her back. Now *that* was sexy. Straight away the sexy images started up again, images as light as feathers but strong enough to uplift her – sex from behind, idle, indolent, anonymous sex, a little wicked, the flesh mortified and pleasured, the spirit vanished altogether. He had his hands up under her shirt. She wriggled round to face him and to get her hands up under his jacket.

'I'm not beautiful,' she said. She was thinking that all these years she had been looking for a man who knew more than her and who was cleverer than her, not thinking that a man who never read could be so sexy.

'It doesn't matter,' he said, 'you'll do nicely.' He was pressing down on her. He had his mouth against her neck.

'And you? Will you do nicely?' she asked, still looking for parity and justice between the sexes.

'I hope so,' he said, with his face now in her shirt and feeling that wonderful I'm-chatting-up-a-woman fluency, 'I hope so.'

38

They parted at the front door of the hotel. 'Which way are you going?' he asked her. She pointed in the opposite direction. 'That way,' she said, and she plunged out into the icy air like a swimmer into the sea. 'I'll ring you,' she called out over her shoulder, and she set off walking very fast, northwards, past Gordon Square in the direction of Euston Station where she caught a train to Hampstead. She was going to her mother's house to collect Ella. She walked down towards the Finchley Road. At the top of Arkwright Road she stopped to look at the lights of West London laid out below her. The night, although it was so cold, had a sweet feel to it, echoing to her thoughts, stretching up for mile after mile, as light as a meringue. Her body, although it was already freezing at the extremities, was warm at the centre from all that good sex. Her boots were ringing on the pavement and with every step she took she was feeling more and more expansive, because it was wonderful to be not just a mother but to live also in another world, of sexual pleasures and delights.

She found Ella asleep on the living-room sofa, covered by a blanket. There was a game of patience on the table, a manuscript spread out on the floor – 'Ella has been helping me count the pages,' said her mother – and Radio 3 playing in the background. Patiently, stoically because of her arthritis, Madeleine's mother bent down and began to pick up the papers. Madeleine got down on her knees to help her.

'Ah no, don't follow *those* numbers, follow these,' said her mother.

'How much is done?' asked Madeleine.

'We're getting there, we're getting there. Ella can count to a thousand.'

'Ella's a genius,' said Madeleine smugly.

'You look very well,' said her mother, peering at her, by which of course she meant that Madeleine looked happy.

'Happy enough, Mum,' said Madeleine, but the fact was that she was feeling very happy indeed, because buoyed up by sexual satisfaction she was forgiving her mother – forgiving her for letting go of Madeleine's father; forgiving her for not having told Madeleine what the world was really like; forgiving her for the defeatism she had always preached in the notion that the world falls short of some other ideal and is therefore best not bothered over . . . I only ever wanted to feel grown-up, she thought. Once you feel grown-up you can forgive them anything.

She took Ella home by minicab. The child woke briefly in the cold air, fell asleep again on Madeleine's lap. 'Sweet, aren't they?' said the minicab driver. 'Very,' said Madeleine. They were coming down the Finchley Road, part of a river of traffic – strings of light in red and yellow and white, and double decker buses sliding past, empty as milk crates, lit up like the façades of houses. She began thinking of novels about London: *The Weather in the Streets*, *Mrs Dalloway*, *The Doves of Venus*. She thought about *Anna Karenina*. Of course it was the shift from erotic to maternal love that so depressed her, if only Tolstoy had understood it. Sexual satisfaction, thought Madeleine – and she didn't mean love because she was very, very far off ever loving George Kaufman – but sexual satisfaction was good for the mind, making it expand with a kind of startled pleasure. 'There,' she said to herself, 'you're more like your mother than you think – utilitarian about everything – even sexual pleasures.' But she wasn't feeling utilitarian, she wasn't feeling utilitarian at all. Her body still felt warm between her legs. It had been disarranged by sex and had not yet retreated back into its usual, cool, secluded privacy. As the car came onto the Chalk Farm Road she saw the crowds going in and out of restaurants and wine bars and massage parlours and transvestite shops – all of them seeking and finding gratification in the navy-coloured night.

As they had been getting dressed in the hotel room he had bent down towards the floor to where her handbag had fallen off the chair. A photograph of Ella lay beside it. He had picked it up. 'Is this yours?' he had asked, as he had examined the little girl's face. She was eating an ice cream, her eyes huge, her gaze tender, almost cross-eyed in its languor, as she drifted very close against the camera lens. 'She's very pretty,' he had said. But Madeleine had snatched it back and tucked it into her bag, and because he had frightened her and she wanted to punish him, she had asked, 'Do you have any children?' for the pleasure of hearing him say, 'No – no, I don't.'

'Why do men want children?' she had persisted, and George who had gone across to the window as he did up his tie, said, 'I don't know, don't ask me,' as he stared out into the night.

When Ella was asleep in bed Madeleine rang Nicola. Downstairs a fight was starting in the minicab company's offices. Nicola lived in a quiet, tree-lined street up in Hampstead. Whilst Madeleine waited for the phone to be answered she pictured those trees gathering up the prosperous darkness in their branches, and pouring all the quietness of those streets down the telephone line towards her. Down here in Camden Town where the streets were full of other people's lives and their stories, it would be many hours before the world grew quiet for a while.

When Nicola picked up the phone Madeleine said, 'I had a drink with George Kaufman.'

'So, now you've talked to him, do you understand him any better?'

'I'm working on it,' said Madeleine, 'I'm working on it.'

39

'George,' said Gina one Friday morning in the first week of February. 'What's happening about the clinic?' Is Oliver pushing it hard enough?'

She was lying in bed watching him get dressed. He had fastened his cufflinks, dealing with each sleeve with frowning concentration. Now he was tilting back his chin to knot his tie. It was the first time in weeks that she had had a chance to ask him about the lawyers. Since Christmas he had worked late every night and over the weekends. He had been to Los Angeles once and to New York twice. He said he was trying to finish the vampire film and also to get funding for a new one. But Gina thought that he must have a new girlfriend, or at any rate be planning one, because on one occasion he'd looked quite elated as he came in through the door but no sooner did he clap eyes on her than he turned remote and absent-minded. And he was shaving with the door shut and leaving for work as early as possible in the mornings. Sometimes he went out with stooped shoulders, the brightness gone from his face along with the old look of cock-of-the-walk, but at other times, for no apparent reason, his step was springy and cheerful.

Today he was preoccupied and gloomy as he scooped up his belongings – wallet, keys, business cards – from the dressing table. She tried again.

'George,' she said, 'what's happening with this business of the lawyers and the clinic?'

'What do you mean?' he asked. 'What business?'

'You know what I mean. The Fountain Clinic. Mr Kalotheou. Whether or not some of my eggs went to another woman.'

'Oliver's dealing with it,' said George.

'But when? What's happening? Oughtn't we to have heard something by now?'

'Leave it to the lawyers,' he said impatiently, 'that's why you employ them. I'm too busy.'

He stood in front of the mirror, brushing his hair. She knew that he could feel her eyes on his back and that he knew what she was thinking. She didn't expect him to mollify her. Reproach always aroused in George a certain stony stubbornness. He turned round at the door. 'Don't give me a hard time, Gina,' was all he said, 'I'll be back late tonight,' and with that he was gone, leaving her to the empty flat and her extravagant nightgown and her beautiful bosom – both wasted at this moment – her body slid like a snake's between the satin sheets, her fingers between her legs idly pursuing orgasms and her mind dwelling partly on memories of France and partly on thoughts of Madeleine Kingdom's daughter.

She gave herself an orgasm. She slept for a while. It was past ten o'clock when she woke and outside the day was fine. The cold weather had given way to something warmer and for several days now the sky had been that innocent blue you see in fifteenth-century paintings of the Madonna's clothing. It was this blue which was reminding Gina bitterly of France – of hot sun on naked trees in town squares – of poplars by the roadside alight with the orangey-yellow leaves of early spring. Memories of France were mingling sharply with thoughts of the egg-child, as George called her, for to have a daughter – and even more so, a beautiful daughter – was a thing of status in Gina's world. When Gina's friends had boys the first time round they kept on trying – one pregnancy after another – until they got a girl, because the difference between boys and girls was that boys might go out into the world to fight your battles for you, but girls went out into the world to *be* you, and thus, like a surrogate, to extend your life for you. A daughter could soften the harshness of growing old and so where once you'd spent money dressing yourself you now spent money on her clothes instead.

Gina wished she'd stolen the photograph of Ella from Madeleine Kingdom's mantelpiece. Her fingers itched in retrospect to scoop up the little girl's picture. She wanted to spur George on with the sight of her, but also to feast her eyes on Ella's face.

Twice in recent weeks whilst driving through Camden Town she had made detours up Madeleine's street in the hope of seeing Ella and today, after her appointment at the hairdresser in Primrose Hill, she knew that she would ask the taxi driver to make that same detour again.

The taxi dropped her by M & S. She walked round by Arlington Road and through to Delancey Street. She was dressed to make men stare in a fuchsia-coloured boiler suit with a flying jacket over it. She stood on the far pavement with the traffic roaring past underneath her nose. Her eyes were on the tall, narrow house opposite her in which was Madeleine's flat. She was looking at the crumbling window sills, the bits of fancy white plaster scrolling over each window, the parapet at the top – in fact, she was half asleep in the warm sunshine – when the door to the street opened and out came a woman and a child. Gina felt alarm, panic, delight in equal measure – panic because the last time she'd seen Madeleine, Madeleine had been cold, contemptuous and angry towards her; but delight also because although at this distance the child was unrecognisable, still she could make out the bright smudge of the face and the mop of blonde hair above it which contrasted nicely with a navy-blue duffle coat. She was hanging on Madeleine's hand with a nervy, skipping movement which turned over Gina's heart.

Gina stepped backwards in alarm: if Madeleine so much as glanced in her direction she would see her. But Madeleine didn't – her eyes were on her child. You could see that her world had shrunk until Ella's blonde head was all it could embrace. As Gina watched they walked off along the street. Soon she felt impelled to follow, taking awkward steps in her tottery, high-heeled shoes. She wished she weren't dressed so noticeably. She had to hang far back. She reached into her bag for her dark glasses, but discarded them when she found that they made her even more conspicuous.

At the top of the road Madeleine and the child turned left. They crossed one, two, three streets whilst Gina hopped along behind. Up ahead of them she saw the entrance to Regents Park. In they went, first Madeleine and then Ella, and then a couple of minutes later Gina. It was a fine, bright afternoon. The sunshine on the naked trees had a voluptuous feel. There were crocuses in the flowerbeds – scarlet, purple and yellow – and a flock of pigeons descending on the path whilst their shadows came up to meet them. The day, although so bright, had a decaying feel about it, because you knew that quite soon its brightness would be folded up by a grey, evening light.

To Gina, who wasn't used to weather, the sky looked enormous. And she was cold too, despite the sun, and tired, because she wasn't used to walking. It wasn't easy following Madeleine and the child. They walked terribly slowly, stopping to look at a tractor or a man chopping trees or a pigeon rustling through the grass. Each time they stopped Gina, who anyway was hanging far back, had to sit down on a bench or even turn round and walk the other way.

They came to the Broadwalk and turned left towards the fountain. Gina thought she heard Ella shout, 'Look, Mummy, water.' So that's what she sounds like, thought Gina. All these years the loved one's voice had been echoing in her head and now at last she'd heard it. They came to the gates and turned right towards the Inner Circle. They crossed the road and went into the Rose Garden. Here the space was so small that Gina didn't dare enter but hung back by the entrance. When she looked inside Madeleine and Ella had gone. A minute later she saw them in the distance by the lake and the willows and the bulrushes and the little Japanese-y bridge. Ella was leaning against Madeleine, feeling in her pockets – presumably for bread to feed the ducks – in such a possessive manner it was like a knife in Gina's stomach.

Gina sat down and waited. Madeleine and Ella walked on. Gina got up and followed. They came to the café and Madeleine and Ella went in whilst Gina hung around outside, behind a hedge, peering through the twigs and waiting. At last, Madeleine and Ella came out with a tray of food and went to sit in a sunny, sheltered corner. Gina went in, hastily bought herself a coffee, and found a table in an alcove, half-hidden behind a screen of pot plants with a view, through a window, of the garden. She put on her dark glasses. From here she could spy on Madeleine and Ella without being seen.

They sat side by side with their backs to her. Ella had a carton of juice and a straw. Her back was very straight but her arms and legs and fingers and toes and face were all wriggling. Soon she got bored of sitting still. She slid down off her chair. Her face floated round absent-mindedly in Gina's direction, and Gina saw a wide mouth, large eyes, a high forehead, again as with the photograph but more so – a familiar face, a face she knew, one which set up echoes of familiarity. She felt every bit of her pause. She felt hot and cold and very tired because it was extraordinary to see oneself duplicated when one had no idea that it had happened; and she felt a kind of exhausted recognition and a feeling of triumph because she'd been right in her supposition, because the likeness was so obvious.

Ella stared back. What she saw in the window was a creature who hardly looked human – hair like a lion's mane, eyes which were two shiny circles of black. She thought perhaps it was a lion. She stared at it for a minute and then her mother called out, 'Ella, let's go,' because even in the sun it was cold, too cold to sit outside. Madeleine had her back to her. She was packing up their belongings. Ella felt herself drawn back into the circle of her mother's body. As she drew away the lion slunk back into the shadows.

After they had gone Gina sat quietly at the table. She forgot about George. She forgot about their marriage. From thoughts of herself and Ella she moved on naturally to thoughts of her parents and herself, and memories of her childhood and journeys through France. Sometimes the inside of her head felt bleak, like a room without furniture, but at this moment it was full, because she was retracing the journey home – the Channel crossing, the streets of Dieppe, the lush meadows and low wooden farmhouses between Dieppe and Le Havre, and then the flat lands as far as Alençon, and then the forests full of hunting rifles and the town squares with their plane trees and the café toilets growing filthier and the fields of maize and sunflowers starting, the noons now intolerable, the southern light jumping and sparkling as you went into Lot, and beyond Lot the mountains yellow with dust and abandoned castles until you came to Narbonne and turned east along the coast, to Montpelier, Arles, Marseille . . .

When she was little her father had driven them. He'd been

in films, and like George had been a flash man, with a taste for Rolls-Royces with sugar-paper blinds and swivelling cocktail cabinets in the back. When Gina was eleven he had died, an event which Gina remembered as uneasy and astounding, fringed with pale, adult expressions and with whispered adult conversations. But it hadn't at the time seemed particularly significant. It was only afterwards that the significance came, as the years passed and her mother withdrew into one marriage after another, the death becoming year by year more harsh, more black and more momentous, until at last it became quite terrible, dividing time utterly in two so that there was before and there was afterwards and afterwards was black and cold and never to be warm again.

Except that at this moment she was quite warm, sitting there in the café watching the evening coming on, and thinking of France as she often did in the spring, because the first warm days always had this effect, taking her straight back, by routes she had forgotten, to her childhood. Sometimes Gina thought that she confused distance and time, that because the house was at the end of a long journey so she believed – she couldn't help herself – that her childhood was there too. She was being pinpricked all over with sharp longings for France. The night before she'd said to George, 'Let's have a holiday, let's go to France, let's drive south to Puissonier' (which was the name of her mother's house). But George wasn't interested. He didn't even properly hear her. 'I've got work to do,' he said. Which was why it was that now she had to go back in her head, again and again and again, as children do who feel they are not loved.

The second time they met she stood in the middle of his hotel room, smiling and looking around her. 'Well,' she said, 'I like it here, it's like playing at houses.' She had taken off her big coat and laid it across a chair. Underneath she wore a pair of narrow-cut, black velvet trousers with tiny rosebuds printed on them and a white shirt with long tails showing underneath a black sweater. She looked like a boy. She looked like the girls who work in films these days, thought George: not the actresses and certainly not the stars, but the production assistants, the continuity girls, the wardrobe department, all quick and brisk and giving as good as they got – sexy if you liked that kind of thing.

'Does your hotel room have room service?' she had asked. 'Couldn't we go straight there? I'm not feeling hungry for a large meal?' – thus pleasing and alarming him in equal measure.

'I thought you weren't going to ring me,' he said, pouring her a generous glass of wine and looking at her sideways. It was nearly four weeks since he had last seen her and her silence had irritated him.

'So did I,' she said.

'So what made you change your mind?'

'I fancy you,' she said, smiling more broadly than ever.

Gina was right to think that George was gloomy and distracted at the moment. Work was difficult. Shooting on the vampire film which should have been coming to an end by now was behind schedule because Siobhan was being tricksy. She was turning up late for work, or not at all, and when they rang her from the studios she was refusing to speak to anyone but George, and to him she was saying that she was unhappy and that she loved him and why didn't he get a divorce? And then, as if that weren't enough, he and Bill had set their hearts on making a children's blockbuster, a fifteen million dollar movie, with all kinds of special effects, something to rival the stuff coming out of Hollywood. They had come up with an idea and a script and he'd been out to Los Angeles and with great care had set up a pick-up deal with one of the studios, so that they would take over the film after it was made. Against this guarantee he had been able to negotiate a loan from a New York bank but in the last ten days the bank had gone cold on him and when he rang the studio for help all he got were temps and doormen, and so the paranoid thought began to haunt him, that perhaps they had never been serious, that perhaps from the start they had been stringing him along? And what with one thing and another he had been awake and worrying for three nights in a row and now he was so tired he felt addled and couldn't tell what was tiredness and what was hunger and what was randiness.

In this situation Gina was annoying him by pestering him with questions about the clinic and the lawyers. George thought she was a typical wife who stayed at home. She didn't understand how hard he had to work nor how many different projects he had to get through in a day or a week. She thought he could drop everything else and concentrate on just one thing, which was getting back the child. And, because she didn't understand this, she thought he wasn't serious about it, although George was always absolutely serious about getting back anything that was his.

This morning he had got up early and, most unusually, Gina had got up early also and had stood in the kitchen doorway watching him drink his coffee. After a while she had fallen into a reverie, her eyes very wide, her shoulders hunched, her body looking bulky. Seeing her standing there a hot, uncomfortable feeling had started up in him which he couldn't at first identify, but which he then recognised as pity. He wasn't used to the feeling. He didn't like it much. With pitying eyes he saw Gina very humbly: the coarse shine of the light on her hair, the bulk of her shoulders like the shell of a tortoise, the pencil lines on either side of her mouth, and, perversely, in his pity he felt an erection starting up inside him.

She needs a child, he had thought, and he'd said, 'Never mind, I'll put a rocket under the lawyers. Maybe by this time next year you'll have your daughter.' But she hadn't been listening because five minutes later she'd started on at him, as if he hadn't even spoken, about how little he cared for her and about how much she wanted a baby.

He rang for room service. 'I have to eat,' he said to Madeleine abruptly. After a few minutes a girl brought up a tray of sandwiches. He took them from her at the door. 'Thanks, love,' he said.

Madeleine was sitting on the bed. 'Do you always call women "love"?' she asked. He looked at her. She wants a quarrel, he thought. 'I don't understand you feminists,' he said. 'You want sex but you reserve the right to quarrel with the person giving it to you.'

'I can like sex but dislike the man,' said Madeleine.

'So do you dislike me?' he asked, and she went quiet, which gave him the feeling that he'd won the point. It was important with her to get the upper hand.

The minute he had screwed her, he rang the office but nothing had come in over the lunch time period. He lay back on the bed, took Madeleine absent-mindedly on his arm, lay there considering the wreckage of his project. After a while he noticed with surprise how light she was – lighter than you'd think, given that she was tall – but that, of course, thought George, was because she was an independent woman and used to earning her own money and going where she pleased. He liked this lightness. Because of it she could lie in his arms really quite companionably.

Sometimes, lately, George had felt that he had passed over the brow of a hill and into a different landscape. And behind him was his youth, where a pretty, frivolous wife could uplift you, but before him was his middle age where something different was required. George would be forty-five this year. He wasn't looking forward to it.

'I don't even know your surname?' he said.

She shrugged.

'Nor where you work.'

She named a couple of liberal newspapers which she guessed he wouldn't read.

'I don't read those,' he said, and he added with a smile to annoy her, 'Liberal crap.'

She shrugged again. 'How's the vampire film?' she asked.

'Lousy,' he said, although it was a principle of his never to tell the truth about work to a woman. 'It's behind schedule and Siobhan's being difficult.'

'Are you going out there every day?'

'No. I've got to get the next project off the ground. In this business you can't afford a gap between one project and the next. If you don't work it's death.'

'And is the next project set up?'

'Up until last week I thought it was,' he said irritably, because it gave him a chilly feeling to talk about work like this to a woman, and yet at the same time he wanted to talk because he wanted consolation from her. He began to tell her what had happened. She listened. 'Do you know for sure that you've definitely lost them?' she asked.

'Not yet, no.'

'Then you'd better get out to Los Angeles and talk to them face to face. You can't afford to let them say no outright, because once they have it will be difficult for them to retract it.'

He looked at her sideways. She likes me, he thought with a jump of surprise, because he was used to women fancying him, wanting him, fighting over him – but *liking* him – now that was a different universe altogether. First she quarrels with me and then she likes me, he thought. 'Let's play cards,' he said.

They sat on the bed and played stud poker. She dealt the cards with a pussy-cat smile. He thought, she's playing to win. He hadn't been expecting this.

'What are we playing for?' she asked.

'Chips,' he said, in an irritable voice.

'But what do they stand for?'

'Ten pees,' he said.

'A pound,' she said.

'OK, a pound,' he said.

He could have sworn that she was peeking at his cards already but he wasn't surprised. He'd played a fair bit of poker – both with men and women – and women, in his experience, would use whatever weapons they could to get the upper hand, showing their cleavage or breathing with their lips apart or tossing back their hair.

The first couple of hands they folded. The third hand she looked at her cards and gave her pussy-cat smile. 'I'll open for two,' she said and put in two of her chips. He had a pair of Kings. 'I'll see you,' he said and put in two chips as well. She discarded one. Only one? he thought, no one discards just one. She's bluffing. He put back three and drew two fives and an eight. Two pairs – all the nice things, he thought. The next round she said, 'I'll bet you four,' and put in four of her chips. Wild cards, he thought. 'I'll see you,' he said out loud and put in four as well which, counting the ante, made fourteen pounds in all. She laid down her cards with a sweep. 'Full house. Three Jacks, two Kings.' 'Two pairs,' he said in astonishment, and she swept up the money from under his nose.

The next game he played more carefully. When she called a smallish raise and put back two he assumed she could have threes or the beginnings of a flush. He himself had a Queen, a Jack, a nine, an eight and a two. He put back the two, hoping for a ten to make a straight but got a five instead and thus was bust. 'I bet two,' she said. 'I fold,' he said. She smirked and laid down – absolutely nothing, a bluffer's hand with not even a pair in it. She swept up the money. Now she had twenty-four pounds.

'Do you always play to win?' he asked her.

'Of course,' she said in amazement at the question, and at that he smiled at her and in his smile there was resentment but also a shade of dazzled acquiescence, the look that men give to powerful women when they fancy them.

George flew to Los Angeles to renegotiate his film deal. It was a twelve-hour flight and eight hours ahead of the sun so that instead of landing in the welcoming darkness that his body craved he came down instead into dazzling heat and sunshine. He went by cab to his hotel. It was in Los Angeles' Westside, which was as close to Hollywood as he could manage because in this city unless you had a good address nobody took you seriously. The hotel was the usual opulent affair, marbled, with Jacuzzis and saunas and faxes, and – like the rest of Los Angeles – full of beautiful women, all limbs and tans and hair and baby-doll appearances. He saw them from the taxi, jogging along the pavements and going in and out of restaurants. As he lay on the bed in his hotel he heard them clack-clack-clacking in their sandals, along the marbled corridors.

He was terribly tired. He tried to defer sleep by freshening himself up with a bath but no sooner had he got into it than he began to doze off, his body sinking deeper and deeper into the warm water until he woke up with a start. He got out and lay down on the bed, turning on the television and flicking through the channels until he found an old movie with Faye Dunaway. He lay there for a while admiring her Hollywood lips. George loved films. Without their richness and romance the inside of his head would have been as bleak as Gina's. But now, though he tried to follow the plot, he was too distracted, not only by his exhaustion but his randiness as well, his cravings for sleep mixed up with a sprinkling of sexual fantasies which at first were focused on the film star but which increasingly fastened on the journalist Suzanne. He thought how bizarre it was that in this city of beautiful women it should be that cool, plain woman who had got inside his head, but there she was, sitting cross-legged on the bed, playing cards with him whilst he stretched out his arms and legs luxuriously at the thought of what was to come.

Madeleine arranged to have lunch with Nicola in a café in Covent Garden. She left her office at twelve o'clock and walked down past the Cavendish Hotel where she stopped and looked in through the ground floor window and saw business men sitting amongst the pot plants and the newspapers, trussed up in their suits. But then she raised her eyes and imagined up above them, on the upper floors, trysts and assignations and naked bodies cavorting in every pose and position. She walked on down to Long Acre and went into the Armani shop and ran her hands along the rails of expensive clothes, putting feet into the gorgeous shoes and torsos into the expensive suits and chests for the ties to lie against and broad shoulders to take the weight – with a swing – of the fancy overcoats.

When she came to the café she looked in through the window and saw Nicola sitting at a table with a scarf around her neck, her long, blue coat draped over a chair beside her, a collection of bags at her feet, an exhibition catalogue at her elbow – and the ghosts of all good, domestic women thronging around her. Madeleine thought, I hope that when people look at me they will see all the resourceful, wicked, sexy women of this world standing at my shoulder.

She went in with a smile, shedding her coat and taking a seat opposite Nicola and running her hands over her cropped hair. 'You look well,' said Nicola.

'That's what my mother says,' said Madeleine.

They looked at the menu. They called the waiter over. Afterwards Nicola said accusingly, 'You smiled at him.'

'So I did,' said Madeleine with a smirk and a downward, complacent sweep of her lashes and she fiddled with the sugar bowl and stretched out her legs and leant forward confidingly and said, 'I saw George Kaufman again. I spent the afternoon with him.'

'You mean – but how could you? How could you even fancy him?'

'I don't know. I just do,' said Madeleine.

'But think what he's done to you,' said Nicola.

'He hasn't done anything to me yet. He's trying to but I shan't let him.'

'Even so,' said Nicola in shocked tones. But then she added, 'Still, I can see it must be nice to be in love again.'

'Not in love, in lust,' said Madeleine.

'All right. In lust. But I can't remember that either.'

A wistful look came over Nicola's face. Madeleine saw it. 'I thought you wanted another child,' she said crossly, because she'd grown used – surprisingly quickly – to the idea that she fancied the enemy George Kaufman, and only sometimes, as now, was the extraordinariness of it all borne upon her, that she should want to sleep with a man who didn't know her name and who, if he did, would want to do her down. After that first time back in January she had decided not to see George Kaufman again, but he had stirred something up in her and now she wanted to go on living in this world he had introduced her to, of sex and good times. Even so, she would have felt better if she could believe that sleeping with George Kaufman was part of a greater scheme. And so she was pleased when Nicola suddenly said, 'You know, maybe you fancy him in order to protect Ella?'

'How do you mean?'

'Well, if he wants you then it wouldn't matter if he also wanted Ella. He could have you both, if you see what I mean – a lover and a daughter.'

She hadn't thought of this. She who liked ideas hadn't thought of this one. But it made her smile, because a good idea was like a present and anyway wasn't this the point of female friends to help explain the other sex to you?

'Or to put it another way,' said Madeleine, 'maybe I'm like

an old-fashioned woman who's making a man less dangerous by giving him sex?'

'Exactly,' said Nicola.

'In which case,' said Madeleine, 'Gina had better watch out, because here's a way in which I could get revenge.'

One day whilst George was in Los Angeles Gina went down to Ella's local school to see if she could see the child coming out at home time. The school stood on a narrow strip of land between two busy roads. The parents were gathered on the pavements in the spring sunshine. Gina wore a green, fitted jacket, belted at the waist, a short white skirt and slingback sandals. She had on dark glasses and her reddish hair lay in a shawl across her shoulders. Some of the mothers stared at her but Gina who had dressed more quietly than usual didn't notice. She had wanted to slide unseen into this world of mothers and children, had wanted to stand amongst the knots of women, smiling vaguely in all directions and letting the talk of school dinners and reading levels wash all over her. She wasn't afraid of seeing Madeleine. She had assumed that Madeleine would be at work and that she would have a nanny of some kind to collect Ella. She began to look around to see if she could guess who this person might be. Gradually she was allowing her shoulders to slump, allowing the soft, blurry effects of mother-love to take their toll; and because she was always conscious of her appearance she could feel it happening and thought in amazement – half-pleased, half-horrified – If I stood here long enough I'd start to look like one of these women from this other world.

And then at half past three a tremor of expectancy passed through the crowd, and people began to straighten up and fidget and take a step forward and look first at their watches and then at the school, where at last the front door opened and the children began to come out. They were laden down with coats and bags. They were scanning the crowd and looking for their parents. And now, as their parents stepped forward and as a dozen different scenes of greeting sprang up across the playground – parents taking bags, parents leaning over to hear what their children said, parents reproaching, coaxing, shouting, smiling – a different thought took hold of Gina: that this was a very poor school, that the parents were shabbily dressed, that the children looked pale and tense, that really was this school good enough for Ella? She hadn't lived with motherhood from the moment of Ella's birth. She didn't recognise the feeling as being a variant on the endless maternal treadmill of anxiety – is this food good enough? Is that car safe enough? Is the childminder loving enough? – and not recognising it, the feeling overwhelmed her, that her child was in a sink school and needed to be saved.

And then Ella appeared. She looked pale and skinny. In the sharp spring sunshine her clothes were worn and faded-looking. She was gripping hold of her bag and trying to keep her footing as the big children jostled her. As soon as Gina saw her the feeling got her round the throat, that this was her child, looking beaten by life, and that now she must save her. Ella meanwhile was scanning the crowd. She stepped in Gina's direction. Closer and closer she came whilst Gina watched and didn't dare turn round to see who it was who was drawing Ella towards her. Now she was so close that Gina could see her in every detail – the pale, set expression, the eyes as large as saucers, the sea of indigo shadows on which they floated. To someone like Gina the loss of Ella's beauty seemed almost more criminal than anything else. And then Ella came up level with her and as she did so gave a start of recognition and Gina thought, she remembers me! All those weeks ago in the park and she remembers me! And then Ella moved on whilst Gina stood there, waiting, counting to the tapping of her feet, waiting some more, and then eventually turning round to see the back of a big, blonde woman, holding Ella by the hand and leading her through the crowd.

They crossed the Chalk Farm Road. They turned left and then right into Parkway, Ella and the childminder walking on ahead and Gina following after them, eyeing up the childminder as she did so and noting the grey tracksuit and the custard-yellow curls. (Gina hated custard.) Ella was exhausted. You could see it in the way she couldn't walk straight but kept pirouetting on the end of the childminder's arm. Halfway up Parkway as she swung round she caught sight of Gina. She stopped in mid-pirouette. Her eyes grew enormous. She opened her mouth to say something, but then the childminder tugged at her hand and Ella swung on round and continued her restless, weary dance up the street.

They came to Mornington Terrace, a row of grubby Victorian houses which fronted onto the railway. A little way down the childminder stopped beside a chipped front door and an overflowing dustbin and began to rummage in her handbag for her key. So this is where my child goes after school, is it? thought Gina. She was shocked by these shabby surroundings. She didn't see the kindness with which the childminder ushered Ella in, nor the relief on Ella's weary face to be where she thought of as home. Instead, she saw the weeds in the pavement cracks, the childminder's downtrodden shoes going slap-slap-slap as she crossed the threshold, the glimpse as the door opened of a dingy hallway and a carpetless flight of stairs. And then the door closed and Gina was left standing on the far pavement, bereft as usual but this time absolutely sure that she would not tolerate this situation any longer for her daughter.

43

The next time they met it was in a pub beside the Thames not far from Hampton Court. George and Bill were still shooting the last scenes of the Victorian vampire movie and George had to be there to hold Siobhan's hand because otherwise she simply wouldn't turn up. George told Madeleine that he could get away for an hour and a half and Madeleine said in a light, indifferent tone that that was fine and that if he gave her the address she could find her own way there. George said, 'Don't be late' – because he was thinking that maybe if there was time he could take the car somewhere private and have her on the back seat – and Madeleine told him not to drink at breakfast because she didn't want him breathalysed before he even got to the pub. George said, 'You sound just like my wife.' Madeleine said, 'I expect wives have a point of view too.' George said, 'You don't really mean that,' and Madeleine said, 'No, no, it's true, I don't mean it at all.'

She left the car in the car park, beside a stream, spring-full, the clear water flowing between the rubbish and the willow shoots. There were couples sitting on the bonnets of cars, the girls in flimsy, chiffony skirts, stretching their necks towards the sun, dropping their shoulders and exhaling in the unexpected warmth. George was inside, in a gloomy Tudorbethan parlour room, sitting at a bar and drinking whisky.

'You're late,' he said.

'Not very,' she said, with that bold smile of hers, seating herself on a bar stool beside him and swinging her legs. 'You've got a tan. You went to California. How did it go?'

'Well. I got the deal.'

'Good.'

'I'm sorry about this,' he said, 'I'd rather have gone to bed with you.'

'So would I.'

'Did you find it all right?'

'I got lost once. Otherwise it was fine.'

'How did you get here?'

She pointed out of the window.

'Christ,' he said. She drove an old brown B-reg Citroën Visa. 'Does it work?'

'Of course,' she said haughtily. 'A Mercedes Estate isn't the only car that goes.'

He opened his mouth. 'You're going to offer to buy me something bigger and better, aren't you?' she said. 'Something grand to make you feel good. Big talk.'

He shut his mouth again. 'Only because I know that you'd refuse it anyway,' he said with a smirk, looking down at the menu. Sometimes he had the feeling that he was a somnambulist and that he was sleep-walking through these smart, abusive conversations that they had together. But the feeling, although peculiar, was pleasant. He didn't talk like this to Gina.

Madeleine asked him about his new film and George began to describe it. It was going to be about a war between children and witches. It would have a grand finale by night, a scene resplendent with special effects, as the witches swooped down and tried to destroy the children and the children fought back under the leadership of their young teacher. First the witches would snatch one of the boys and when they pulled him back to safety would take instead the teacher's girlfriend and carry her off on a terrifying midnight ride, seen through her giddy eyes, as they swooped and shrieked between the tower blocks and tried to drown her in the Thames – but she would cling on to them, screaming with fear, as the water came up to meet them, shining hungrily in the darkness and the lights.

'How old is the audience?' Madeleine asked.

'Eight. Nine. Ten. That kind of age.'

'So why bring into it romantic love? Aren't they too young for all that?'

He shrugged. 'Children like that kind of thing. You may not but they do.'

'I've got nothing against romantic love. I just don't see that it's relevant here.'

'You know your trouble,' he said crossly – because he hated to have his film attacked – 'your generation of women, you're all of you loveless, you just don't believe in love.'

'Yes, I do,' she said, 'I love my child.'

'Ah, but that's different. You love your children all right. It's the men that you don't love. I bet you don't love your husband.'

'Are men so lovable?' asked Madeleine sulkily.

'As lovable as you are,' he said.

And then he stopped, for standing by their table and watching them was a child of eighteen months or so, dressed in a navy padded suit decorated with scarlet strawberries and yellow apples. He had dark curls, glossy but rather thin so that you could see the ghostly scalp beneath. His eyes were the colour of tea which has been left too long to brew and his red lips were a little apart so that you could see the silver bubbles of spit forming over his teeth.

George and Madeleine stared. 'God, he's beautiful, isn't he?' said George sentimentally.

'I expect he cries,' said Madeleine brutally, but she kept her eyes cast down so that George wouldn't see the lie in them.

'Does your child cry?' he asked.

'No, not any more. She's beautiful,' said Madeleine, raising her eyes again, and for a moment, sitting there, they were united by the beauty of children, by this little boy and by Madeleine's memory of Ella, as she had been last night, sitting at the kitchen table, threading beads onto a necklace whilst Madeleine read a book.

The little boy turned on his heels and started to run. He hadn't gone three steps when he tripped over his feet and fell. George jumped up. Out shot his hands. They seized the little boy round the waist, swinging him over with a crane-like movement until he was standing on the ground once more. George's hands lingered. Madeleine saw how neatly they fitted into the curve of the waist and she felt – with an unwilling intuition because she didn't really want to know what went on in his body – how his fingers felt the inner organs under the skin, felt how warmly they were packed together. Oh, for God's sake! he wants a *baby*, Madeleine thought, and George looked up and caught the thought, but thought it had to do with sex. First came insults, then came lust. Desire hung between them like one of Ella's necklaces.

They bolted down their lunch and drove to a country lane where, on the back seat of his car, he screwed her. From where Madeleine lay she could see a bank of trees, sprigged and hazed with fresh pale green. She could see pink blossom, speckling a sky already speckled with shreds of clouds, white on blue, like a bird's egg. George was kneeling on the seat above her, dressed in one of his glorious shirts, but naked from the waist downwards. He was putting on a condom and as he did so was looking down at himself – as men do, thought Madeleine, tenderly, as if they like what they see. But the condom wouldn't go on. He threw it away and reached for his trouser pocket for another. 'I could get you pregnant,' he said suddenly. 'Sod off,' she said, but still she put her head back sweetly for him to kiss her lips because she was thinking that what could be more sexy than to have George Kaufman's baby, to be George Kaufman's lady with a bun in the oven, and how else to be fucked, when you are pregnant, than on your hands and knees like an animal? – that wicked, pornographic pleasure?

44

Mr Chatoo wrote to her. He said that he had now had a chance to talk to the other side and to get some idea of the evidence they had accumulated – 'which unfortunately is quite impressive'. As well as this, he had learnt that two more children born in the clinic had been DNA-tested and had been found not to be their parents' children. In the circumstances he was now advising her to have a DNA test done on Ella. He said that he was absolutely sure that if the Kaufmans went to court – which they showed every sign of doing – that the judge would accede to their wishes in this matter. He said that it was important not to waste their efforts fighting battles they were going to lose, and besides they had to remember that costs might be awarded against them. Better by far to concentrate on what really mattered which was keeping Ella. He still hoped that the DNA test would show that Ella was Madeleine's. But if not, the Kaufmans might still drop the affair and if they didn't, it wouldn't be difficult to show them up in court as unfit parents.

Madeleine rang him up. She was in tears. 'Now Mrs Kingdom,' he said, 'you've been through many hard times and I know you can get through this one too.'

'But I don't want my child going into hospitals and having needles stuck into her.'

'Oh, it won't come to hospitals. A blood sample is all they need and that can be done at your local GP's surgery. We will definitely push for your doctor to do it. Anything else could upset the child and Ella's welfare is paramount. Of course you too will have to provide a blood sample.'

'Me?'

'Because the DNA test works by revealing family similarities. If Ella is your biological child then it will be revealed in similarities between your samples.'

'But suppose they cheat? Suppose they fiddle the results?'

'That won't be possible because two sets of tests will be done. Their lawyers will request blood samples and they will organise the testing on those samples. We will send our samples separately to the forensic laboratory at Oxford which I always use and which has the best reputation in this field.'

Madeleine stopped crying. Had her father spoken to her like this when she was little?

Madeleine took Ella out of school for the morning and took her to the doctor. They had recently changed surgeries and the new one was on the other side of Regents Park. They walked along the Outer Circle. Ella was skipping beside her, her stick-like arms and legs flying in every direction, their shadows making an intricate pattern. She was pleased to be missing school. She was looking around her and observing the unfamiliar daytime world. The strangeness of it all made her chatty. 'Mummy,' she said, 'I saw a lion at the school gates the other day.' 'Did you?' asked Madeleine absent-mindedly, 'what did it look like?' She was walking beside Ella with a heavy heart. She felt as if she were going to a funeral. This answer wasn't at all what Ella had been expecting. If Madeleine had been looking downwards she would have seen a puzzled look come over the child's face. But Madeleine was watching a couple of men going the other way and staring at Ella with what seemed to Madeleine to be covetous eyes. Madeleine thought that everyone wanted her child.

The doctor was a locum. He didn't ask what the samples were for. He smiled at Ella and Ella simpered back. Gloomily, Madeleine watched the blood flow up into the syringe. She thought it was one thing to speculate that your child might not be yours, quite another thing to know it for certain. When Madeleine gave a sample Ella peered very closely. 'Have you got green blood like Doctor Spock, Mum?' she asked, and Madeleine smiled faintly.

Afterwards they went to an Italian restaurant in Goodge Street and ordered pizzas and ice cream and milkshakes. 'What? All those things?' asked Ella, who was accustomed to having to choose. She was half-slumped against her mother, whispering to herself as she wrapped a strand of hair across her mouth and round her nose. 'Zippidy doo-da, Zippidy day,' she was whispering, 'My, oh my, what a wonderful day. Why is a pizza called a pizza?' she asked.

'It's an Italian word. I don't know what it means.'

'I wish you hadn't called me Ella. I wish I had a different name.'

'Like what?'

'Clare.'

'You don't want to be called Clare. Whatever for?'

'It's more ordinary,' said Ella. 'Did you like your name when you were little?'

'No,' said Madeleine.

'Tell me about your childhood, Mum,' said Ella.

Stories gave Ella a dopey, soupy look. They soothed her mind which otherwise was full of regrets, always wishing her life had been different. Madeleine talked and Ella licked the back of her ice cream spoon and listened. Each time she dug the spoon into the ice cream her eyelashes swept down and settled against her skin like moths. In her near-seven-year-old face Madeleine could see embedded an older face, gawky and adolescent, the cheekbones higher, the eyes though still enormous now tilted upwards at the corners, the nose longer, the mouth wider, and the expression, that neat but stony expression! – Oh God, she looks like George, thought Madeleine. It came to her in a flash what she should do, a sudden, vivid, guilty image of herself and Ella throwing themselves on George's mercy, revealing who they were, begging him to take them on, to look after them, to take them under his wing – a seductive, guilty, weasel hope that a man might solve their problems.

45

But as it happened events overtook them.

That Sunday morning George and Gina quarrelled. He quarrelled out of habit but she quarrelled from a dull dreariness that bordered on despair, because today she was fed up with her life and with George and with her endless, ongoing infertility. Everything about her body was slow this morning, except for the words in her mouth – quarrelsome responses to George's quarrelsome remarks – which surprised her by leaping straight out of her mouth as easily as if they had been greased with butter.

They quarrelled over the cost and the colour of Gina's highlights and how far it was to California and the time difference between there and here. They quarrelled over Julia Roberts' house in Hollywood, although neither of them knew anything about it, and what the doormat was made of and the cost of Harrods' bedlinen. They quarrelled over who played the lead in the film *Pretty Baby* and what the word 'paedophilia' meant, each of them appealing to the Greek roots of the word, although what either of them knew about *that* could be written on the back of a postage stamp; and George made comparisons with the word 'gynaephilia' or did he mean 'homophobia'? and 'what's that got to do with anything?' asked Gina. She wants sex, thought George knowingly, but he was damned if he was going to give it to her.

They were due to go out for Sunday lunch. The day was fine and warm, the grass in the park an acid green, the sky a tender blue, the blossom trees stepping forth in the palest of ice cream colours. But neither George nor Gina noticed the weather. They were far too busy quarrelling. They quarrelled as they got into the car, quarrelled as they drove along Prince Albert Road. As they passed the entrance to the park the car engine suddenly cut out and in a startled silence they glided to a halt beside the road. They sat there for a minute in dumbstruck astonishment and then Gina started blaming him for failing to maintain the car and he started blaming her for putting a spell on it. Then George saw the petrol gauge and that the answer should be so simple made him angry and he started to shout some more and this made Gina so angry that she got out of the car and flounced away on her tottery high-heeled shoes. George ran after her. He seized her by the arm, so tightly in fact that he hurt her and she thought he'd done it on purpose so she swung round and gave him a resounding slap across the face.

He raised his hand to his cheek in amazement. She felt a champagne shot in her veins. She even smiled through her tears and thought she saw an answering spark in his eyes and perhaps they would have started slapping each other like a couple of clowns in a comedy routine, but at that moment George – with his hand still on his cheek – turned his head and his expression was so astonished that Gina turned to look as well. Her hands dropped to her side. She seemed as amazed as her husband. They resembled a couple of guilty children caught in a quarrel. For what George had seen, not five yards away and walking along the pavement towards them, was the journalist Suzanne holding a child's hand, whilst what Gina had seen was Dr Madeleine Kingdom and the beautiful Ella, over whom the three of them were quarrelling.

They had been out for a walk in Regents Park. First, they had been to the playground and, because this was Ella's treat, Madeleine had schooled herself to be patient, as Ella swung and slid and whirled around on the roundabout, to feel the slow passing of time as luxurious, not frustrating. Afterwards, they had walked on in the direction of the Broadwalk. The trees were still leafless. Long, black shadows lay across the grass. On either side of the path the lower halves of the bushes were buried deep in shadows, although the sunlight shone on the upper twigs. When they came to the Broadwalk they turned right in the direction of Primrose Hill, beside the zoo's perimeter. The wolves were sunning themselves in their enclosure. Ella stopped to stare. 'Are they dogs?' she asked.

'No, wolves,' said Madeleine.

'But they've got yellow eyes. Why won't they look at me?'

'Because they're wild animals, I suppose, and human beings just don't interest them. They're not like pets, you see.'

'Can we have a wolf at home?'

'What do you think?' asked Madeleine.

'All the other children at school have got pets,' said Ella and Madeleine opened her mouth to answer but Ella ran on down the path – ten, twenty, thirty yards ahead – making the tie between mother and daughter longer, looser, as loose as Ella dared.

But when they came to the park gates she took her mother's hand and together they turned left towards the crossing and Regents Park Road because Madeleine wanted a coffee. It was as they were walking up Prince Albert Road that Madeleine saw the dark blue Mercedes Estate, all shiny in the sunlight and the Kaufmans quarrelling beside it.

She was long-sighted and besides she was not distracted by emotions as they were, and so she saw them long before they saw her. If they hadn't looked so ridiculous, fetching each other slaps in the middle of the street, she might have been alarmed. As it was, although her heart jumped up in her throat and she held Ella's hand more tightly, she carried on walking – right up to them – whilst they stopped their fighting and stood and stared at her. 'Hello, Gina,' she said, 'Hello, George,' with a smile and a nod to each of them, and then she led Ella round them and carried on walking.

One, two, three, Madeleine counted – ten paces for them to stand and stare – eleven, twelve, thirteen, fourteen – twenty paces for Gina to turn to George and hiss, 'It's her. It's her and the little girl,' and for George to open his mouth guiltily – 'What do you mean, it's her?' – and then to shut it in confusion as Gina said, 'Madeleine Kingdom. The woman who's got our baby.' Twenty-seven, twenty-eight, twenty-nine, thirty paces for George to open and shut his mouth in gobsmacked astonishment, to wrestle with his emotions, to struggle to reconcile Suzanne the journalist with Dr Madeleine Kingdom, whilst Gina began to cry and shout, 'That's our child, George, I swear that is our child.'

At forty paces she turned. She couldn't help herself. There

they stood on the pavement, Gina clutching at George's arm and George staring after her. She felt triumphant – she knew she did and knew that even at forty paces Gina could see it. But she was also panic-struck. Suppose they came after her?

'Who are they, Mum? You're hurting my hand,' said Ella.

'No one,' said Madeleine. She had quickened her pace. She was suddenly afraid that George might have a temper.

'Why are we hurrying, Mum?' asked Ella.

'Never mind,' said Madeleine and she began to march the child towards the path which led down to the left, across the grass and over the canal towards the Outer Circle.

'Can we go down on to the canal path?' asked Ella.

'No.'

'Oh Mummy,' Ella wailed.

Madeleine was half-pushing and half-pulling her up the path. As they came up on to the Outer Circle Madeleine saw to the left and down the road the entrance to the zoo. 'We're going to the zoo,' she said.

They passed the balloon sellers and the ice cream vendors. The zoo was nearly empty. There were weeds and grass growing up between the pavement cracks.

'Can we see the monkeys?' asked Ella.

'In a minute,' said Madeleine. 'First I want to see the fish,' and she took Ella into the stony, cave-like darkness of the Aquarium. They passed the crocodiles, the freshwater fish – the bream, the perch, the eels. They passed the tropical fish swimming in their brilliantly-lit windows. They passed the turtles and the piranhas and the tiger sharks swimming ceaselessly in circles. There was a small turtle in the bottom of a tank. 'Is it a baby?' Ella asked.

'Yes.'

'And is that the mother?'

'Yes.'

'Does the mother love the baby?'

'Yes,' said Madeleine. Ella nodded. She was going from tank to tank, peering closely into each, a look of enchantment on her face. Gradually the darkness was beginning to soothe Madeleine, but even so she was still panicking, still jumping each time she bumped into someone in the darkness, still clutching Ella's hand.

46

On Monday morning when Madeleine went into work the departmental secretary said, 'There's a man here waiting to see you.'

'Where?'

'Down there' – the secretary nodded down the corridor – 'he's sitting outside your room.'

She wasn't at all surprised. It was only what she had expected. She found him sitting with his elbows on his knees, face turned away from her and dressed in a cream-coloured suit. In the dustiness and the dowdiness of the Victorian corridor he looked quite absurdly dapper, camp even and theatrical. She came up quite close to him before he turned his head and saw her. Slowly he got to his feet. There was a look of reproach on his face. No sooner did she see this than she forgot her fantasy in the Italian restaurant about throwing herself on his mercy. It was as if she'd never had it. Instead all she wanted to do was abuse him. She opened her mouth to begin but he got there first, saying, 'You lied to me.'

That threw her. Well, isn't that amazing? she thought. He cares about *that*. Isn't that just like a man to care about sex when a child is at stake?

'I *lied* to you,' she said, 'what the hell do you think you did to me?'

'I didn't do anything to you,' he said in bemusement.

'Didn't do anything to me? You tried to take away my child?'

He gave a shrug as if to say, Oh *that*. 'I don't want your child,' he said.

'Tell that to your wife, tell that to your lawyers.'

'So you knew all along who I was,' he said, 'and I thought you fancied me.'

'I wanted to know everything there was to know about you,' she said brutally. 'I wanted to know just exactly how unfit you are to be a parent. Think about it – the overdraft, the designer drugs, the girlfriends. I've told my lawyer everything. No one is going to put you in charge of a hamster.'

At this he looked dumbstruck. 'So you never fancied me?' he asked for a second time. Well, she wasn't answering that. 'You tried to take my child away,' she said.

'I don't want your child,' he repeated wearily.

'I don't believe you. If that's the case why haven't you told Gina?'

'I have,' he said, 'I told Gina so yesterday.'

That took the wind out of her sails. They stood staring at each other. 'What did she say?' asked Madeleine curiously, and George replied with a shrug, 'She said.'

'Good,' said Madeleine after a pause, 'in which case there's nothing more that we need to say to each other.' She turned to walk away.

'No, wait a moment,' he said, 'you could still have me' – his eyes were naked and hopeful – 'we could still have each other and Ella too. You must have fancied me a bit. What about those times in bed together? I'll tell Gina it's all over. We could see if we could make a go of it – you and me and Ella as a family.'

She shook her head. Again she felt a desire to abuse him, to put the boot in, to make him suffer. 'Forget it, George Kaufman. I never fancied you. I never even liked you.'

Visibly he crumbled before her. He shrank in size. It was hugely satisfying for her to see this. He paused. He was searching for words. 'Then there's nothing more to be said, is there?' he said uncertainly.

'No, nothing,' she said brutally, and after another hesitation he turned round as if looking for the way out. 'That way,' she said with a nod of her head and obediently he walked in the direction that she'd indicated.

After he had gone she went back to her room. She felt weak and tearful because she was being uplifted by a very pure love for Ella. At the same time she was thinking, I beat him, I put the boot in, what a baby he really is – why was I ever frightened of them? – like a six-month baby. For the first time in months she felt she could see past the blockage that had been the Kaufmans and into her future with Ella.

On Mondays she worked late and didn't collect Ella until seven. At a quarter past six she stopped work and because the evening was fine and a feeling of expansiveness had been growing inside her all day, she decided to walk home across Regents Park.

She cut across Fitzrovia. She walked up by Portland Place and across the Euston Road and into Regents Park by the Park Square Gate. The weather was fine but it was still early in the year and the formal gardens were deep in blue twilight as she walked northwards towards Camden Town. She passed a forsythia burning in the gloom. She saw the last of the crocuses spread voluptuously beneath the still naked trees. She saw a woman, well-dressed, wearing dark glasses, a tourist perhaps, sitting on a bench, and was reminded of Gina. Very cheerfully she began an internal dialogue with her enemy. 'You see,' she said, 'it's quite fair really, you get the man and the money and the sex – and I'm sure he screws you as exquisitely as he screwed me – but I get the child, because Ella is mine, and because you've never been a mother – not really, not truly – and so you can't understand what it feels like when someone threatens your child. But it's all very fair – in fact, it's more than fair – because there's a lot of women out there who'd think that you'd got the best of the bargain by a long, long way.'

She was smiling as she crossed Chichester Road and continued up the Broadwalk. She looked to her left and through the trees she saw an ocean of grass rolling and undulating away towards the northern edge of the park. So bright and shining did this ocean of parkland seem in the evening light that she began to think of the future, to remember that it was the better half of the year that lay before them, the half of the year with the summer holidays in it, and that perhaps this year, if she was careful with the money, they could go abroad – maybe on a beach holiday? maybe to Italy? – and from there they could go inland and see the pictures in Florence, which was what she'd always planned to do with Ella.

On and on she walked, dreaming her dreams – up as far as the fountain, right and past the playground where she'd played for years with Ella, out by Gloucester Gate and across the Outer Circle towards the top of Parkway. As she waited for the lights to change she remembered George's words, not this time but the last time that they'd met: 'Your generation of women,' he'd said, 'is a loveless generation. You don't love men at all. It's the children that you love.' It's true, thought Madeleine, it's absolutely true. A thousand years of romantic love and we've given it all up and instead we love the children; and at the thought of her skinny child, with her long, tangled hair and her raspberry-coloured lips and her green eyes and the smooth, brown backs of her legs Madeleine began to hurry.

She crossed the top of Parkway. She went round by Delancey Street and turned right into Mornington Terrace. On her left was its long, grubby, Victorian façade. On her right beyond a high wall was a deep, deep cutting from where she could hear the zip and tear of high-speed trains. She began to think what she and Ella would have for supper and what book they would read in bed tonight. She came to Norma's house and first rang on the bell and then looked up to see what lights were on. When she saw that the front room with its bay window onto the street was in darkness, the first faint whisper of anxiety arose because normally after supper this was where Ella sat with Norma and watched television. And yet at the same time her mind felt too buoyant and too hopeful to permit of any anxieties and so she told herself that they must be in the kitchen and she rang the bell again. She heard footsteps in the hall. The front door opened and there stood Mandy, Norma's teenage daughter. 'Ella?' began Madeleine and as she did so the whisper of anxiety took on a louder tone because Mandy's face was surprised, bemused, puzzled to see her.

'Ella?' said Madeleine again.

'Wait a minute,' said Mandy and she turned back down the corridor. 'Mum?' she shouted. The door to the kitchen opened. Norma stood in the yellow electric light. Madeleine's feet had already carried her over the threshold and down the corridor.

'Where's Ella?' she said to Norma, pushing Mandy aside, and now because Norma's face was so puzzled and confused the whisper of anxiety had turned into a shout and cold fingers of fear had got Madeleine round the neck – a mother's terror – the child slipped out of your grip and gone, lost somewhere out there in the vast, vast world.

'Your sister came for her,' said Norma in a terrible, hollow, fearful voice – because of course the knowledge of her mistake was now written all over her face – 'Your sister came for her at half past three.'

47

They had gone out for Sunday lunch with four other couples to a Chinese restaurant in Hampstead. After the shock of seeing Suzanne/Madeleine Kingdom outside Regents Park, George had told Gina in the car that there was no way he was going to spend good money pursuing through the courts a child who might – or might not – be theirs, and who anyway they'd never met. This was his decision and he slapped it down, brooking no excuse, no argument, no explanation. She couldn't believe what she was hearing. Of course she started on at him. She asked him how he could even think of abandoning his child? But he answered her curtly, 'Listen, Gina, I don't want an argument – I'm not interested – do you understand?' And then she stared tearfully out of the window, because she had started to think of herself as a mother – look at me, the mother, she had begun to think – and the idea had afforded her great satisfaction. But now he was taking that away from her.

He parked the car in silence. He walked off into the restaurant as if she didn't exist. She didn't understand why he was suddenly so angry. He sat down on the far side of the large round table to avoid her but quite soon she saw an empty seat and she sidled round and they began a covert argument in low, vehement voices. He told her she was hysterical. She told him he was heartless. She asked him how he could even think of abandoning his child. He said, 'It's only an egg, for God's sake.' She said, 'What do you mean, only an egg? The egg is everything,' and she accused him of not caring about the one thing that mattered to her and he accused her of only caring about babies, of not giving a monkey's for him.

After that she sulked for a while and then she looked tearful again and then she seemed to be casting around the table for support from the other women so he said, 'Just don't start, Gina, right?' and at that she burst into tears. He got to his feet. 'Why would I want a baby with you, anyway, you old witch?' he asked, because in for a penny, in for a pound, he could hardly make things worse, and besides he felt better for abusing her. As he walked out of the restaurant the last thing he saw was Charlie with her arms around Gina whilst the rest of the women stared after him reproachfully, but he thought that the men had a look on their faces as if to say, 'Good for you, mate, you show her.'

He went straight from the restaurant to the office and didn't come home until late that night. Lying on her own in bed that afternoon Gina rang Charlie in the hope of comfort; and Charlie tried as best she could, but what else could she say other than that life was a bugger, darling, life was a bugger? And then George came home but hardly saying a word and left again early the next morning, still silent, so that all her tears and protests were thrown back upon herself.

She lay in bed until late. At midday she got up and put on a shift dress of red taffeta, very plain – as suited her mood. She swallowed a couple of pills and went out to meet Charlie in a wine bar in Belsize Park. She sat down at a table outside. The sky was a powder blue. The clouds over Haverstock Hill were very high and white and innocent-looking. The leaves on the trees were just coming out, each leaf like an umbrella half-erected. The wine bar made her think of France – as of course was the intention – of chestnut trees and green-painted doors and wrought-iron balconies. Le Tabac. Bar. Le Frommagerie. La Boulangerie. The dank smell of cheese. The trussed-up rolls of meat. And then Charlie arrived and over a cocktail she asked, 'So do you mean that you just bumped into her by chance?'

'That's right,' said Gina.

'But I don't understand why that should have changed his mind?' said Charlie.

Gina shrugged. As she drank down her cocktail a yearning had started up in her. She wanted to see Ella again. She wanted to look at her just one more time, to feast her eyes on the familiar

features, to feel again that flash of certainty, that this child –
without a doubt – was her daughter.

She ordered another cocktail and the yearning hardened into
something definite. She asked Charlie if she'd come with her
because of course she wanted to show off her daughter, but
Charlie looked embarrassed and unwilling – she said she'd rather
go shopping and why didn't Gina come too? – but Gina said
no, because her mind was made up, she was quite suddenly
absolutely fixed on what she wanted to do. And so she went
alone, catching a taxi to Camden Town and getting out beside
the Jazz Club at the bottom of Parkway and walking through
and reaching the gates of the school by twenty past three.

The school was of the old, Victorian board-school design, three
storeys high, of reddish brick, with a gabled roof and tall windows
divided up into smaller panes and decorated with friezes and
pictures painted by the children. There were two doors with the
old lettering still above them – 'Boys' and 'Girls' – an old, white,
enamel fountain in the playground and a high wire-mesh fence
surrounding it all. Standing there in the spring sunshine Gina
was suddenly bitter that by an accident, by a chance and nothing
else, she had been excluded from all this. And then the doors
opened and the first of the children came out, and among them
Ella, dressed in a mauve sweatshirt and shorts and showing such
a bony couple of legs they looked like a pair of broomsticks while
her sneakers were so large against her skinny ankles that they
resembled a couple of boats. She was half-carrying, half-hauling
her bag and she looked – if this was possible – even more tired
than before, because she was tripping herself up with her bag
as she walked.

She came across the playground in Gina's direction. Gina
looked around. There was no sign of the childminder. Ella
came closer. Gina stepped forward. Ella saw her and hesitated, blushing and smiling faintly in recognition. Gina held
out her hand and with this movement – which was like a
cat scooping a goldfish from out of a bowl – she fished Ella
ever so smoothly and simply from out of the pool of children.

'Here,' she said, as she took Ella's bag, 'you'll trip over it.'
The childminder came pushing through the crowd. 'Ella,' she

said in tones of anxious alarm. Before Gina could think the words slid out of her mouth:

'Hello,' she said, 'I'm collecting Ella today. I'm Madeleine's sister.' Now why did I say that? thought Gina.

The childminder looked doubtful. Her eyes were going from Gina to Ella and back to Gina again. Now all of Gina's will was bent upon erasing this uncertainty. She smiled more widely. She willed the childminder to be defeated by her, Gina's beauty and graciousness and money.

'Have you got your reading book?' she asked Ella, as she'd heard a dozen other parents ask today already. 'We're going down to college to collect Mummy.'

Still the childminder looked uncertain. 'She didn't say . . .' she began.

'Didn't she?' asked Gina. 'Oh dear. Would you like to give her a ring? I'm over in London and I said I'd pick up Ella and take her down to college and we'd go out for an early meal but nothing too late because Ella's been looking tired. She does look pale, doesn't she?'

'She gets tired,' said the childminder, falling into a comfortable, maternal role.

'She needs a holiday,' said Gina fondly.

'That's what I said,' said the childminder, but she was still looking worried.

Gina smiled at Ella and then Ella did it. She must have felt she knew Gina because of the times she'd seen her. She put her hand into Gina's and smiled. This is the best moment of my life, thought Gina.

'Well then,' said the childminder, satisfied at last.

'Say goodbye,' said Gina to Ella. (It's easy, this maternal talk, she thought.) 'Say, see you tomorrow,' and with a smile and a wave from Gina they walked away.

Gina was walking on air. She was remembering every scene she'd ever watched from film and television of mothers and daughters together. She had slowed her pace right down to Ella's. She was feeling with her hand each of the four, long, skinny fingers, one of them with a scab on it. She was looking down at the top of the head, thinking this is the view you mostly have of your children, how well you'd get to know the top of this head. She was watching herself proudly and thinking, a mother at last. And then they walked onto the Chalk Farm Road and here Gina hesitated because time, which had shrunk right down to the present moment, was now opening up again before them – *what now*? – but at that moment a black taxi cab came sailing slowly in their direction so out went Gina's arm and the taxi came to a halt. 'St John's Wood,' she said and bundled Ella in, and thus the deed was done.

As they came up the Adelaide Road something terrible happened. Ella, who all this while had kept her eyes cast down, now lifted them up and Gina saw panic in the child's face at her unfamiliar companion. Ella began to scream. Gina had never seen anything like it. All Ella's body – the eyes, the mouth, the arms, the legs, the torso – all was swept up in it. The body went as tense as steel. The arms and legs flew in every direction. The mouth turned huge and square. Wet tears began to drip from the eyes and snot from out of her nose. A howl began which she couldn't stop and a strand of hair got stuck in it. In one minute the child had become so ugly that Gina could hardly believe it. The howl was bouncing round the inside of the taxi cab. It was hurting Gina's ears and head. She gaped in pain and disbelief. She started to shout in protest. She wasn't stricken by the tears as Madeleine would have been. Instead, although she was upset, she was also cool, astonished and even a little embarrassed.

The taxi driver was shouting above the din. 'Is she all right?' he was shouting.

'She just doesn't like school,' Gina shouted back and then she looked out of the window and saw – thank God! – that they were in Acacia Road so she tapped on the glass and the taxi stopped and out she tipped herself and Ella, onto the pavement. The sudden change of scene silenced the child. She stood there, drenched, knock-kneed and exhausted. It was a street of bijou modern houses, very sunlit and prosperous and silent.

'Come on,' said Gina briskly – Christ! she thought, that tone of voice, just like my mother – and not daring to meet Ella's eyes for fear of starting her off again she marched her in the direction of the flat.

She led her up the stairs into her Neff kitchen, that grand, childless-woman's creation, in which surroundings Ella looked even more ragged and dishevelled. Inspiration came to Gina – what a mother does in these circumstances. She felt like an actress working her way into the role as she asked, 'Would you like something to eat?' and she found Ella a Diet Pepsi and half a box of Harrods' chocolate truffles. She also swallowed two more of Charlie's pills – just a little pick-me-up number, Charlie had described them ('Listen, darling, you get them from the health-food shop, they're called Heaven and they're not even illegal') – because all that crying had given her a headache. Ella was in a trance. She allowed herself to be lifted up bodily and placed at the table. Gina had been wanting to do this for months – but how thin she was! – Gina could get her arms around her and hardly know that she was there. Gradually Ella allowed Gina to push the chocolates into her mouth. As she swallowed them down the sweetness began to revive her. She said, 'I want my mother.'

'Soon,' Gina reassured her, 'soon.'

Time was opening out again – what now? thought Gina – and then another inspiration came to her, because the pills were making her feel better, they were clearing her head no end, and she said, 'Come into the bedroom and let me show you my clothes.'

Ella sat on the edge of the double bed, which was the size of a field and covered with a sprigged and flowered counterpane. She was watching with huge eyes as Gina opened the wardrobe and with a flourish began to draw out her amazing clothes, raising one knee and laying the clothes out against her. 'You see,' said Gina again and again, 'isn't this lovely? And this? And this?' She wanted Ella's approval. She wanted them to be a mother and daughter together. A warmth was beginning to flow through Gina, and not only warmth but pity, for the milk-faced child who sat on the edge of the bed and watched. More inspiration came to her. In the back of her wardrobe was a bag of children's clothes left over from the days when she'd tried her hand at charity work. Out came the bag now and the clothes were tipped across the bed. 'Look,' said Gina, 'look at this and this.' Blouses frilled at the neck, a suede jacket with a fur-lined hood, a child's sunglasses, a blue silk dress with a white sailor's collar, flounced skirts, a quilted dress in pinks and reds, Victorian-style boots laced up past the ankles and a long, navy coat to match, with a full skirt and a huge hood.

Ella reached out a hand to touch the mother-of-pearl buttons down the front of a pink cardigan. 'Would you like to try it on?' asked Gina, growing bolder, and she drew the sweatshirt, the T-shirt and shorts from the unprotesting child, checking the labels as she did so – *John Lewis, Oh, for God's sake* – and in their place slid onto the bony, straight-up-and-down body the sailor's dress and the cardigan. 'There,' said Gina, 'you look lovely,' and emboldened further she took a hairbrush from the dressing table and began brushing Ella's tangled hair. It was soporific work. When the hair was as smooth and as shiny as she could make it she took a hairband and wound and twisted Ella's hair up and through it. Now you could see the child's neck and ears. 'There,' said Gina contentedly.

And yet not altogether so, because with each movement of her hand she had been catching sight of the jewelled face of her watch – a quarter past five, it said – and was thinking that very soon George might come through the door. She didn't want to see him. Since their quarrel the day before she'd gone off him absolutely. And besides he would be bound to pick a quarrel in front of Ella, not even thinking of the poor child's feelings. She looked up and saw the two of them – mother and daughter – in the mirror.

How pale they looked. 'We're as pale as each other,' said Gina out loud, 'what we need is the sun' – and then it came to her, such a sharp, strong longing that it couldn't be resisted; a plan, all laid out and settled in an instant; a picture of the two of them, driving south between the rows of poplars, their strong, white, sinewy trunks, the dazzling light upon them, the miles of French roads running into the sun whilst Ella – and this was the bit that pleased Gina in particular – grew brown and pink and golden as health and happiness returned.

48

She rang the ferry company. The next boat left from Dover for Boulogne at half past eight. She stood beside the telephone making calculations. At this time of day the journey by car from London to Dover would take at least two hours, so she didn't have much time. She ran around the flat gathering make-up, shampoo, a hair dryer, even an adaptor for the French sockets. She took armfuls of silk shirts and trousers, high-heeled shoes, fancy lingerie and satin jackets and shoved them into a holdall. She scooped up all the posh, second-hand children's clothes from the bed and put them in the holdall also. She remembered deodorant and suntan lotion. She took a bottle of gin, the camera, her passport and George's passport – which didn't make much sense, she knew it, but she was in too much of a hurry to be rational – and of course all the credit cards in her bag.

Ella meanwhile sat there in a trance. Seeing her staring eyes Gina had an idea. She went to the medicine cabinet and took down a sleeping pill. She chopped it into quarters – one of which, she calculated, ought to be enough for Ella – and stirred it into a glass of orange. Ella drank it down. Gina was pleased. The child so clearly needed sleep. She even remembered to take an old jacket of her own for Ella to wear if they went up onto deck. She was proud of the way she was managing. She marvelled at how easily she took up motherhood. 'You see,' she said out loud for all the world to hear, 'I can do it too.' The last thing she grabbed as she bundled Ella out of the flat was a duvet – to keep Ella warm in the car. 'I want Mummy,' said Ella as they went down the stairs. 'Not long,' said Gina, 'not long.'

As they drove eastwards towards the M25, Ella fell asleep in the seat beside her. Gina was a good driver, fast but safe. To see her drive like that would make you think that her true nature was to be efficient and that it was only circumstances that had made her so dizzy. She drove south round the M25 and took the Dover turning. The motorway was choked with traffic and twice she had to leave it and take off down the back roads. Just short of Dover she stopped the car and transferred Ella to the back seat, covering her with the duvet from head to toe to keep her warm.

She reached the ferry terminal by five past eight. The man in the terminal looked at his watch and shook his head and sighed. Boarding was at seven thirty, he said, but Gina pleaded with him – she said her mother was waiting for her on the other side – and after a minute he relented and picked up the phone and rang the ferry. 'You're the last one on,' he said, 'how many?' 'One,' she said. 'Passport?' he asked, so she passed across her passport and her credit card and thus she got on board.

She was indeed the last car up the ramp. As soon as she had parked they hung up some orange ticker tape behind her. She got out and stretched her arms and legs. When she looked back through the open doors she saw the jetty and a scrap of brownish water and a patch of shiny evening sky over the town, and she began to feel excited. It was the prospect of abroad, of foreign-ness, of running away, of doing a bunk. And then someone shouted out, 'Can you go up to the passenger decks?' and suddenly she remembered Ella on the seat beneath the duvet.

She wouldn't stop sleeping. For such a skinny child she was appallingly heavy. She slept as stiff and as straight as a board and though Gina tried to bend her at the waist and knees to get her through the narrow gaps between the cars she wouldn't go, so in the end Gina had to carry her bolt upright like a tree trunk. Two crewmen lounged and watched her. 'Can you help me?' she begged and then one of them stepped forward and took Ella and carried her up the flights of narrow, metal ship's stairs until they reached the cabin deck.

She was pleased now that she'd thought to get a cabin. The crewman put Ella on the lower bunk. As soon as he had gone Gina got her bottle of gin from out of her handbag. Against the white sheets Ella was sleeping rosily. The ship's engines had come on. Seagulls were wheeling and mewing outside. The vista of docks and cliffs and warehouses was slowly beginning to alter as the ship moved off from its moorings. Ahead of them lay the Continent.

Sitting there and drinking gin Gina fell to dreaming happily of foreign-ness, of the Abroad, the wonderful Abroad, which had been and always would be a backdrop to all kinds of pleasures and adventures. She was thinking of trees pollarded into unfamiliar shapes; of mansard roofs and napkins folded in the foreign way and sweet, fizzy juices in bottles of a squat, un-English shape. She was thinking of the trussed-up rolls of meat – how did they do that? – in the butchers' windows; of strange-looking sweets and foreign signs and cars in town squares parked beneath the chestnut trees. She was thinking of town houses with peeling stucco and big, square windows, and suburbs and roundabouts of municipal flowers in crude and violent colours; and beyond these the roads running north and east and south, but especially south, to towns which grew ever hotter and more dusty until you came to the Mediterranean Sea.

She must have sat there for quite some minutes drinking gin and dreaming, for when she next looked out of the window she saw that they were well out to sea and she realised that she was hungry. Now came her first problem. She didn't want to leave Ella for fear that she might wake and panic in these unfamiliar surroundings. On the other hand, she didn't think she could sit here without food for the rest of the voyage. She hadn't thought of bringing food. She searched in her handbag but she couldn't even find any chocolate. In the end she left Ella, pulling the door shut and checking and re-checking that she had the key as she ran to the cafeteria and loaded food onto a tray and carried it back, tottering and wobbling, to the cabin.

She was only just in time. Ella had woken up. She was staring around her with huge and crazy eyes. When she saw Gina she started to scream. It was worse than the tears in the Adelaide Road. It was a sound as loud as a road drill which beat against the walls of the tiny cabin, hammering against the inside of Gina's head. It was as if the scream itself, as well as the child, was trying to escape. Gina made a feeble attempt to take Ella into her arms, but Ella kicked and scratched her and Gina retreated, clutching at her stomach where Ella's shoe had caught her. After that she could only put her hands across her ears in a vain attempt to protect herself from the din. She saw Ella come flying off the bunk and hit the floor. She saw her feet beat crazily against the side of the bunk. She wondered how many people were complaining to the purser and how long it would be before he came knocking at the door. She was amazed and horrified at the spectacle. But also curiously disengaged, even censorious. How could the child *stand* to make such a noise?

And then gradually it began to diminish. The feet beat less frantically. The tears, the sniffs, the crying was now audible in the gaps between the screams. She raised a drenched and snotty face and looked for a moment into Gina's eyes before she hid it again. Gina held out a croissant. Shakily she took it and began to eat. Gina held out juice, a biscuit, an apple. Her hands wouldn't work so Gina had to hold the apple up against her mouth so that she could bite it. She allowed Gina to pull her into a sitting position, to straighten down the clothes and wipe the hair from off her face. Now Gina wanted to get out of this cabin before who-knows-who came knocking at the door. She took one of her jackets and wrapped it round Ella's shoulders. 'Come on,' she said, 'we're going out on deck to see the ships.'

She had to half-carry, half-drag Ella up several narrow flights of steps. When they came to the heavy outer door she put Ella trembling on the floor whilst she set her shoulder to the door and pushed. Outside night had fallen. A full moon was floating over France and the air was so cold you could see the mountains on its flat, penny surface. The black sea was full of ships' lights, bobbing and tossing on the water, but the night sky was high and hushed and churchy. Gina, who was wearing only the red shift dress from lunch with a thin jacket on top of it, began to shiver. The cold had got into her stomach and her throat and her lungs. Ella shrank against her and Gina was touched by this sign of affection although she knew the child only did it because Gina was slightly less frightening to her than the vast and empty night. 'That's where we're going,' she said, pointing to the lights of Boulogne. 'It's darkness there right now but when the sun comes up tomorrow you'll see how warm it is and how we'll eat ice creams and croissants and grow tanned and see the sea.'

When they passed the harbour lights, flashing red and yellow, they went back down to the car. The ferry was only a quarter full and it didn't take long to unload. They waited in a small queue for passport control. It was when they were only a car or two from the front that Gina realised her mistake, for here sat Ella in the seat beside her for all the world to see and here was her passport with no child, no dependent of any kind, written into it.

She thought this was it. She thought that in two minutes flat the two of them would be sent back to England *tout de suite*. She sat forward in her seat as far as she could. Ella, thank God, was nearly asleep, slumped down and looking tiny with her chin upon her chest. And then the car rolled level with passport control and there sat an official with round, dark, truculent eyes – a high-bridged nose, an official's hat worn like an American baseball cap, a stroppy, so-what-can-you-do-for-me? stare – and straight away she knew what to do. She tilted up her chin. She showed her long and beautiful throat. She tucked one hand under her deep and pillowy hair and flipped it out. She sighed and cast her eyes up sideways towards him. He took her passport but his eyes were on her, not it.

'*Bonsoir*,' she said. He wouldn't answer. His manner said that even her *bonsoir* was impudent. But although he wouldn't smile she could see that he was pleased.

'You are going on holiday?' he asked.

'That's right,' she said, and she added, 'to see my mother.'

His style was of long, brooding silences. Really? said his silence. So, in the meantime, get your clothes off. At last he flipped her passport shut. '*Bonnes vacances*,' he said.

'*Merci*,' she answered and then the car rolled forward into the French night, and it was done.

They called the police who came twenty minutes later in a couple of cars and took statements from Madeleine and the childminder. They listened to Madeleine's story and rang George and Gina's home number but nobody was answering, so then they tried George's work number where a ponderous, know-nothing janitor said that George had left the office but no, he didn't know where he'd gone. It took them an hour to track down George to a restaurant in Great Portland Street, a further fifteen minutes for him to drive them home, and another fifteen minutes to find out that the passports and the car were missing, to ring Charlie and to piece together what Gina had done. It was nearly nine fifteen before they began ringing the ferry companies, nine thirty before her name came up at the terminal in Dover, nine forty-five before the message got through to passport control in Boulogne, and by that time Gina had been gone a full ten minutes, vanished into the vast continent which stretches from Boulogne to Vladivostock and which encompasses lakes, mountains, deserts, rivers – a hundred languages, ten thousand cities, and a hundred thousand towns and more.

49

They took her to the police station in Kentish Town, in past the reception area and the high metal grill behind which a policeman sat, and into a room with dingy walls and cracked linoleum on the floor where she sat with them whilst they made their phone calls. In fact, she could hardly sit still but perched on the edge of her chair, her eyes following their every movement, her skin crawling with anxiety for her absent child. Whilst they waited for their phones to be answered they tapped on the table with their fingers and asked her questions: So how old was the child? and where did she go to school? and who was this other woman? and what claim did she have on the child? Madeleine was absent-minded. She kept interrupting them and talking out loud to herself. She was distraught for Ella but she was also incensed that anyone could do this to her. She kept remembering more and more outrageous facts: that Gina knew nothing about children; that she had tried to use money and smart lawyers to steal a child; that George Kaufman had humoured his wife in all this; that Gina had thought that some spurious biological claim could outweigh the years of love and toil and sleepless nights. The detective in charge was tall and youngish, with hair bleached blond – (surely that can't be right, thought Madeleine) – and a bone-white look about him, his grey eyes very steady. Madeleine looked at him and for one moment her grief receded and she thought, if I were my mother or my grandmother, I might think those steady eyes represented wisdom. But this of course was the nineties, not the thirties . . . Too steady, thought Madeleine. Dead more like it.

She was there when they rang the ferry terminals. She was

there when they discovered that Gina had boarded the eight-thirty boat for Boulogne. The thought of her child vanished over that black sea beyond the reach of her hands was too terrible and she began to scream, at which they hustled her out, calling for a woman constable who put her in a police car and drove her home.

She had thought that she wanted to go home but when she got there she found the flat curiously and terribly becalmed in an earlier life: the breakfast things still on the table; Ella's books strewn across the floor: the duvet from Ella's bed wrapped into a nest in the corner of the sofa where Ella had sat this morning. She knew she had to pick up these things, that she had to tidy away this terrible evidence of their earlier life, but her hands were stiff and her feet were stuck and she couldn't get her body to move. She poured herself a gin and lit a cigarette, but nothing, it seemed, could stop this terrible worry that crawled across her skin. She began to cry but it didn't help, so then she screamed, on and on, the scream bouncing and leaping inside her head and outside round the room until at last her voice gave out and she started to cry instead. She heard knocking on the door – the neighbours presumably – but she took no notice.

At half past ten she rang the police station and they told her in weary, cautious, regretful tones that they hadn't picked up Gina in Boulogne; but – and here their voices grew manfully optimistic – they were very hopeful of picking her up soon, because Gina was making no attempt to disguise herself and because the number and the appearance of her car and herself had been distributed across Europe.

She didn't want them to ring off. She told them that unless she was absolutely sure that they would ring her the moment they heard anything she would feel obliged to ring them every ten minutes. She heard alarm in their voices, the universal male alarm at an hysterical woman. They told her not to ring them, that she must keep calm and let them sort it out, and then they rang off – although she begged them not to – and left her to her terrible fears. Her anxiety for Ella was diffused across the room. In an attempt to focus it she picked up a knife from the table and began to saw at her little finger. She screamed with pain and rage. She put her finger into her mouth and sucked and sucked and sucked it like a baby.

She began to pace the room. She decided she wouldn't go to bed. She decided she would never sleep again until she had found Ella. Up and down the room she paced until it grew cramped and confined so then her feet carried her to the door and down the stairs, past the minicab office – the open door, the fug of smoke, the plastic beakers and ringing phones and coffee spilt – and then out into the street, coatless, childless and distraught.

The moon was up. She stood on the corner of Delancey Street and saw it tucked down beside the tower blocks at the bottom of Arlington Road. It was, although she didn't know it, the same moon that Ella had seen from the deck of the ferry. Standing there she became convinced that if she went round to Mornington Terrace she would find Ella sitting on Norma's doorstep waiting to be let in. Vividly, she saw Ella's soft flesh and the wasteland of brick and concrete all around it and the stony light of the moon pouring down on top of it. She set off at a run towards Mornington Terrace. She turned the corner and saw the façade of houses, crooked and tumble-down, in the moonlight. She saw a single tree in leaf outside Norma's doorstep, a street lamp at its centre, burning from the inside outwards, like a pumpkin lantern. She stared and stared but she couldn't see Ella anywhere. In despair she went on, round into Arlington Road. She passed a building site and a high wire fence behind which there lurked the shadow of a dog. She saw two men on the far pavement, shoulders hunched in shared conspiracy, and her habitual sense of the danger of these streets began to soothe her. She crossed over Parkway and started down Regents Park Road in the direction of Primrose Hill and as she did so she began to think more calmly and to realise what she had to do – which was of course to go home and get some sleep because tomorrow she would have to go to France and get Ella back herself.

She packed a bag – money, passport, change of clothes. She got out an atlas and stared at it, trying to work out what would be in Gina's mind. South, she thought. South into the sun. A woman like her loves heat. She lay down on the bed because although she didn't expect to sleep she needed rest. And yet after a few minutes she did sleep and slept indeed for six hours, waking the next morning to a terrible knowledge that bloomed and blossomed all over again, that Ella had gone.

First she was astonished, then she was terribly angry. It was her anger that made her think of it, that before she left for France she would ring George Kaufman and tell him exactly what he had to do because he was otherwise too stupid to understand it. At a quarter to eight she rang his home phone number. There was no answer. She was amazed. She couldn't believe that in the circumstances he could simply have gone to work as normal. She rang his work phone number and got the know-nothing janitor. She shouted at him a bit and then there was silence and then on to the phone came the cautious voice of George Kaufman. 'Listen,' she said, 'you go out to France and find your wife and my daughter now, because otherwise I'm coming round with a knife to kill you.'

50

They spent the night in Dieppe in a hotel overlooking the harbour. Gina took a room with a television and a balcony because she thought they might amuse Ella. Downstairs in reception there was a fish tank with a couple of crabs and an eel inside it, fighting in slow motion as if through treacle, and these too were noted as things to amuse Ella. Right now though she was asleep. She had to be carried up the stairs. *'La petite,'* said Madame La Patronne, brisk and sentimental, as she climbed the stairs ahead of them in her stout, sensible shoes. It was half past eleven and Gina was tired. Her back ached from carrying Ella and she was fretting over her crumpled, soiled clothes. But even so she stood at the window, curtains half drawn back, looking down at the town – at the lights out on the water, at the traffic and the street signs. Their room was just above the sign which said 'Hotel'. It flashed in a sequence of colours, bathing Gina's bare toes in her strappy high-heeled sandals, first in pink then green then blue. Like a scene from a film, thought Gina happily and she took off her clothes and lay down beside Ella, reaching out one hand timorously to touch her before she fell asleep.

When she woke the next morning Ella was awake already, sitting up in bed and watching her. She was still in yesterday's clothes. Oh God, I forgot to undress her, Gina thought. The eyes, staring at her so unwaveringly, were embarrassing. 'Hello,' said Gina, 'we're on holiday. Shall we buy you some pyjamas? Have you seen out of the window? Look,' and she went across and drew the curtains. There were nets on the other side of them. The room was suddenly filled with a subdued dazzle of sunlight. Ella didn't move. She didn't speak. 'Perhaps you should put on some new clothes,' said Gina, and she rummaged around in the holdall and pulled out a flounced skirt and a sweater appliquéd in suede and leather. Still Ella didn't move, although she allowed Gina to lift her bodily off the bed and onto the floor and permitted her to draw off her existing garments and to put the new ones on. 'There,' said Gina, 'how delightful,' but she didn't mean it. The sweater was an orange colour. It made Ella's skin look sallow.

There were maroony-coloured stains on the thin skin underneath her eyeballs and if you weren't used to children her pole-like body looked extraordinary. Gina took out a hairbrush and began to brush Ella's hair. Finally she took each foot and pushed it into its shoe. 'There,' she kept saying, keeping up her encouraging commentary, but inside she didn't feel encouraging at all, she felt brisk and impatient. That orange sweater, she thought, she can't wear it a minute longer, she looks dreadful – and then, for a second time in twenty-four hours, she thought, Oh Christ, just like my mother.

She didn't dare linger over her usual routine of bath and make-up. She thought that unless they were quick Ella might start to cry. 'Breakfast,' said Gina with false gaiety and she pulled on the first clothes that came to hand, and led Ella downstairs. She felt stale and crumpled. She wasn't used to the feeling but then she saw the breakfast things, the coffee cups, the pats of butter and soon a plate of croissants and a jug of coffee – all the pleasures she had grown used to in her childless life – and she began to feel better. 'And how is the little one this morning?' asked Madame La Patronne, looming over them. 'Fine, fine,' said Gina, pushing scraps of croissant into Ella's mouth. '*Quels beaux yeux*,' said Madame La Patronne, looking at Ella – an older woman's admiration for a young woman's beauty. 'Aren't they!' said Gina proudly.

They left Dieppe by eight o'clock – a full three hours earlier than Gina was accustomed to leaving home. They took the road which runs south along the clifftops. These were green and wooded and large parts of them were given over to the gardens of suburban-looking mansions which could be glimpsed behind high walls and wrought-iron gates. Flowering azaleas and rhododendrons lined the drives. The gardens were speckled and rumpled with blossom. Every ten miles or so the road dipped down to seaside towns with cafés and boulangeries along the seafront, and telegraph poles and pollarded trees and restaurants with plate-glass windows and little strips of yellow sand upon which a few children and some dogs were playing.

South of Fécamp they left the coast and went inland. The landscape grew even lusher. Banks of woods and deep green meadows lined the road. Wooden farmhouses stood roof-deep in grass and flowering orchards. Ella sat in the passenger seat. She was completely silent. Gina tried to make conversation. 'Oh look,' she kept saying, 'a cow. Oh look, a church spire,' and later on – as her attempts at motherliness grew thin – 'Christ, we're nearly out of petrol,' and 'Where's that bloody map?' Still Ella said nothing. Gina realised that she'd scarcely said a word since half past three the day before, that her hysterical tears of yesterday had given way to a trancelike remoteness.

When they were nearly at Le Havre she stopped the car and struggled with the map. Up until now she'd been following a familiar route but now she saw that since she'd last been here they had built a bridge across the Seine just east of Le Havre. She started the car again. She struggled with road signs, the names of towns, the points of the compass, which way round the roundabouts you should go, until she found herself on the road to the bridge.

It was a huge structure, arching up as steeply into the sky as the back of a bow which has been bent almost to breaking-point. 'Look,' cried Gina involuntarily and Ella turned her head a little. 'That's where we're going,' said Gina and once she'd paid the toll she put her foot down on the accelerator, pointing the car's nose upwards and making it climb faster and faster into the warm, blue sky. The steel cables flashed past. The air opened out beneath them. The aeroplanes grew bigger. The light from the sea leapt in a white radiance to meet their eyes. Even Ella felt the drama of it, wriggling forward in her seat and lifting her chin above the level of the window. She was looking less tense and strained. If only she'd smile, thought Gina. They came down on the far side and now Gina saw signs for Trouville and Deauville, towns which she remembered from her past, and an idea came to her and she said, 'Let's buy buckets and spades and go and play in the sand.'

They skirted round Honfleur and took the road along the coast, through Trouville and Deauville, past long, yellow beaches and wooden promenades and expensive restaurants and bijou women's clothes shops. Trees blew in the chalky-white sea wind and high-stacked apartment blocks, built at the turn of the century, turned seawards their elegant façades. The season didn't begin until June. The windows were shuttered, the beaches almost empty.

Gina had come this way more times than she could remember – when she was very small, with both parents, on their way south; on numerous occasions when she was adolescent in the running-away days; once or twice on mother-daughter jaunts when she was twenty, the two of them going shopping, buying shoes and dresses, comradely, as beautiful, idle mothers are sometimes comradely with beautiful, idle daughters.

The past came back to her in showers of sensual fragments – the hem of a cotton jacket, sun-warmed, blowing against her face as she walked along the promenade; the dress she had bought with her mother, sewn with jet-black beads, long and hollow like little pipes; the sand in the cracks in between the wooden planking of the promenade; the sense of being herself at twenty – two arms (a little heavy round the top), two legs (very nice), good breasts, a pretty head, a great many men at her feet. 'Look,' Gina kept saying to Ella, 'Look, we'll go and play there soon,' and it seemed to her that Ella, who hitherto had been as still as a statue, gave a little twitch of pleasure.

She parked the car in the square beside the church at Villers. They went straight to the bucket and spade shop and bought red and blue spades, a purple rake, an orange sieve, flags and moulds of a pink elephant, a blue horse and a purple mermaid. Now Gina thought she saw the faintest smile on Ella's face. On the far side of the road were a dozen café tables in a concrete piazza. 'Let's have an ice cream,' she said, and she ordered a coffee for herself and an ice cream for Ella. The ice cream was enormous. It was so big it stung Ella into speech. She turned it round and round. She held up her spoon against it. 'It's bigger than my spoon,' she said, and her voice sounded piping and unfamiliar.

'If it gets any bigger it will go up your nose,' said Gina, and Ella gave the faintest giggle.

There was a clothes shop on the far side of the piazza. After the beach we'll go shopping, thought Gina, and I'll buy her some dresses, a hat or two and make her look pastoral.

Down by the seashore the tide was out and the beach was at its hugest. Ella sat down on the bottom step and took off her sneakers. They were the same ones she wore back home in Camden Town. She looked out at the yellow emptiness of the beach and hesitated.

'Let's go over there,' said Gina and when Ella was settled she tipped out the bag of beach equipment. Ella made herself at home. It was as if to play on a beach were bred in her bones. Even this small amount of sun had turned her skin from sallow to brown. The wind blew a strand of hair across her face. 'Don't move,' said Gina and she reached into her bag for her polaroid. 'Is that me?' asked Ella in amazement when she saw the photograph. She had come out looking like the heroine of a shampoo ad. and for one moment Gina's cravings for beauty were appeased.

Gina thought how peculiar it was to sit here with the next generation come into being, so that she was no longer the first but the middle generation. It made her think of her mother, made her want to see her mother again, made her think how happy her mother would be to see her granddaughter, although even as she thought this another part of her knew that this was nonsense because her mother wasn't the maternal type and had never before been pleased at the sight of a child. But even so she couldn't help thinking, why don't I ring her? Why don't I tell her that there's a surprise in store for her? Why don't I tell her that we're coming to Puissonier? There was a phone box up on the promenade. Gina could see it from where she sat. Ella was filling up the moulds, expertly slapping them out onto a smooth expanse of sand. 'I'm just going to make a phone call,' said Gina, 'I won't be a minute.' Ella didn't look up but Gina could see that she had heard her. 'All right?' Gina insisted and Ella shifted her head in what might have been a nod.

Gina stood up. She walked awkwardly across the sand. When she got to the steps she looked back and saw that Ella hadn't moved, that she was still slapping out sandcastles in a circle around her. Up the steps went Gina and across to the telephone kiosk. She searched in her bag for the right change. She tapped out the number but her fingers were clumsy and she tapped the wrong digit. She tapped it again and this time the phone rang, and rang, and rang, whilst Gina held on and pictured the house in Puissonier, the walnut tree and the *balancier* and her mother's mules in the grass and the stone wall where the scorpions lived. She must have stood there for a minute or two with the receiver warm against her ear. She began thinking of the clothes that Ella needed – pale colours, ice cream colours, raspberry and pistachio, but not navy, not orange, not black. She put the phone down. Later, she thought, later, and she stepped back across the promenade to the top of the steps. The wind blew in her face. The sky was blue and the beach was empty. She took a step down. *The beach was empty.* She stared. She thought she must have got the wrong steps. She ran to the bottom and out past the beach huts to where you could see for half a mile in each direction. There were dogs, a man and a woman holding hands, a couple of children. She saw a pile of beach equipment – the purple rake, the orange sieve, Ella's castles, Ella's shoes. She was disbelieving, too disbelieving yet to panic. She began to examine the beach more carefully, mentally dividing it up and examining each portion. She even whirled round to see if Ella was straight behind her, and all the while the wind came blowing and tossing out of the blueness, fluttering the flags and Gina's shirt and a kite along the beach, giving Gina the curious idea that it was the wind that had kidnapped Ella.

51

She had meant to leave by nine o'clock that morning but when it came to it she couldn't tear herself away from the phone for fear of not getting news of Ella. She kept looking at the telephone. She kept waiting for it to ring. Every time she moved away she drifted back towards it. It was the focus of her anxieties. Just to look at it made her heart jump and her stomach lurch. Her fingers itched to pick it up and its ring – which wasn't a ring but a silence – kept echoing inside her head. To and fro she went from the phone to the window, where she stared up and down the street begging for a sight of Ella. Time passed terribly slowly, each minute served up and stretched out to its limit before another one was put down in its place.

At nine o'clock she rang the police who told her that the crew of the ferry had been interviewed, and that Ella and Gina had been seen together – going from the car to the cabin, and then up onto deck – and that Ella seemed unharmed. For one moment Madeleine was hugely relieved, but then relief gave way to anxiety because the news was already out-of-date, because no one had seen Ella since nine o'clock the night before, and that was twelve hours ago. Those twelve hours seemed like a black well into which Ella had fallen. Every bit of Madeleine itched and twitched with worry for her child. She knew that she ought to go to work, ought to sit down and mark some essays, ought at least to walk to the newsagent's and buy the newspapers, but she couldn't, she couldn't do anything, and though she knew that time would never move on again until she stopped thinking about Ella, still she was helpless in the face of her anxieties, pinned and trapped upon the point of Time.

She rang the police again. She asked them what they were doing and they told her that they had circulated Gina's description throughout France, that they were getting in touch with every hotel within a hundred miles of Boulogne, that Gina Kaufman's husband George was confident that she was heading south to her mother's house on the Mediterranean. 'But have you remembered what Ella was wearing? Have you included that in the description?' Madeleine asked, and then she thought, George Kaufman, that bastard George Kaufman.

At half past eleven there came a knock on the door. She ran down the stairs. She flung it open and there stood the bastard, dressed in a fresh white shirt and a suit, and carrying his briefcase. He stepped inside. He closed the door behind him. 'I'm sorry,' he said, smiling with embarrassment, and that did it. Up shot her hand to get the blow in quick, but he must have been expecting it, because although she was quick, he was quicker. He caught her wrist, and then her other wrist. They began to sway and struggle. She was shouting. He was shouting. She was crying and trying to bite his hand. He pushed her backwards up the stairs. 'Just shut up,' he was shouting, but even through her distress she could see that this was how he was used to women – anguished, weeping and hysterical.

When they came to the top of the stairs she tripped and fell backwards. She felt empty space behind her and then she crashed to the floor. He fell on top of her and winded her so that for several minutes she couldn't do anything and then – instead of shouting – she started to cry. She felt something hard pressed up against her and the last scrap of her which was rational thought: of course – tears and erections – like sex and funerals – they go together.

When Gina found that Ella had gone she stood there helplessly for a couple of minutes and then she noticed two *gendarmes* walking along the beach. She ran across to them and showed them the photograph of Ella. She spoke in a rapid, anxious voice, her eyes shooting all over the beach: 'This is her but I can't find her anywhere. But she was here only a minute ago so she can't have gone far, I swear it.' The *gendarmes* had blue eyes and baby faces. Even in her distress she noticed that they were men and smiled at them. But they were staring at the photograph and then speaking to each other in French. 'She is your child?' asked one of them. His English was halting and uncertain. 'What is her name?' the other enquired. 'Ella Kingdom,' said Gina impatiently, and then she realised that their half dozen words were probably the only English that they knew. 'This is no good,' said Gina out loud – she couldn't waste time with these two – and she snatched back the photograph and began to hurry away along the beach, calling out 'Ella, Ella,' in a distraught voice.

But the two *gendarmes* came after her and one of them took her courteously but firmly by the arm and when she swung round to remonstrate with him the other whisked the photograph out of her fingers and then took out a radio and began talking into it. '*Anglaise*,' Gina heard, and 'Ella Kingdom,' and at that the astonishing idea occurred to her that she had misunderstood the situation, that they had been looking for her as well as she looking for them and that having found her they did not intend to let her go.

They led her away across the beach. She struggled in her spikey sandals across the shifting sands. Her head was full of unpleasant thoughts which slowed her progress even further: the realisation that news must have come from England – that people would misunderstand – that George would be angry with her. She wasn't used to so many uncomfortable ideas. She wanted to raise a hand to rub her forehead but the *gendarmes* had her by the arms so she kept tossing back her head instead.

They put her in the back of the car and climbed into the front. When they started the engine she panicked at the thought of Ella lost somewhere out there on the beach and now being abandoned by anyone who knew her. She began to scream. She tried to clamber out but the doors were locked. The policemen no longer looked so baby-faced. A confident self-righteousness had settled on their faces – as if they now knew how badly she had behaved – and this was making them look older and more remote. They took no notice of her screams but drove her away across the town, leaving the sea behind. She felt as she used to feel when she was a teenager and dreamt of running naked through Victoria Station – horrified at the situation which she had got into, powerless to get out of it and so hoping to wake up and find that none of it was true.

The police rang Madeleine at half past twelve, London time. She was lying on the floor after sex, too exhausted and deranged to move. George had fetched her a drink and now he was standing over her, saying, 'Puissonier, we must go to Puissonier.'

'What?' she said.

'Puissonier,' he said again, 'she'll have gone to Puissonier. It's her mother's house. If we catch the ferry today we could drive all night and get there by tomorrow morning.'

Tomorrow morning, she thought. To see Ella again by tomorrow morning! She wished now that she'd never suggested that they went together. She'd rather go alone because Ella was her child and nothing to do with anyone else. But on the other hand he knew the way and she would need him as her guide.

And then the phone rang. Slowly and tiredly she sat up. George passed the phone across to her. 'Yes?' she said. It was the bleached-blond inspector with the grey eyes. He said that he had news, that Gina had been picked up by the police in a town called Villers, but Ella – unfortunately – had been lost somewhere in the town. Long before her mind understood the words she heard herself say, 'Lost, oh God, she's lost.' It was as if the words were wandering around inside her head looking for a foothold. 'Lost,' she said again, winding the telephone cord round her fingers, and still the words couldn't seem to find a perch inside her.

'What is it?' asked George.

'Your wife,' said Madeleine, 'your wife has lost my daughter.'

He didn't understand. 'Puissonier,' he said, 'we need to go to Puissonier.'

'You don't understand,' shouted Madeleine, dropping the receiver, 'your wife has – lost' – she was talking very slowly now – 'my – daughter – somewhere – in – France. Gina has been picked up by the police but Ella is lost.'

She noticed with satisfaction that now at last he looked duly awestruck by what his wife had done. 'Oh Christ,' he said, 'that silly cow. Is she still out there? I'll have to go out and talk to her myself. If they're trying to talk French to her they won't get anywhere.'

52

The woman who had stolen her got up and walked away and left her alone on this field of sand. The sun was a yellow eye which squinted at her over the sea. She didn't like it. It made a lump in her throat and gave her a headache. When she narrowed her eyes to shut it out her eyelashes made black picket gates which covered each eye. The sun was a long way away. She knew she would have to walk a whole day to reach it. The woman who had stolen her didn't come back. She buried her feet and her toes came up like pink sweets through the grains of yellow sand. She made two more sandcastles then took a length of her hair and chomped it. She had been growing her hair. It was nearly the longest hair in the class. Her hair slid between her teeth. It tasted dry and salty. A man walked towards her. He was very tall, like a tree. He wore white, cotton jeans and the shadows in the creases of these jeans were very black. She noticed that each time he put down a foot, it buried itself nose-down in the sand. He smiled at her and stuck out his tongue. It was the shape and the colour of a raspberry ice-lolly. He walked past her and on along the beach whilst she stared after him. She thought that he was like one of the men downstairs in the house back home. She liked those men. She stood up and knocked over one of her sandcastles. It fell in a soft heap and she walked right through it and on, after the man. She was hoping of course that he would take her to her mother.

He didn't notice her. He climbed a flight of concrete steps and Ella followed stealthily behind him. Fifty yards along the beach was another flight of steps and down these Gina was descending as Ella climbed up hers. Ella reached the promenade. The sun had heated up the wood and it was pleasant underfoot. The man in the white trousers walked down the promenade, then turned left across a car park and into a café. She hesitated. She didn't like to cross the car park. The cars were as big as boats. She wasn't meant to go near cars. A black cat walked past and she tried to grab his tail and let him pull her but he whisked himself away and jumped up on a car. She drifted slowly and nervously for twenty yards until the sound of a car behind her made her jump and she ran towards a wall. She thought she was lost. She began to back along beside the wall until she turned and found that she'd reached the café anyway. The café walls were made of glass. She could see inside to chair legs and the underneath of tables. But she couldn't find the door. The glass went on forever. Now she was at the entrance to an alleyway which ran up beside the café. The black cat sat and looked at her. 'Puss, puss,' she said and she ran after him and in one minute found herself at the far end of the alleyway in a narrow street.

Opposite her was a terrace of grey stone cottages. She saw a jam of cars and a chequer of cold shadows and bright sunlight. The cold shadows were pleasant. She skipped through them for a while until she turned a corner and saw the piazza where she had eaten an ice cream with the strange woman. She saw an ice cream on an empty table and sidling up she reached out to touch it. A voice shouted, 'Hey'. She jerked her hand away. She knocked the ice cream over and ran off, but not before she had got her knuckles covered with ice cream which she licked off as she ran.

She passed the bucket and spade shop and came to the church. This reminded her of the strange woman who had stolen her. She went round the church and looked down another street and saw a fragment of bright sea at the end of it. Its blueness seemed like home. She was lonely. She thought hungrily of the strange woman with the hair and she set off running down the road and the sea grew bigger and bigger.

She ran across a road and came back onto the promenade. If she'd gone on down to the beach she would have found Gina weeping and distraught, trying to make herself understood to a couple of *gendarmes*. But as she crossed the promenade she saw, to her right, a man beside a barrow selling pancakes. The smell of the pancakes drew her, and so did the man. She came up close and saw a narrow face and two enormous eyes, crammed together lopsidedly. Behind him was a backdrop of blue sky and sea. On the side of his barrow was a picture of a laughing girl, all teeth and hair, and a sizzling pancake. Ella fixed the man with her eyes, sewing them on as tight as she could in a way that always upset the adults. At first he smiled, then he grew anxious. '*Allez*,' he said, '*allez*,' but she didn't. She just stood there until he rolled up a pancake and shoved it in her direction. She ate it ravenously. He was packing up his barrow. He kept giving her irritable glances. He stamped his foot in her direction as if to frighten away a flock of birds and she sidled back down the promenade, then stood and watched him.

He set off walking and she followed him. They were walking into the sun, the man first, then the trundling barrow, then Ella. The sun was enormous. Its rays poured down in a golden tower. Twice the man stopped and turned and shouted at her. Twice she stopped and stared and when he started walking again, doggedly walked after him.

They came to the end of the promenade. Here the grand blocks of flats and fancy shops had dwindled away and instead there was a concrete wasteland and some municipal dustbins. They turned off across this wasteland. She felt that he was no longer trying to get rid of her, that though he didn't like her being there he had accepted her. She trotted up until she was level with him. He smelt of sweat and sugar pancakes. The lady on the side of the barrow smiled as she followed after them. Inside the barrow the pots and pans were crashing and jumbling together.

They came to a street of bungalows, concrete yards, wilting trees and chicken-wire fences. He turned in at a gate. He made one last attempt to slam it on her nose but she slipped in too quickly for him, and at that he shrugged and let loose a stream of words, incomprehensible and yet at the same time expressive of all his frustration, his disbelief, his outrage at this ghost of a silent child who had got her claws into him and wouldn't let go. She stood there under the waterfall of his words until gradually her eyes cleared and she registered where she was: in a concrete yard with a trellis overhead entwined with an ancient grape, a peeling door, a barred and shuttered window, a rusting table and chairs at which there sat a collection of heads – eyes, locks of hair (a great amount of these), or none at all, teeth, lips, dark glasses – and underneath the table a forest of legs and naked feet, entangled together.

The heads stared at her. The man who had brought her here started to talk again. He was voluble and outraged. The heads began to laugh, first at him and then at her. Their laughter was like sharp glass. She shrank back. But where was she to go? One head rose up and turned into a tall and skinny woman with a long face and long hair plaited into dozens of locks. She stretched out a hand over the table and gave Ella a lump of bread. She was neither kind nor unkind. Ella squatted down and began to eat.

The heads began to talk again. It was clear that they were talking about her. After a while Ella realised that they were frightened of her, which struck Ella as peculiar, because of all the frightening things about this situation, surely she herself was the least so? Eventually another head rose up and came round the table, turning into a plump woman who took Ella's hand and led her round the side of the house and in through a door into a room with a heavily shuttered window which let in only a drain of brownish light. By this light she could make out a table, a scrap of ancient flowery carpet on the floor, a stove, a sink with a flowery curtain underneath it and shelves above with storage jars arranged along them.

The woman began to prepare a meal. She bent down to find saucepans. She reached up for storage jars. Ella sat on the floor and watched her. The woman bent and reached and bent and reached until Ella fell asleep. When she woke up she was lying on a heap of coats and blankets in a narrow corridor beside the open door to the kitchen. From where she lay she could see the heads sitting round the table, talking animatedly, hands reaching across the table in pursuit of lumps of bread and glasses of wine, long, knotty legs communing under the table.

And then it happened. There came a banging on the side door, more banging from the front of the house. The heads at the table fell instantly quiet and looked at each other. Someone tapped a spoon on the table. Someone else half rose with an uncertain movement, scraping back their chair. And then, with a deafening crash, the door burst open, and hard upon the

heels of this flying, crashing movement there came an uproar
of bodies moving forwards, voices shouting, asserting, protesting
– a head at the table screaming in a woman's voice – and two
middle-aged men stepping forward. They were stealthy and quiet
as gentlemen. They were obviously in charge.

No one saw Ella. She got to her feet and crept along the wall.
By the way that the eyes of the newcomers skated over her, fixed
on higher things, not seeing her, Ella knew that it was not her
that they were looking for. A policeman stood guarding the door,
his face lifted up, watching the scrimmage in the kitchen and the
corridor, hands clenched with nervous fear not far from Ella's
head. She slipped past him. She saw the blue evening sky, very
dense and pure, the grapevine curling against it, the moon like a
potato print entangled in its leaves. She turned to run down the
passage way beside the house. She glimpsed police cars out in
the street, splashing their yellow lights through the blue air. A
young policeman came down the passageway towards her. His
head was bare. His hair was blond where the brightness from
the sky had settled on it. When his eyes lit on her he first looked
startled and then he reached out and grabbed her. He marched
her into the concrete yard at the front of the house, showing off
his catch to the others. When they brought the heads out one
by one Ella could see that they were being asked to whom this
child belonged, and – by their shrugs and their looks of innocence
and indignation – that they were denying all knowledge of who
she was.

They drove her to the police station. They took her down a
long corridor, past the room where Gina had been sitting since
twelve o'clock midday. All afternoon she had cried and tried
to explain herself and asked to ring George and begged to be
released so that she could go and look for Ella. But even the
policemen who spoke English didn't seem to understand so that
now she was sitting quiet and longing for George to come and
rescue her.

Ella meanwhile was taken into another room where a police-
woman asked her in English what her name was. But Ella had
heard so much French in the last twenty-four hours that she
could no longer distinguish French from English, and so she
sat mute until they gave her a pen and paper whereupon

she wrote, in large, uncertain handwriting: Ella Kingdom, 53 Delancey Street, London. I want to go home.

The news came through to Madeleine on George's mobile phone as they were on their way to Dover. It was half past seven and they were hoping to catch the same ferry that Gina and Ella had caught twenty-four hours before. They had stopped in a lay-by and were arguing over the quickest route. 'Listen,' said Madeleine, 'why don't you map-read and I'll drive?' but George couldn't do that. The car was his beloved machine and he never allowed women to drive it. He looked at her – helpless, resentful, admiring as usual – and then his phone rang. He passed it across to her. 'Are you sure?' Madeleine asked, 'are you sure?' and impatiently they said, 'Of course we're sure. She's given her name and address and she's asking for you,' at which Madeleine felt a sudden, giddy shifting of the cosmos as she ceased to be the mother of a possibly dead child but became again the mother of a living one, that sunny and ordinary experience.

53

The summer after Ella came home was nearly as hot as the summer that Madeleine conceived her. The heat began early. It was well set in by May, the days growing hot and hotter and hotter still until mornings bloomed at five o'clock and noons were brazen-blue and burning (although the evenings were cool and dusty-golden, the parks jamful of revellers and twilight never coming until ten or later). Such a burning summer it was that by day the pavements grew oppressive and Madeleine's thoughts turned to greenery and to gardens, to fantasies of shade and running water. But at night she slept with the window open, her nightgown rucked up around her waist to cool her heated legs and although the days were hard and Ella wilted and grew pale and picked at her food, the nights were wonderful, the air so warm outside that people talked and laughed all night as if it were broad daylight, whilst the dossers, who were usually so sad, smiled at Madeleine in the early mornings when she passed them.

One Saturday morning Martin and Angelina went out walking in the cool of Highgate Woods. It was early but the woods were already full of people, the trees overhead eighty or ninety feet tall and hugely swollen with summer foliage. Martin and Angelina walked in a small procession. Dominic who was five ran on ahead. After him came Charles who had just turned two. Martin came next, a tricycle in one hand and a bicycle in the other. Lastly there came Angelina pushing the pram in which the baby lay. The pram was laden with bags and bottles and hats and nappies and sun cream. Up ahead of them was the playing field. The shadows on the grass were a strident black, the sunshine a brilliant green. Angelina wore a white dress. The light through the trees was green and gold. When Angelina stepped into a patch of sunlight her white dress turned her into a blob of light.

As they walked Martin and Angelina were quarrelling, in the way that parents of small children do, obliquely and with long gaps in between whilst they cared for the children.

'If you drag that tricycle you'll break it, Martin,' said Angelina.

Martin raised it by one inch, then looked around for Dominic. The little boy had hung back and was now creeping up on Angelina.

'Don't headbut your mother,' said Martin in a tone of voice as if to suggest that this was exactly what he should do.

'It's hot,' said Angelina with distaste.

'It's hotter in France,' said Martin.

Angelina looked disbelieving. 'It would save a lot of money if we went skiing at home,' she said, because this was what their quarrel was about – as well as the heat and their tiredness – that Angelina wanted to take their skiing holiday in January in her parents' hotel in the French Alps, and Martin didn't.

'I thought home was here, in London, where we live,' said Martin.

Angelina looked impatient. 'The children would like to see their grandparents,' she said.

'We've only just got back from seeing them,' said Martin. 'Maybe the children would like to go somewhere new.'

'Swing,' said Dominic, 'I'd like a swing,' and he took their hands and 'One, two, three,' they went, swinging him higher and higher.

'Swing me too,' shrieked Charlie, 'swing me too.'

They came to the sports field. They sat outside on the grass so that the children could play. Martin went inside and fetched a tray of food and drinks.

'But I asked for a cappuccino, Martin,' said Angelina. It was true.

'I thought you didn't like cappuccinos,' said Martin. 'Filthy Italian muck.'

Angelina looked at him. She moved the tray away from

Dominic's flailing feet. The gesture said, 'Careless fathers. It's mothers who have to think of everything.'

'Drink your apple juice, Dominic,' said Martin. The little boy drank up.

'Football,' he said, 'I want to play football.'

'You play football, Martin,' said Angelina, 'I'm tired.'

'No, Mummy play,' said Dominic and Martin lay back and shut his eyes to hide the look of triumph on his face.

Angelina looked at him. 'I need to think,' said Martin deprecatingly, and he let his thoughts drift off into oblivion. As he vanished beyond her reach he was picturing to himself the marital bed, with the babies on one side and Angelina on the other and the years drifting down on top of them, and he thought: she won't give an inch on anything and I'm trapped in domesticity and will anything ever change?

When he opened his eyes again she was sitting with her legs stretched out, her arms behind her, her hands flat upon the ground and her head thrown back so that her face was lifted up towards the sky. Charlie and Dominic were standing side by side, looking at him. 'I thought you were going to play football,' said Martin sternly, although really he was revelling in his sons' good looks, because they were plump children with thighs like hams, mop-haired, pink-and-gold, with rude good health lying just beneath the tight and shiny covering of their skin. They had seen a programme on television the night before about a family of lions. Now they began to roar like wild animals. 'Roll, Daddy, roll,' they screamed and they put their hands with their rosy-coloured nails against him and began to push.

But Martin was a big man and he didn't move because something else had caught his eye. Thirty yards away across the grass and walking in the direction of the café he saw Madeleine. At first he thought she was alone but then he saw a child on a bicycle weaving and swooping and flashing around her. Madeleine looked tired. She wasn't wearing summer clothes, just fewer winter ones: a navy-blue T-shirt and dark-coloured leggings. Her shoulders were hunched. Her face was unmade-up. Her hair had lost its short, sharp cut and had grown long and shapeless across her shoulders. The child was dressed in shorts and a T-shirt with a hat on her head which shaded her face so that all Martin could see of her was her knock-kneed skinniness, as she pedalled madly against the spinning wheels.

So that's what happened to Madeleine, is it? thought Martin. Over the years he had not forgotten her, but remembered her in the way that you remember cold weather in a heatwave, thinking to yourself that next time you'll be more grateful for its bracing, sustaining qualities. He dwelt in particular on memories that revealed her sharpness, such as the dinner party where they had first met, an extravagant, complacent affair which would have passed in an atmosphere of velvety complacency had not Madeleine been there – twenty and all alone and defiantly arguing the rights of women to a bored-looking, handsome young man in a dinner jacket. Or so Martin remembered it, a sharp image to bring into discontented focus all Angelina's soft femininity.

But now he was horrified to see how stern and shabby Madeleine had become. All these years she had been the beguiling alternative that perhaps he should have stayed with but now she had turned into the sad, shuffling, downtrodden alternative that, thank God, he had avoided. I never expected her to turn out like that, thought Martin, although on reflection it wasn't surprising – in her plainness and her austerity she reminded him of her mother, or even of her mother's house. He turned his head so that he could watch her walk away. He kept his eyes half-closed and his face blank so that Angelina, who had sharp eyes, couldn't see what he was thinking.

As she vanished into the distance he heard the children squealing close beside him. They were falling over and over each other with their slippery limbs. Angelina stood up. She towered over him, her dress very white with the blue sky behind it. She had an itch in one foot. She had slipped the foot out of its moccasin and was rubbing it against the other shoe. Angelina spent money on pedicures. Her feet had a softened, painted look. She scrunched up her toes, giving the foot a blind look as back inside the shoe it went.

Martin thought she might be cross with him. He called Dominic over. 'Go and ask Mummy what she's thinking,' he whispered, but Dominic wasn't listening. He and Charlie had hurled themselves upon him and were butting him with their heads. At last he rolled over and as he did so, with squeals, they spilled from off him and rolled across the grass. A lion pride, thought Martin. A pride of lions. A pride. A pride. How proud I am.

A man walking past stared at Angelina. In Martin's mind Angelina's clothes fell off her. He perched dark shades upon her nose. He painted her fingernails scarlet to match her painted toenails. He saw the bones of her feet splayed out as fine as chicken bones. He felt an erection starting. The children were slipping all over the place as if they were coated in butter. A pride. A pride. A pride of lions, thought Martin, who, although deeply, was also pleasurably mired in domesticity.

54

That same Saturday morning Mr Chatoo, the lawyer, was in a garden centre not far from Highgate Woods, seeking out Bishop's Hat and Blue-Eyed Mary to plant in the shady borders of his cottage in the country. As he stepped patiently amongst the plants, picking out the healthiest and the most vigorous speci-mens, he was thinking about Madeleine Kingdom and the long, buff-coloured envelope that had arrived on his desk by second post on Wednesday afternoon. Inside were the results of the DNA tests which had been done on Ella, Gina, George and Madeleine. He had read the letter through. He had read it through a second time. He had put it down on the desk and thought about it. He had read it for a third time but there could be no mistaking what it said. Comparisons between Ella's DNA fingerprints and those of Madeleine, George and Gina had revealed absolutely no familial relationships whatsoever. It was 99 per cent certain that Ella was not the child of any of them and thus it had to be concluded that an egg and sperm from some other couple being treated in the clinic at the time had been used inadvertently.

Mr Chatoo thought about it. He weighed up Madeleine's relief at knowing that the Kaufmans had nothing to do with her child with her shock at discovering that some other couple did. At length he tucked away the envelope at the back of Madeleine's file. He did it in the same way that he would hide an unprepossessing plant at the back of his herbaceous border where the other plants would conceal it. Mr Chatoo liked people to be happy. It was why he grew flowers.

Oliver Hewitt was not so sensitive. He sent the results straight on to George and Gina along with a bill, the two bits of paper in one envelope floating down through George and Gina's letterbox that Saturday morning. When the letter arrived George had got Gina up against the bathroom wall and with one hand entwined tightly in her hair was screwing her from behind. As he did so he was calling out to himself with involuntary delight. George rarely lost himself in love-making. He liked to remain objective so that he could calculate triumphantly that this would be another lay, fuck, screw, shagging and shafting, to be added to all those other lays, fucks, screws, shaggings and shaftings that he had enjoyed in his life. But George now found some silky path of pleasure and for once lost himself in Gina and shouted out with joy.

Afterwards, he took a shower and then shaved, smiling to himself as he did so and standing very straight. He could feel that the hard, ambitious corners of his nature had ceased for a moment from knocking uncomfortably together and had fallen into a blessed repose. 'Gina, love,' he called out through the bathroom door, 'Coffee,' and Gina, slayed and sweetened by orgasms also, rolled out of bed and pulled on a wrap and padded through to the kitchen, a big, lush woman, not yet rank – though nearly so.

As she passed the hall she saw the letter lying on the mat. She stopped. She picked it up. She turned it over. She knew at once whom it was from. Oliver Hewitt, she thought. It's probably his bill. Much good that he did us, that rip-off merchant, and taking the letter into the kitchen she threw it into the bin.

Meanwhile, in the bathroom, the sharp, cool image of Madeleine Kingdom had jumped into George's head. It was not the first time that this had happened to him. He found that he was remembering her quite often, that she would get into his head as he was driving home from work or late at night as he sat drinking whisky and watching films from his collection of videos. 'Oh, you cow,' said George out loud to the mirror, and he smiled, because of course she did it on purpose, affording him both pleasure and pain with her appearances, but a little bit less of the first than of the second.

Madeleine, on the other hand, didn't remember George at all – or so she would have said if you had asked her. And yet perhaps it wasn't true because sometimes she woke in the morning with the luxurious and sensual feeling that in her dreams she'd had sex and although afterwards not one scrap of the dream remained, except for this feeling of lingering pleasure, even so when she tried to name the person who must have screwed her so delightfully it was always George Kaufman that she thought of; although there again, thought Madeleine, maternal love is like erotic love – it gives you a feeling of repletion – so perhaps it was not George Kaufman screwing her but Ella walking through her sleep that caused her to wake so happily?

In years to come George would pity Madeleine, thinking that she must miss him and yearn for him just as he missed her. But George got Madeleine wrong, as Martin did as well that Saturday morning when he saw her looking so shabby in Highgate Woods (she had left home in a hurry and was indeed looking dishevelled), thinking that this shabbiness must go all the way to the core. Neither he nor George had any idea how the inside of her head was lit up like a Christmas tree with love for Ella, nor how idle and companionable and loving was the conversation that they made that day in Highgate Woods when Ella had slowed her bike to a wobbling halt and they were walking across the grass together.

This is how their conversation went:

'Can I put on tomorrow's clothes tonight, Mum?' asked Ella.

'Why?'

'So I won't have to get dressed again tomorrow?'

'Why not just keep on today's clothes? That would be even quicker.'

'Can I?'

'No,' said Madeleine, 'no, you can't.'

'Oh.' Ella clicked her tongue.

'Don't tutta,' said Madeleine.

'What's tutta-ing?'

'Clicking your tongue.'

'Like this?' Ella gave an example.

'That's right,' said Madeleine.

'Do you tutta?'

'Sometimes. When people drive me mad.'

'Ah.' Ella nodded with satisfaction. 'Mum?' she said, 'is there such a thing as clothes you can eat?'

'I don't know. Why would you want clothes you can eat?'

'So you can eat them.'

'You mean, stupid question. Like chocolate T-shirts?'

'Strawberry leggings.'

'Vanilla socks?'

'I ate Shaun Long's socks at school.'

'You didn't. What did they taste like?'

'Disgusting.' She put her finger down her throat to signify vomiting. 'Can we go to the café?' she asked.

'I should think so,' said Madeleine.

As they queued beside the counter Madeleine said, 'I can see Shaun Long's socks up there. They're one of those sandwich fillings.'

'You can't,' said Ella, 'don't be silly, Mum.'

'You're right,' said Madeleine, 'I am silly.'

They bought two chocolate ice creams and took them out into the garden. Ella sat on Madeleine's lap, swinging her legs proprietarily on either side. 'You're heavy, sweetheart,' said Madeleine but she made no attempt to push Ella off, because a multitude of voices was speaking up inside her, voices loving, clever, naïve, astonished, voices which felt the sun and loved Ella's knees and remembered an Andrew Marvell poem and thought of the plan which her mother had divulged to her the day before, to sell the house on the Finchley Road and to give some of the money that accrued from it to Madeleine to buy a bigger flat. 'Because you'll never get a bigger mortgage on an academic's salary, my dear,' her mother had said, and Madeleine had been startled but pleased that her mother was worldly enough to understand this. In which case, thought Madeleine, we could move to a different catchment area and Ella could go to a different school, somewhere gentler and less stressful?

'Mum,' said Ella, 'why don't you wear that white blouse you bought at Christmas, the one with the frilly neck?'

'I don't know,' said Madeleine. 'Why? Do you like it?'

'Yes.'

'Then for you,' said Madeleine, 'I'll wear it.'

'Would you do anything for me, Mum?'

'Why? Did you have something in mind?'

'No. I just wondered if you'd do anything for me?'

'I rather think,' said Madeleine, yawning and stretching and tipping her off, 'I rather think I might.'